Seduce Me Tonight

KRISTINA WRIGHT

mischief

Mischief
An imprint of HarperCollins*Publishers*
77–85 Fulham Palace Road,
Hammersmith, London W6 8JB

www.mischiefbooks.com

A Paperback Original 2013

First published in Great Britain in ebook format by
HarperCollins*Publishers* 2012

Copyright © Kristina Wright 2012

Kristina Wright asserts the moral right to
be identified as the author of this work

A catalogue record for this book is
available from the British Library

ISBN-13: 9780007534784

Set in Sabon by FMG using Atomik ePublisher from Easypress

Find out more about HarperCollins and the environment at
www.harpercollins.co.uk/green

CONTENTS

Contents

Diamonds and Pearls

We made it to pearl. As I packed my half of the kitchen, I just kept thinking, we made it to pearl.

I was keeping the china and the punch bowl, not because I was fond of gold leaf or crystal, but because they had been wedding gifts from my mother. My mother made it to gold. No – I shook my head at the chip in the plate I held, the gold leaf damaged – she made it to *until death us do part*.

People will tell you that it's smooth sailing if you make it past the seven-year itch. Those are the people who didn't make it past the three-year breaking-in period. Other people will tell you that twenty is the tough year – when you've spent two decades with the same person and realise your best years are behind you. Those are the people who crapped out around ten years, only to get remarried and go another ten with someone else. As if a decade per spouse is somehow better than two decades with the same person bitching about your inability to remember to pay the electric bill or put your dirty clothes in the hamper.

Our silver anniversary had come and gone and my co-worker Janine said, 'Twenty-five years! Holy shit! You've been married for ever!'

At the time, I'd laughed and agreed with her, but in the back of my mind I remember thinking, it doesn't feel like for ever. It feels like we just started and then got tired before we reached for ever.

Everyone knows twenty-five years is the silver anniversary, but no one knows what represents thirty years together. Traditionally, it's pearl. The modern is diamond. I like diamonds better, but I have a jewellery box full of both from birthdays, Valentine's Days. Anniversaries, too. He'd given me diamonds or pearls for many anniversaries. A strand of pearls for our eighth anniversary (traditional: bronze; modern: linen) and a gold watch inlaid with diamond for our fifteenth (traditional: crystal; modern: watches – so I guess he was paying attention). Other gifts in-between and after, gifts I admired and enjoyed and put away for some future special occasion.

There were diamond earrings and pearl hair clasps and diamond-and-pearl baubles for the twenty-sixth through twenty-ninth anniversaries, the ones no one has bothered to put on the anniversary gift lists, as if those years between twenty-five and thirty don't matter at all. As if what Janine said was true: being married twenty-five years was for ever and there was no need to acknowledge another anniversary for at least five more years, and every five years after. I guess we took that to heart. Those years between the twenty-fifth anniversary trip to the Greek Isles and the thirtieth anniversary trip to divorce court were a blur of pot roast dinners, political talk over waffles at our favourite brunch joint and mediocre sex a couple times a week or whenever we were both in the mood and awake at the same time.

The traditional gift for every anniversary should be sex. It's hard to complain about his snoring when he's fucking you. Suddenly every noise he's making is a turn-on. It's impossible to complain about her lousy cooking when you're going down on her and your mouth is full of the sweetest juice you've ever tasted. Or maybe I'm wrong. Maybe two people can fuck every day for thirty years and still end up where I was, packing away ugly thirty-year-old plates and a dusty punchbowl.

'What are you smiling about?'

Nathan and I were civilised people. We didn't fight and scream, we didn't throw things, we didn't pull childish immature acts on each other. No, we were a couple who had been married for thirty years, raised three children and had mutually decided a divorce was in both our best interests. And now the years were gone, the kids were grown and had their own lives and we were a divorced couple packing up our mutual belongings at the same time in the same house we'd shared for over two decades.

I shook my head as I used several sheets of newspaper to wrap a gravy boat I couldn't remember using in a decade. 'Just thinking that if people fucked every day of their marriage, maybe there wouldn't be any need to get divorced.'

Nathan had his hands full of some bubble-wrapped thingy from our shared home office. Probably that ugly snow globe I'd gotten him as a last-minute anniversary gift last year. I'd seen it in one of those mall stores you see everywhere and been stricken with a bout of bad taste, buying this hideous glass and wood creation depicting Chicago in winter. I'd even gotten the damned thing engraved with our names and wedding date.

'So, if we'd had sex every day, we'd still be together?' he asked slowly, the consummate professor repeating the information he's been given, looking for a different interpretation.

I shook my head. 'Who knows? Maybe we'd be fucking right now instead of packing up all this – *fucking stuff* – and going our separate ways.'

I don't know why I said that. Hell, outside of when

we were actually fucking, I never even used that word. OK, not even when we were fucking, unless I'd had a couple of drinks first. But something about signing my name – *his last name* – to a divorce decree seemed to have loosened a knot of tension inside me. There I was, standing in the kitchen, packing our wedding china, barefoot in a sundress on a warm summer evening, saying *fucking, fucking, fucking.*

Go *fucking* figure, huh?

I felt suddenly, inexplicably weary. I put the plate I was holding on top of the already wrapped stack of matching plates and leaned against the counter, studying my husband. My ex-husband, I mentally amended.

The years had been kind to Nathan. He didn't look much different than the kid I'd met at Berkeley as an undergrad. The dark hair was turning silver, the lines around his eyes and mouth were more defined, like water etches stone after a millennium; there were a few more pounds on his always lean frame, but he was otherwise exactly the same as when I met him thirty-five years previous. Still quick to smile and slow to anger. Still stubborn as a mule and gentle as a kitten. Still kind-hearted and thoughtful. Still sexy as hell in well-worn jeans and an old Yale T-shirt.

There is a moment when every newly divorced person looks at his or her former spouse and doesn't see their partner, lover, friend of X number of years, but a stranger.

I felt like I was having an out-of-body experience looking at Nathan standing in our kitchen. He was everything I had ever wanted. Still was. And yet ... and yet, here we were, packing up our fucking stuff and going on our merry separate ways.

'What do you see?' he asked, that gentle tone of a teacher trying to coax the student to find the answer on her own.

I shrugged and turned away, fingering the single strand of pearls I wore, one last birthday present before it all went to hell. 'I see a life together that's fallen apart. Time to start anew, I guess.'

I sounded more carefree than I felt. Much as I'd wanted this – and I had been the one to file the divorce papers when it dawned on me that Nathan wouldn't, no matter how much we fought or withdrew from each other – I really didn't know what I was going to do now. The house had gone on the market once we started the paper-work for the divorce and we had gotten a more than generous offer just days after the realtor listed it. Our 'separation' involved Nathan moving into the guest room. It wasn't that we couldn't afford for one of us to move out, but it seemed silly when the house was more than big enough. Our paths rarely crossed except in the mornings for a few minutes before we both went to work. It made sense for us to live together as roommates until the house sold and we could each take our half and find something new. It was civilised this way. It was also bitterly depressing to realise that after thirty years together we could live in the same house for months without talking other than to pass on phone messages, without touching because we made such a wide berth around each other, without one of us caving in and climbing into bed with the other, one late night. Depressing as hell.

I slammed the poorly wrapped plate down on top of the stack and heard an audible crack. I gasped. The tears started coming even before I unwrapped the plate and saw it had been cleaved in two. I felt Nathan's hand on my shoulder, that gentle, familiar squeeze to comfort me. But it didn't comfort me. It made me angry. For the first time in at least six months he was touching me and it was because he felt sorry for me.

I shrugged him off. 'Leave me alone!'

'I was just trying to be kind, Rachel,' he said. 'It's not as if you ever liked that old ugly china.'

I whirled on him then. 'It was my *mother's*!'

'Well, it's not as if you liked her much, either,' he said, evenly. 'And she was old and ugly, too.'

I knew he was joking. Sort of. Nathan was a lot of things, but he wasn't cruel. He was trying to make me feel better. Trying to lighten the mood. He never could stand to see me cry. I knew all of that, but my first reaction wasn't to laugh. Or even to stop crying. I sobbed

– and slapped him hard. The diamond in my engagement ring glinted in the overhead light, as hard and cold as I felt.

'Go to hell, Nathan Davis.'

He recoiled, as much from the shock of it as the pain, I think, and stared at me. The look of utter horror on his face was comical. I'd never so much as raised my voice or slammed a door, much less slapped him before. I was the quiet, angry type, more likely to hide in the bedroom nursing my wounds than to vent my emotions and risk hurting someone else's feelings. It was, I thought, a good quality. But standing there with my hand stinging and my entire body practically vibrating with anger while the tears dried on my cheeks, I felt pretty good. Furious and violent, clearly, but *good*. Alive.

As quickly as the feeling came, it faded, shrivelling up inside me like it had been deprived of oxygen. I was ashamed of myself.

'I'm sorry.' I watched him rub the red mark on his cheek and felt small. And sad. 'I don't know where that came from.'

'I do.'

He picked up the sugar bowl from the counter, the one that went with my mother's china, examined it for a minute, then dropped it. I gasped in horror as it hit the tile and fractured into several smaller pieces, scattering shards across the kitchen floor.

I blinked at him, certain it had been an accident, but he proved me wrong by picking up a salad plate and doing the same thing. The sound of breaking porcelain seemed to echo even as he reached for a third piece. I was frozen in place, unable to move to stop him as another salad plate crashed to the floor.

I finally found my voice when he picked up the serving platter. 'What the *hell* are you doing?'

'Breaking your mother's china,' he answered, as if that made all the sense in the world.

I looked at the fragments of the seventy-five-year-old dishes littering our pristine kitchen floor – not even *our* kitchen floor any more, as the house was officially sold – and felt … nothing. I took a deep breath, waiting for the indignant anger to explode out of me again, and simply exhaled. There was no emotion there, no sense of loss. All I saw was a mess to clean up and a few less things to pack.

Nathan seemed almost as shocked when I started laughing as he had when I slapped him. It started small, just a twitch of my lips as I mentally replayed his comment about my mother and her china, and built from there. First a giggle and a shake of my head at my own audacity – laughing at something that wasn't funny in the least – then an open-mouthed guffaw at the idea that I should feel bad for giggling. I looked at Nathan, at his gaping 'have you lost your mind?' expression, and completely lost it. I was doubled over with laughter, clutching at the kitchen counter to keep me upright.

'You're right,' I managed to say between fits of giggles. 'I *hate* this china. It's ugly and tacky and has to be hand washed. Good god, *hand* washed! Who has time for ugly hand-washed china? I don't!'

Nathan nodded sagely. 'I know.'

'Unbelievably *fucking* ugly.' I was like a kid discovering the power of dirty words. 'Right?'

'Right.'

It was contagious, Nathan's baritone chuckles joined my own girlish-sounding squeals and soon we were holding onto each other, laughing like fools. And maybe we were. Fools, that is. The two biggest fools in the world – and we had to hold onto each other because no one else would.

I kissed him then. It was an open-mouthed, awkward, laughing kiss, but it was the first kiss we'd shared in at least a year. His mouth felt both new and familiar. A couple of days' growth of beard scraped against my cheek as I cupped the back of his head and held him to me, as if he might pull away otherwise. But he didn't. He didn't even hesitate before he was kissing me back. He fisted his hands in my hair, kept long even now because that's the way he liked it and I had never thought to cut it, and held me as tightly as I held on to him.

All traces of laughter gone, I tentatively nipped his

bottom lip. I heard – and felt – his moan. It had been so long since we'd even kissed, I didn't know how to proceed. I couldn't think straight, didn't *want* to think at all. I wanted to feel. His act of destruction had released something inside me, something tight and coiled, and now I was reaching for more, hungry for something more than anger and hurt. His tongue swept along mine and I whimpered softly at his teasing. This was all familiar too, distantly so, as a recurring dream feels familiar in the light of day.

I don't know how long we stood there, leaning against the counter, pressed together and making out like teenagers. The tick-tick of the kitchen clock counted out the seconds of our mad descent into wherever this was leading and the hardness of his erection pressed against my hip corresponded to the wetness between my thighs that he couldn't feel. Yet.

That thought, as much a memory as anything else we'd shared, made me whimper again. I could feel my long dormant arousal awakening within me, blossoming like the heat had blossomed in his cheek where I had slapped him. I cupped his face in my hand, remorseful and anxious to set things right. I kissed the spot where I'd hit him, feeling his skin warm and rough beneath my lips. I trailed kisses down the line of his jaw, along his neck, to his collarbone. I breathed in his scent, clean and masculine and all Nathan. All mine.

Mine. Where had that come from?

I didn't have time to consider it because he was pulling me up against him, one hand still tangled in my hair, the other wrapped firmly around my hip. He nestled the bulge of his erection against the soft swell of my belly and we both groaned. I ached for him to fill me. To fill the emptiness between my thighs, yes, but also to fill the hollowness behind my breastbone.

We stared into each other's eyes, so close I could see his pupils dilate when I wiggled against him, pressing even closer. He pulled his hand from my hair, anchored it on my other hip and slowly scrunched my dress up in his hands. I shivered as he revealed me, so slowly I thought I would scream with the anticipation of it.

'Are you wet?' he asked when the hem of my dress was up to my hips.

My breath caught in my throat as I nodded.

'Take your panties off for me.'

I did the best I could with him holding onto me. I hooked my thumbs in the sides of my panties and tugged them down over my hips. They slipped down my legs and I stepped out of them. Then I waited for what he would do next.

He didn't make me wait long. In one smooth move, he picked me up and sat me on the edge of the counter. He pulled my thighs apart, baring me to his gaze. He stared between my legs without speaking. The kitchen counter was cool against my ass, but that wasn't what made me shiver. He looked angry.

'What's wrong? We don't have to –'

I moved as if to slide off the counter and he held me in place, his fingers digging into my upper thighs.

'Don't move,' he all but growled at me. 'I want you so much.'

This was most certainly *not* familiar. What were we doing? We weren't the types for sex in the kitchen, Nathan wasn't ever demanding and I was never this passive and agreeable. But here we were, with him pushing my thighs even wider apart and me whimpering in expectation. He licked his lips as if in anticipation and then dipped his head between my legs. The first swipe of his tongue along my pussy made me squeal in a very unladylike manner. I had only a moment to contemplate the utter ridiculousness of the situation before he did it again.

Then I stopped thinking.

Nathan took his time licking me, using the broad flat of his tongue to take long, slow swipes along my pussy. I knew I was drenched, I could feel the wetness and smell my arousal. I braced my hands on the edge of the counter and jutted my hips forward to his mouth, suddenly shameless. If we were going to do this, I was going to enjoy it.

Nathan made an appreciative grunt and used his thumbs to spread my lips. I trembled in anticipation,

13

waiting. Wanting. Needing. He let me wait, simply staring at my pussy open before him, as if he had me right where he wanted me and was in no rush to let me get away.

I didn't examine that thought for too long. I didn't want to think about what happened after this crazy little tryst. I didn't want to think at all. I'd spent months, years, thinking and planning and wondering where it all went wrong. I was tired of thinking. I wanted to *feel*.

'Do it,' I urged. 'Lick me. Please.'

It was the 'please' that did it. I could see the way his expression softened and he became the Nathan who would do anything for me. He stopped teasing me then and lowered his head between my legs. There was no hesitation, no need for me to beg, there was only sensation – his tongue dipping inside of me, his fingers sliding into me. He wet my clit with my own moisture, then licked it away. I cried out, gripping the edge of the counter and draping my legs over his shoulders. I dug my heels into his back, urging him on, afraid he would stop. He didn't.

Whatever had happened between us in the past, Nathan still knew what I liked. What I needed. He held me open before him, like a feast for his pleasure alone, and then he ate me like a starving man. We both were starving. It had been so long, too long. I couldn't even remember the last time, but there had never been a time quite like this. I clung to the counter and to him, feeling my orgasm building low in my belly. Muscles taut, body aching with the need for release, I didn't think about anything but the feeling of Nathan's tongue on my clit as I sat there bare-assed naked on the kitchen counter that didn't even belong to me any more. And that thought – that wholly inappropriate, completely naughty thought – was what sent me careening over the edge.

I screamed, open-mouthed, uninhibited, raw with the need to vocalise what I was feeling. Holding Nathan between my plump thighs, riding his mouth in an effort to prolong my pleasure, I spiralled down into that blissful state of utter sensation where nothing mattered at all. I cried out my passion, my need, my frustration. My sadness. I pushed my hips against Nathan's open mouth as he devoured everything I had to give. I slid around on the counter, its surface slick with the proof of my arousal.

I was still crying when he tugged me forward, over the edge of the counter and onto his cock. I was still coming, my pussy still contracting as he slid into me, knees bent, and pressed me against the counter, filling the emptiness inside me in a way that no finger or toy ever could. I hadn't realised how badly I had missed him – or how much I wanted him – until he was buried inside me, staring into my eyes as he thrust into me, hard and fast. His jaw was clenched, a vein pulsing at his temple as he struggled to maintain control. I felt a surge of feminine power at knowing he was as needy as I was.

I was standing on my toes, my calves quivering with the effort to hold steady under the onslaught of his thrusts. He hooked his hand under my thigh and draped it over his hip, and we both groaned as the angle made my pussy narrow around him and brought my clit up tight against his pubic bone. In the aftermath of my orgasm his cock felt huge and every thrust sent little aftershocks of desire pulsing through me. He still wore his jeans, had tugged them down just far enough to free his thick erection, and the open zipper scraped against my slick, sensitive skin while the sharp edge of the counter dug into my back. I didn't care. Pleasure with a side of pain, I thought fuzzily. It was entirely worth it just to hear him grunt my name.

I could feel his cock swell and twitch inside me and I clung to him, hands fisted in the fabric of his T-shirt, my leg wrapped high on his hip and holding him close. I nipped at the taut corded muscle in his neck, hard enough to hurt, which made him jerk against me. He went still and quiet, only his ragged breath and racing pulse letting me know how hard he was coming.

We stood like that for an endless moment, holding tight to each other, unwilling to move away and lose contact. Finally, he pulled back just far enough to look at me. Crow's feet framed his laughing blue eyes and silver strands sparkled in the tousled chocolate-brown of his hair. Had it really been thirty years?

'Rachel. I love you, Rachel.'

Staring into his eyes I had the sense that time had melted away. Suddenly, we were standing there the day we'd moved into the house, when we had a four-year-old and I was pregnant with our second, but didn't know it yet. We'd scrimped and saved for a down payment on our dream house and finally it was ours. It was one of the happiest days of my life.

I blinked and it all came rushing back, reality knocking the breath out of me. Tears stung my eyes and rolled down my cheeks. Nathan watched and held me, never saying a word. Then he bent and kissed a tear away as it followed the curve of my cheek.

'Now what?' I put a hand in the centre of his chest and gave him a firm push, my wedding rings flashing in the light. Mocking my moment of weakness. 'Was that just one last time, for old time's sake?'

'Is that what you want it to be?'

'Damn it, Nathan, could you for once in your life answer a question without asking a question?'

I sounded angry and bitter. But what I was really feeling was overwhelming loss. The anger was familiar, comforting. I clung to it the way I'd clung to him moments ago, using it as a protective barrier against the words he was about to hurl at me. But there was no angry retort. He simply laughed.

'I do that, don't I?'

'You just did it again!' I said, smacking his shoulder in exasperation. 'Just answer the question.'

'I will if you stop hitting me, woman.' He pulled me close, trapping my hands against his chest.

'OK. Sorry.'

He laughed again, shaking his head. Then his smile faded. 'I don't want it to be the last time, Rachel,' he said, sounding all growly-voiced like he had earlier. 'I don't want it to be over.'

'But we're divorced! And we sold the house.' I pointed out the truths, but I neglected the most important truth of all – I didn't want it to be over, either.

'So what? We don't have to be married to give it another go,' he said, making it sound completely reasonable. 'Let's start over. Somewhere else. Someplace new. Let's be new together.'

'Let's fuck on kitchen counters, you mean?'

'Yeah. Let's figure out where the hell *we* went –' he shook me gently for emphasis '– and where we want to go now.'

I gazed at the kitchen floor, littered with remnants of my mother's dishes while we stood half-naked in front of open kitchen windows that looked out on the street. My thighs were sticky with his desire and mine, too. It was crazy. Ridiculous.

It felt right.

'OK,' I agreed. 'But we have to clean up this mess.'

'Why? We're not done yet.'

I wasn't sure whether he was talking about the mess or the sex, and I didn't care. I knew what had to be done.

I twisted out of the circle of his arms and unwrapped one of the dinner plates I'd already packed. Turning it over in my hand, I examined the tacky gold trim and the faded scene of pheasants in a field, and shrieked with laughter. It really was hideous. Maybe if we got rid of all the bad, the only thing left would be the good. I made a sound most often heard in karate class and flung the plate against the wall.

'Rachel!' Nathan said, as if shocked. But he laughed with me as I unwrapped and smashed another plate. 'If the neighbours didn't already get an eyeful and think we've gone stark raving mad, they're definitely going to call the police now.'

'I don't care!' I said, giggling helplessly and swiping at tears between bouts of destruction. 'Help me! This will take all night.'

I froze in place as he cupped my breast through the bodice of my dress and ran a callused thumb over one bra-less nipple. 'When we're done, I'm going to fuck you good and proper in our bed.'

It was a promise I believed and the only vow that mattered right now. We'd take it one day – or ugly plate – at a time and see where it went. Who knows? Maybe we'd cobble together something even better from the shattered pieces of our life together.

'You've got a deal,' I said, flinging a teacup to the floor and feeling something hard and brittle inside me give way. 'And I love you, too.'

We destroyed every dish long before the sun came up. And then he kept his promise.

The Story of Us

Some fairy tales don't end happily ever after. And sometimes happily ever after is in the eye of the beholder.

My boyfriend and I have what some people would call a volatile relationship. I used to call it dysfunctional and addictive. Late at night when I couldn't sleep and I was replaying our most recent fight, I called it fucked up. I hated him for bringing out the worst in me – but I loved him for it, too. And he felt the same way about me. We were on a path to destruction and neither of us was in a hurry to put on the brakes because it felt too damned good.

It's not like Brian beat me or something. Nothing like that. The only bruises he ever left on me were during sex and I didn't mind at all. But we fought a lot and we had broken up at least five times in as many years, maybe more if you counted the number of times I had thrown him out of my apartment and told him not to come back. But he always came back and I always let him. It is what it is, you know? It was just hard to say exactly *what* it was. It took me a long time to realise that the label was less important than the emotions.

My friends who have overheard some of our fights, or heard about them in the aftermath, ask me why I don't just dump his ass and find a nice guy who will treat me right. I could. I know I could. I'm attractive, if not gorgeous, and I have a lot going for me personally and professionally. I'm not lacking self-esteem over here, trust me. But those nice guys my friends talk about leave me cold. I've dated those guys. The ones who won't raise their voices when they're angry, the ones who will take a few days to 'cool off' and then act as if nothing happened. The ones who remain even-tempered and good-natured no matter how many of their buttons you push. I hate those guys. They are as dull in bed as they are to fight with. Brian, on the other hand, is anything but boring.

What I don't tell my friends, what I don't even tell Brian because he'd say I was the one with the problem and I don't need to give him ammunition, is that I *like* the fighting. It gets me hot. Yeah, I guess that is fucked up, isn't it? But I think he likes it as much as I do and won't admit it either. He pushes me and I push him and we fight. And after we fight, we make up. And the making up is hot and sexy and sweaty and rough. I fume for days after a fight, but the longer the wait, the hotter I get to make up with him.

The other thing I don't tell anyone is that sometimes I have to change my panties after one of my screaming, throwing, slamming fights with Brian. I'm just wired that way, I guess. He pushes my buttons to piss me off and that does something to my other button. My clit stands at attention when we're going nine rounds over who was flirting with whom at the bar or whatever. I hear myself say things I never thought I would ever say to someone I love, with my hands balled into fists at my side, not sure whether I'd rather slap his face or stroke my clit. Maybe both. Yeah, there's something wrong with me. Right?

I've slapped him a few times, pushing him, taunting him. Waiting to see what he'll do, hoping he'll do what a nice guy would never do. When I started dating, while my friends were being told by their mothers that boys didn't hit girls, my mother was practical and told me not to slap a boy unless I'm prepared to be slapped back. The threat of being hit by a boy scared me when I was thirteen but the thought of being slapped by Brian excites the hell out of me at thirty-three.

I guess I could just ask him to slap me. But that seems

a little twisted. Nice girls don't ask to be hit and I'm a nice girl. Except with Brian. He brings out the bitch in me. With everyone else, I'm this super-controlled, calm, rational, together woman. The female counterpart to the guys I've dated who keep their voices modulated and never swear during an argument. People who know me wouldn't recognise me when I'm fighting with Brian. The problem is, I think I'm my truest and most honest self with him – when I'm longing for him to call me a slut and slap my face. Why else would I stay with him and fight with him? He brings out the worst in me – and I love him for it.

'You're a stone-cold bitch, you know that?' he asked me once during a particularly gruesome battle. I don't even remember exactly what we were fighting about – I only remember the fight itself.

Brian is a writer and works in advertising, so he's always careful with how he uses language. He'll say I'm *being* bitchy or I'm *acting* like a bitch, but that was the first time he'd called me a bitch outright. My head snapped back like he really had hit me. Hot tears pricked my eyes, but I furiously blinked them back. I didn't want him to think he had gotten to me. If he thought he'd penetrated my 'stone-cold' exterior, he would stop taunting me. And I didn't want him to stop. I wanted more. A *lot* more. So I just smiled. That's something else my mother taught me. No matter what horrible insult someone hurls at you – smile. It makes them crazy. I knew for a fact that it made Brian crazy.

'Only to you, baby,' I purred. 'Only to you.'

The veiled meaning was that there was some other guy who I treated better. I could practically see Brian imagining me fucking another guy, or a string of other guys. Jealousy twisted Brian's face into something ugly and unfamiliar. I should have been scared, but that primal female part of me that loved the fighting and wanted more thought it was hot as hell. He looked like a brute – and I wanted him to unleash that brutishness all over me. I ached for it in a way I couldn't explain even to myself.

'What are you saying?' His voice was quiet. Almost sinister.

I took a step forward, the threat of tears long gone, and smiled sweetly. 'It means I know how to treat a *real* man.'

Lightning fast, he was on me, one hand grabbing my arm to push me up against the wall, the other hand coming up in an arc. I thought he was going to slap me. I really did. Even though I wanted it, was ready for it, I flinched just a little.

He blinked, as if touching me had shocked him and let me go so abruptly, I nearly fell. *Damn.* It was my own fault. This time, the tears came and I couldn't stop them.

25

'Go on, do it,' I taunted him, though my voice sounded wobbly with emotion and had lost its previous heat. 'You were going to hit me, you know you were. Go ahead and do it!'

I was screaming the words, like a child throwing a tantrum because she hadn't gotten what she wanted. It sounded like a plea rather than a taunt. Brian just stared at me as if seeing me for the first time.

'You thought I was going to hit you,' he said, something different in his voice. 'I was going to hit you. Swear to God, I was.'

It finally dawned on me why he sounded different. He sounded sad. I took a step towards him, tried to touch him. 'Just do it,' I begged. '*Do it.* You want to.'

He shook his head. 'I'd never hit a woman. I'd never, *ever* hit you, Jules.'

I said what had been hanging in the air between us, the truth that I couldn't hide from any longer, the reality that maybe was starting to dawn on him. 'But I *wanted* you to.'

He rocked back on his heels as if I'd punched him in the stomach. 'What the hell is wrong with you? Seriously, Jules, who says that? Who *wants* that?'

My first reaction was shame and embarrassment. I was messed up, something was wrong with me. He'd just said it. My shame was followed by white-hot anger. I said the other truth that was between us, the truth I'd always suspected and was now willing to put into words. 'You want to. I know you do. It's why we're still together. It's why you fight with me and push me and let me push you. You want to take it farther, you want to, but you can't.'

His hand came up to my face, but too slow to actually be a blow. Instead, he tucked a lock of my dark-brown hair behind my ear and gave me another sad puppy-dog smile. 'Maybe. But I can't do that. I'm done, Jules.'

I thought he meant done fighting, but he fished his keys out of his pocket and took my apartment key off his ring. Then he laid it on the table by the front door and walked out. The door closed with a finality that echoed inside me. I didn't start crying for another thirty minutes, but once I started, I couldn't stop. Some time later, it started to rain.

* * *

Some time after 2 a.m., after tossing and turning for hours, I finally got up, threw a raincoat over my short nightgown and headed out into the night. I had only intended to go for a drive, but I found myself driving to Brian's town house and parking on the street. I sat there, windshield wipers dashing away the heavy rain, staring up at his darkened windows and wondering if this was wise. I'd already gone this far, I decided, I might as well see it to its bitter conclusion.

He'd given me his key back, but he hadn't asked for mine. I let myself in the front door, shushed his friendly Labrador Charlie, and made for the stairs to go to his bedroom. Brian's voice caught me up short.

'I'm in here,' he said, calling to me from the living room just off the front entrance. 'I figured you might show up.'

The room was dark, so it took my eyes a moment to adjust and see that he was lying on the couch, one arm tucked behind his head. He didn't seem like he'd just woken up, nor was he surprised to see me. I took a hesitant step toward him, not at all sure how to read his relaxed body language or his quiet, neutral tone.

'Brian, I –' I stopped, not even sure what to say. 'I'm so sorry,' I finally said, though I wasn't sure what I was apologising for. 'I don't know what's wrong with me.'

'You want me to hit you.'

It wasn't a question, but I didn't know what to say back to him. Did I? Maybe. Yes. In the right context. When I wanted it, but only then. But I didn't want to have to ask for it, I wanted him to just do it. Shit. How could I explain it to him when I didn't understand it myself?

'Not hit,' I whispered, my throat raw from screaming and sobbing. 'Not like that.'

'Like how, then?' He sat up and clicked the switch on the lamp beside the couch. A warm glow illuminated his face. He looked exhausted, a five o'clock shadow on his

28

high cheekbones, his black hair tousled like he'd been running his fingers through it in frustration. I knew this face, this man. I knew him and I trusted him. I owed him as honest an explanation as I could give him, even if it didn't make any sense to either of us.

I raised my shoulders in a shrug. 'I don't know. A slap, I guess.'

'Like a spanking?'

'Yeah, sorta.' It felt surreal to be talking about this. 'But more. More than a spanking, more than my ass.'

'Your face?'

I nodded. 'Yeah.'

'You want me to slap your face when we're fighting – or when we're fucking?'

'Both,' I whispered.

'Do you push me to fight so I'll do that, be that rough with you?'

I nodded. 'Yeah, I think so. I think I do. It's messed up.'

He moved to the edge of the couch and rested his arms on his splayed thighs. 'Come here.'

I went to him without hesitation. I wasn't sure of his mood or what was happening between us, but I knew I trusted him. Despite the fights, the angry words, the years of feeling like we were never connecting, I still believed in him. In us. And I knew he would never do anything I didn't want him to do.

When I was standing in front of him, he looked up at me. 'You're not messed up,' he said softly, pulling me down in front of him until I was kneeling on the carpet between his legs. 'I think I wanted the same stuff – well, wanted to do it to you. But that's even more fucked up.'

I couldn't help myself, I laughed. He was sitting on the couch, I was on my knees in front of him like I was going to go down on him, but instead we were talking about our mutual desire to do the one thing we couldn't do. 'Oh, baby, what the hell have we been doing all this time?'

He shook his head. 'Hell if I know. The fighting – it's been off the chain, right? I mean, I have never, ever fought with anyone like I fight with you. *Never*. It's weird.'

'Dysfunctional,' I agreed.

'And I hate myself when I'm saying those things. Hate you when you're screaming at me. But I can't resist it.' He stroked my hair absent-mindedly, as if he was petting Charlie. 'I try to ignore you when you start pushing me, but I can't fucking resist it.'

'You crave it,' I said, running my hands up and down his thighs to the same rhythm as his stroking of my hair. 'You need it.'

'Yeah,' he said starkly, self-loathing in his expression. 'What's wrong with me?'

'What's wrong with us? I need it, too.'

We sat there like that for awhile, touching each other as if we couldn't help ourselves – and maybe we couldn't. Maybe this was love, even if it was not what we thought love should be.

He looked at me, searched my face as if seeking some elusive answer. 'What now?'

I took a deep breath and let it out in a long, ragged sigh. I felt as if a great tension had gone out of my shoulders. Something in me had opened up. For better or worse, he knew my darkest secret. And I knew his.

'It's on the table now. Let's see where it goes.'

'You're going to have to take the lead here,' he said, as he pushed my hair behind my ears again and cupped my face. 'This is so outside the realm of my experience I don't know what to do. It feels ... wrong.'

'But I want it,' I reminded him. 'I'm *asking* for this.'

He just shook his head.

'But I said I want it.' I was louder, more forceful. 'Slap me. Slap my face.'

He went very still. 'No.'

I could feel the familiar anger beginning to rise. He was teasing me now, playing with my emotions. 'Slap me, Brian. Stop messing with my fucking head. *Slap me.*'

'Why should I?'

'Because I want you to.'

He laughed. 'Not good enough. Why should I do what you want, when you've been such a bitch to me?'

'And a slut,' I said, putting that taboo word on the table, too. In for a penny, in for a pound.

He blinked at me, his breath catching in his throat. 'Yeah? A slut?'

'Yeah.'

'What else?' he asked.

It was my turn to taunt. 'You tell me.'

'A little whore,' he said, the word sounding foreign on his tongue. 'Whore.'

I was wet. I could feel the wetness gathering between my thighs, soaking through the cotton crotch of my panties. 'You *want* me to be a whore.'

'Yeah, I do. But that doesn't mean I'm going to slap you just because you want me to, you bitch.' There was a note of anger in his voice, as if the resentment of the past five years of frustration and miscommunication was bubbling up in him, too.

'Fine,' I said. 'Slap me because *you* want to. You've always wanted to. You want to slap the smile right off my face, don't you? You want it so bad you can taste it like you can taste my pussy on your tongue.'

His hand cracked across my face before I even had time to blink. It wasn't hard, less sting than shock, but it shut me up. I gasped, or maybe he did, and we sat there blinking at each other. I instinctively raised my hand to cup my cheek, but he pulled it away and put it on his bulging crotch.

'That's what you want, isn't it?

I nodded, swallowing hard. 'Yes.'

'Want me to fuck you, little slut?'

'Oh God, yeah,' I groaned. I pulled off my raincoat, stifling under the weight of it. Still kneeling in front of him, I stripped my gown over my head. 'Fuck me.'

'I'm not done yet,' he said.

This time, I was prepared for the slap across my cheek. Same spot as before, so I really felt it this time. Felt the heat in my face, the throb of the sting corresponding with the throb between my thighs. I stared at him, naked except for my soaking wet panties, thinking I didn't even know who he was. Thinking I loved him, wanted him, needed him. Thinking, if he stopped now I would die.

He grabbed me by my hair and pulled me down to the floor with him. 'Little bitch,' he growled, dragging me across his lap by my hair and smacking my ass hard with his other hand. 'You fucking little bitch, driving me crazy all this time.'

I whimpered, my ass burning with every hard slap. 'I'm sorry,' I said. 'I didn't know how to tell you!'

He flipped me over on my back and palmed my pussy through my panties. 'Your pussy is so fucking wet. You love this.'

'Yes,' I gasped. 'I do.'

'Good,' he said, roughly stripping me of my panties

33

with one hand while he got his pants undone and his cock out with the other. 'So do I.'

He was in me with one quick thrust. I gasped at the onslaught, the sudden sensation of fullness. He sat up, taking me with him, so that he was on his knees and I was wrapped around him as he buried himself inside me. He caught my hair in one hand and pulled it back until my neck arched painfully. Then he slapped me again – not my face this time, my breasts. First one, then the other. I gasped at the sensation, my nipples tingling in pain and pleasure, my clit throbbing, his cock hitting just the right spot.

I came, moaning, crying, as he slapped my face, then my breasts, then pinched my nipples hard, once, twice, all the while whispering filthy, nasty things to me. Telling me what a whore I was, what a fucking slut, what a nasty, dirty girl. I eagerly agreed to all of it as I came on his cock. I even gave him a few more words to use, which only made him fuck me harder.

As my orgasm ebbed, he lowered me back to the floor gently – gently, after all he'd said and done to me – and covered my body with his. He fucked me with hard, steady thrusts to get him where he needed to go, to bring him to where I already was. His breath coming in fast pants, his cock swelling inside me, his balls slapping my ass. Brian. Solid, dependable Brian. My boyfriend, my love. I wrapped my arms and legs around him, holding him to me, clenching my pussy around him, surrounding him with my passion.

'Fuck your slut, baby.' I whispered the words like a love poem again and again. 'Fuck your little whore. Fuck me, fuck me, fuck me. Fill me with your come.'

He came with a bestial moan. Body tense as he arched up over me, he thrust into me one last time before putting his full weight on me, our hot, damp bodies pressed together in a way that was so familiar, after an experience unlike any we had ever shared.

He whispered something in my ear, so soft I couldn't hear him.

'What, sweetheart?'

'I said, I love you,' he whispered again. 'I love you, I'm in love with you, I've never loved anyone more than I love you. Whatever this is, however fucked up we are, I love you. You need to know that. You need to believe it.'

I cradled his head against my shoulder, shifting my hips so that I could bear his weight for as long as he needed to lie there. 'I do, Brian. I know it. I really do. And I don't think we're fucked up.'

'No?'

I pulled his head down and kissed him hard. 'No. We were made for each other. I have never loved you more than I do right now.'

And as I said the words, I realised how true it was.

It didn't matter if everyone else thought we were fucked up. I didn't believe that any more and I would make sure he didn't believe it either. He was mine, I was his and whatever 'this' was, it was our story and ours alone.

And that was all that mattered.

Cherry in a Glass

Leo started coming in my bar a couple times a week after he got out of the police academy. He was a baby-faced rookie with silver-rimmed glasses and a shiny utility belt not even broken in yet. He looked like a kid playing dress-up in his daddy's uniform. He'd sit at the end of the bar and order a club soda. Thirty minutes later, he'd give me a nod, throw down a five and be gone.

I know all the cops from the Third Precinct. They come in during their shifts to check on me and shoot the breeze while pretending not to notice the array of shifty characters sharing the bar with them. They come in after work dressed in their civilian clothes so they can throw back a few shots before heading home to their wives or girlfriends or Playstations. They're good guys, most of them. They treat me with respect and keep an eye on the place when I'm not around.

I'm no badge bunny, but I've taken a few of them home. Usually the single ones who've had a rough shift and would rather sit on a bar stool all night than go home to an empty apartment. I've done my part as marriage counsellor and sex therapist, too. Being a cop is tough on a relationship and wreaks havoc on the sex drive. Sometimes a man just needs a good no-strings fuck to remind him that he's alive, that there's something worth living *for*. Call it my pro bono contribution to society. Not that any of the wives or girlfriends would thank me.

I never thought of Leo like that. He just looked too damned *young* for me to go dipping my fingers in that particular pie. He came in one night with a look I've seen on a hundred cops' faces before. That bleak, empty-eyed stare of a man who has seen something he wishes he hadn't. It's a hazard of the job and it fades with time, but a little bit of their soul gets replaced by a hard edge of cynicism in the process.

He claimed his usual seat at the bar and gave me a wobbly nod of acknowledgement. I sidled up in front of him, wiping down the already clean mahogany bar.

'Bad night?'

He nodded, studying his hands as if they contained the secrets of the universe.

'What was it? Homicide?'

He jerked his head up. 'How'd you know?'

I shrugged, almost embarrassed by my own nonchalance. Everything I knew about police work was secondhand information. I'd feel differently if I'd been the one standing over the body. 'Seen that expression before. First one, huh?'

'Yeah. Never seen a ... dead person ... before.'

'That sucks,' I said, filling a beer glass with seltzer. 'What's your name, kid?'

'Williams,' he said. 'And I'm no kid.'

'Yeah, I know. What's your first name?'

'Leo, ma'am.'

'Well, Leo, I'm no ma'am. My name is Kayla,' I told him. 'This is my bar.'

'Yeah, I know. The guys told me.'

I wondered what else the guys had told him. Cops talk. They're more gossipy than a bunch of housewives drinking the kitchen sherry. I knew more about their lives than their own families did.

I fished a couple of maraschino cherries out of the container under the bar and dropped them into his glass, sending little tendrils of syrup spiralling down into the carbonated seltzer. I pushed the glass in front of him. 'There you go.'

He held the glass up to the light, studying it. 'What's with the cherries?'

'For your first homicide. You broke your cherry, kiddo.'

He rewarded me with the first smile I'd ever seen on his face, which served to reinforce how young he looked. 'Thanks. You just made my night.'

I felt something spread through my belly the way the cherry syrup spread through his glass. 'Any time,' I said, putting more meaning into the words than I intended.

I left him alone to drink his cherry-flavoured soda, but there wasn't quite so much tension in his shoulders as there had been when he walked in. That made me feel good. Bartending is about more than serving up drinks – it's about understanding people and what they need. Or maybe I'm just trying to justify having the hots for a young cop.

After that, we were on a first-name basis. Some nights, he'd walk in with that familiar dejected expression and say, 'It's cherry time, Kayla.' Then, if the bar was slow, he'd tell me what he'd been through that night. Sometimes he'd wait for me if I was busy and that gave me a little thrill, even though a part of me believed he only saw me as his bartending therapist.

I was there when Leo made his first suicide call and I listened without comment as he described the knife wounds on the woman's wrist and how she looked almost happy in death. He told me about his love of animals and the first time he had to put a bullet in the head of

40

an injured deer hit by a car. I dared to pat his hand when he told me about his first experience with a car full of drunk teenagers, half of them dead on the scene after a collision with a tree. That one brought tears to my eyes, thinking about my own two sons.

They weren't all traumatic events; some were good career firsts. His first search warrant, his first drug arrest, the first court case he won. Other firsts were just plain embarrassing and he'd relate them in hushed tones, looking over his shoulder to make sure none of the other guys overheard his shame. Some things he could laugh at, like the first time he caught a couple going at it in the backseat of a car. That one made him blush and his blushing turned me on.

'They didn't even care that they were sitting there naked,' he said, naïve incredulity in his voice.

'Lust makes people do crazy things.' I thought back to some of my antics, not all of them in the distant past. 'Lust is the devil.'

He shrugged, as if he didn't have a clue. 'I guess.'

We had an easy camaraderie that wasn't quite like what I had with the other guys in the precinct. There was no swagger to Leo, no macho bullshit to peel away like layers of an onion. At night, after I locked up the bar and headed home alone, I thought about Leo in ways that would surely make him blush. Naked, sweaty, hard. Part of my heightened lust was the fact that I wasn't taking anyone home any more. Not for a lack of trying on their part – I just wasn't interested. I tried not to dwell on the reason I wasn't interested.

Then one night Leo came in looking like a man who'd lost his best friend. The lines etched into his exhausted, stricken face aged him by ten years. The bar was hopping more than usual that night, so it took me a good five minutes to make my way down to him.

'Hey, what happened?'

'Dead kid. Five years old,' he said, as if giving a report. 'Wandered off and drowned in the lake.'

'Fuck. I'm sorry.'

He bent his head. I thought he was crying, but then I saw that he cradled something on his lap. 'It was his,' he said, holding up a bedraggled orange and white kitten in his big hands. 'Parents said he was in the yard playing with the cat, last they saw. Thought the father was going to strangle it, so I took it.'

His words were punctuated by rough strokes of the cat's fur. That little furball was all that was holding him together but a kitten wasn't company enough to fight off his demons once the lights went out.

'Let me get Quentin to close up shop for me and I'll get you home.'

'Oh, I'm fine,' he said, a little too loudly.

I ignored him and walked to the other end of the bar. I snagged Quentin as he went by on his way to serve a round of beer to a bunch of rough-looking bikers. 'Can you close for me? I've got something I need to do.'

Quentin looked from me to Leo. He's been with me for seven years, as rough around the edges as some of our customers, but he's a decent bartender and had become a good friend. 'Got yourself another rescue?'

'Something like that.'

He winked, but there was no humour in his knowing expression. 'Just watch yourself, girl. That one's liable to break your heart.'

I laughed. I knew about lust – lust could twist me six ways to Sunday. But love was for other people, and so was heartbreak. I hadn't had enough time to fall in love before I'd fallen pregnant and love wasn't a privilege I'd had as a young wife or a single mother. I hadn't been heartbroken when my abusive ex-husband took off with one of my barmaids ten years ago and left me to finish raising two rambunctious boys. Love sure as hell wasn't a luxury I could afford now. The idea of this sweet young kid breaking through my protective barrier, much less breaking my heart, was ludicrous.

I shook my head and made my way back to Leo, who was trying to keep a hold on the mewling kitten. 'C'mon, rookie. Let's get you home.'

'I haven't had my cherry soda yet.'

I knew he was in shock, so I humoured him. 'I'll make you one at home.'

I guess that's when it dawned on him that I wasn't taking him to his house. 'Oh,' he said, long and slow, drawing it out like a deep, relieved sigh. 'OK.'

Out in the parking lot, I sized him up. 'Are you OK to drive?'

He nodded.

I wasn't convinced, but I let it go because I only live a couple miles from the bar. 'Good. Just follow me.'

My house is on a quiet dead-end road. It's not much, just a little two-bedroom bungalow. The place had seemed cramped with two six-foot teenagers eating me out of house and home, but now with them gone – Ty off to the Army and Nate off to college – it felt huge and lonely.

I waited to get out of my car until Leo's truck pulled in on the gravel driveway behind me and he shut off his engine. He met me at the front door, the kitten tucked in the crook of his arm.

'Hey,' he said, as if we hadn't just seen each other at the bar.

He was nervous, I realised. That didn't surprise me, really. The short drive had given him time to think and nervousness was cutting through the shock. What surprised me was that I was nervous, too.

'Come on in.'

I let us into the darkened house and turned on the lamp by the window, filling the room with a peaceful amber glow. I could feel Leo close behind me, his grief so large it felt like a third person in the room with us. The kitten let out a wail and that seemed to break the nervous tension between us.

'Let's get the little guy some food,' I said. 'I've got tuna and milk to hold him until you can get him some cat food.'

'Thanks. That's really nice of you,' Leo said, his voice thick with a range of emotions. Fleetingly, I wondered if any of those emotions had my name on them.

I took the kitten and gave Leo a little nudge toward the couch. 'Sit. I'll be right back.'

The kitten was a cute little thing. I dumped tuna in a cereal bowl and sat the kitten in front of it while I found a box to line with newspaper for a makeshift litter box, and an old towel for a bed. Once I had everything set up by the radiator in the corner and the kitten was purring over his windfall, I returned to the living room.

Leo didn't look as forlorn as he had at the bar, but he sure as hell didn't look happy. He looked lost. Sad. I sat down next to him, our knees bumping.

'Are you going to be OK?'

He nodded slowly. 'Yeah. It was rough, but I think I'll be OK.'

I nodded along with him. I only knew of one way to get over this nagging feeling that I was robbing the cradle and going to hell for it. I put my hand on the back of his neck and pulled him down for a kiss. I half expected him to resist; I wasn't entirely sure he knew my intentions or would even want what I had to offer. But his lips parted and he kissed me back, a quiet sigh whispering across my mouth.

The funny thing about older men is they forget how to kiss properly. They're all about the fucking. They may spend some time on the foreplay to get a woman ready, but kissing takes a back seat to all the rest. Leo kissed like he knew it was as far as he was ever going to get with me and he was determined to get his rocks off that way. His lips were velvety soft, softer than any man I'd ever been with. It was like kissing a woman except for that little hint of invisible stubble above his upper lip. I moaned when he nibbled my bottom lip, nipping it with his teeth before sweeping his tongue over it to soothe the pinch of pain.

I slid my hands down to his broad shoulders, feeling the muscles bunch under my touch as if he was showing off his gym work. But no, he was just reaching for me, pulling me up against him so he could dip his tongue in my mouth. It was awkward, with him still dressed in his uniform and that damned utility belt getting in the way. I made an anxious little noise in my throat and he pulled back, searching my face.

'Did I hurt you?'

I laughed. 'It's going to take a lot more than kissing me to hurt me, but we need to get you out of that damned uniform.'

I stood and took his hand. He followed me willingly to the bedroom. I didn't turn on the light.

He tried to pull me into his arms once we were standing by my bed, but I slipped away from him. 'First things first.'

I saw a flash of white teeth in the darkness. 'You're not teasing me, are you?'

'Oh baby, I'm no tease,' I said, my voice sounding a little breathless. 'I just want you naked.'

He had no response to that.

I got his utility belt unfastened while he stripped off his shirt, then his vest, with a loud rip of Velcro, then his undershirt. I unfastened his pants and felt the bulge of his erection against my hand. I gave him a squeeze and smiled at his deep moan.

I yanked his pants and underwear down in one swift motion as I slid to my knees. His cock hung heavy in front of me, a shadowy outline of his arousal. I inhaled deeply, revelling in that musky masculine scent. That's all I did, just kneel in front of him and wait.

'Please,' he said, so softly I almost didn't hear him.

'Please, what?'

I *was* teasing him now, trying to ratchet up his arousal – and mine. I like a man to tell me what to do. To make him quiver until he's insistent and rough in his need. I didn't know if Leo had it in him, but I was going to find out.

'Don't make me get the cuffs.'

Despite the threat, the way he said it told me he had no idea how to use handcuffs in a sexual way. The boy might have had the accoutrements for kinky sex at his disposal, but I'd bet my bar that was one cherry he hadn't busted yet. I hadn't been thinking beyond that night, but the possibilities excited me.

'Hmm, you just might have to do that,' I said, knowing he wouldn't.

'You *are* teasing me.'

'Yeah, baby, I am.' I waited a beat. 'This time.'

I heard his sharp intake of breath at the promise of the future. 'Suck it, Kayla,' he said, his voice dropping an octave to become a demanding growl. 'Now.'

I murmured my appreciation of his new-found dominance before I took him in my mouth. Without using my hands, I sucked the head between my lips and listened to his corresponding groan of approval. His erection jerked in my mouth and I took another inch of that velvety warmth.

He caught my long hair up in his hand and moved me gently along his length. Slowly, as if he had all the time in the world to fuck my mouth and intended to enjoy every second. I cupped his balls in one hand, feeling their heavy weight in my palm. He thrust harder into my mouth when I did that, giving my hair a little tug just the way I like it.

I used both hands then, one on his balls and one on his shaft, feeding his erection into my hungry mouth. I had only intended for this to be an appetiser for things to come, but he jerked his hips forward and his dick slipped to the back of my throat. I wasn't ready for it and I gagged, the sound turning me on in my submissive haze of desire. Then he was coming and I was swallowing as fast as I could to keep from gagging more.

I nursed his dick as he came, my hands braced on his thighs to hold him still. I felt a flood of disappointment, my aching pussy still untouched and needing to be filled. But I held him in my mouth until he went soft, the bittersweet taste of him thick on my tongue.

'Damn, baby.' He still held my hair in his hand, moving my head slowly back and forth on his dick. 'That was amazing.'

What was amazing was that his dick was hardening, just moments after his orgasm. I pulled back to look up at him. 'You're getting hard again.'

He just laughed, a full-bellied laugh of masculine pride.

'Oh, hell,' I said in wonder, stroking his rising erection. 'Praise God for younger men.'

Leo pulled me up from the floor and tugged my T-shirt over my head, then thumbed my hard nipples through the thin fabric of my bra. I moaned, feeling a corresponding zing of sensation in my clit. I worked the zipper of my jeans down with trembling fingers. Then it was a frenzy of four hands on my body, with him trying to unfasten my bra while I got my jeans off.

He turned me towards the bed and stumbled, his pants and underwear wrapped around his ankles. He hadn't even taken his work boots off yet.

'Why don't you get yourself undressed and I'll take care of myself?'

I was stretched out naked on the bed by the time he unlaced his boots and got the rest of his uniform off. He stood beside the bed, hesitating.

'What?' I said, afraid he'd changed his mind, even if his dick hadn't.

'Can we turn on a light?' he asked. 'I want to see you.'

I flipped the bedside light on, the amber glow showing me his hard, muscular body. He had an expression of near awe on his face, the wire rims of his glasses winking in the faint light as he stared at me.

'Damn, you're beautiful,' he said. 'I want you so bad.'

Then he did something that made me catch my breath: he slowly and deliberately took off his glasses and put them on my bedside table. Then he climbed on the bed and knelt between my spread thighs. I could feel the wetness pooling at the opening of my pussy, I was so ready for him. I reached for his hips to pull him into me, but he leaned back.

'Who's teasing who now?'

'I've never –' he started, then paused and looked up at the ceiling. 'I mean, I haven't been with a –'

'Oh, fuck.' My whole body tensed up. 'You're a virgin?'

Damn. He really was as cherry as the drinks I made for him. It was one thing that he was a decade and a half younger than me, but I didn't think I could deflower a virgin. Never mind that I'd just blown him, it didn't seem right to do the deed just to scratch an itch, especially after the rough night he'd had. I was so wrapped up in my moral dilemma that it took me a minute to realise he was laughing at me.

'God, I know I look innocent, but I'm no virgin,' he said, shaking his head as he laughed. 'I just meant, I've never been with an older woman before. All my girl-friends have been my age. I just don't want to screw this up.'

To punctuate his comment, he ran his hand up the inside of my thigh, so close to where I wanted him that I gasped. I didn't feel older than him. I didn't feel like the one with more experience. I didn't feel in control of the situation at all. My body was humming with a need only Leo could satisfy.

'It's OK,' I managed to say as I wrapped my hand around his wrist and brought it to my pussy. 'I've never fucked a boy so much younger than me.'

Taking his dick in his other hand, he ran it between my legs, wetting the tip with my juices before rubbing the head against my swollen clit. 'I'm no boy,' he growled. 'I'm a fucking man.'

And then this *man* was *fucking* me. He didn't take his time like he had with my mouth; he pushed the full length of his dick into me in one swift stroke. I went from aching emptiness to almost painful fullness in an instant.

He stayed like that for a minute, buried inside me so deep we were breathing in unison. This was round two for him and his control was better, but I was just as hot for him now as I had been when we left the bar. I pressed my feet to the bed and raised my hips, hoping he'd take the hint.

His soft laugh was indulgent and knowing, with no trace of the tender young rookie I knew. Or thought I knew. 'You want my dick?' he asked, giving me another quick thrust.

I whimpered, raising my hips again to meet the next thrust. 'Oh, yes, baby.'

He stretched out over me and I wrapped my legs around his muscular back and gripped his ass, pulling him deeper. He rocked his pelvis, bottoming out inside me, giving me another twinge of pain that fuelled the ache of desire.

I'd expected hard fucking with no subtleties, but this was something else. Slow and wet, our bodies pressed together in anxious need, with all night to get there. He kissed and sucked my neck, trailed kisses down between my breasts before licking my nipples until I whimpered. He sucked my nipples in time to his thrusts, my pussy making wet slurping sounds as he slid in and out. The sheet beneath me felt damp and the room smelled of sex.

My orgasm built slowly, spiralling out from low in my belly. I felt the first tremors and rocked against him. He sat back on his heels and pressed my knees to the bed, with just the head of his dick inside me. I was splayed open before him, on the verge of coming hard. I writhed on the bed while he watched me.

'Fuck me, Leo,' I gasped. 'Please.'

He thrust into me like he had that first time, the whole length of his dick pushing into me in one startling stroke. He pulled back to the tip and slammed it home again. His deep, unrelenting thrusts started slowly and built to a pace that made it difficult for me to catch my breath. I gasped and screamed as I came and kept coming, clutching at the pillow beneath my head.

'That's it,' he coaxed in that gravel-rough voice. 'Come on my dick.'

He kept saying it, demanding it, his voice and his dick beating a rhythm into my body that was merciless and impossible to ignore. My orgasm seemed to go on for ever and he kept fucking me in long, slow strokes that rubbed against that sweet spot in my pussy. I arched up, taking him as far as I could, then pressed against the bed

53

when it became too much to bear. He reached under me, gripped my ass and pulled me up so I couldn't escape.

'I'm so close, baby.'

'Come for me,' I said, as demanding as he was.

He was quiet, his body going still and tense as his dick throbbed inside me like a separate entity. Then he let out a soulful groan. I rocked my hips to milk every last sensation from his sweat-slick body, my hands soothing the muscles in his back.

We lay like that for a long time until he got too heavy for me and I nudged him off. He had that self-satisfied smile of a man who knows he's done it right. I couldn't argue with that.

He rested his head on my shoulder, his eyelashes tickling my cheek. 'That was so ... nice.'

I laughed. 'I think "nice" is an understatement.'

'Yeah, but my brain is scrambled and I can't think of anything else.'

'Well, if I'm your first older woman, I think maybe I need to make you another cherry soda, huh?'

'Yeah, I guess so.'

The kitten meowed plaintively just then from somewhere in the house. I'd forgotten what had brought us here tonight. Leo had too, judging by the way his body jerked against me at that lonesome cry. The wails grew louder until I heard the snag of claws in fabric and felt the soft press of fur in the small of my damp back.

'He thinks you're his mama,' Leo said.

'They all do. So, are you going to keep him?' I didn't know what else to say. What could I say to this young guy I had nothing in common with but a couple of mind-blowing orgasms?

'I can't have pets at my place. Maybe you could keep him?'

'Sure.' I yawned, feeling the tug of sleep. 'I'm used to taking in strays.'

'And maybe I could come back and visit him?'

He hadn't caught my double meaning, but I caught his. I sighed, but it was a sigh of acquiescence. I'd gone this far, I might as well go all the way, I told myself. I was in no hurry to get rid of him.

'Maybe, but you've got to promise not to fall in love with me. That wouldn't go well for either of us.'

Curling a leg over my hip, he nuzzled my neck the way the kitten was nuzzling my naked back. 'I won't fall in love with you.'

I turned my head and stared at Leo's contented expression, a smile playing on those soft, full lips. He would fall in love with me and it would be messy and emotional and it wouldn't be good for either of us. I closed my eyes and decided I would deal with it when it happened.

Hell, maybe this time I'd fall in love. With a cherry on top.

Fixing What's Broken

Bang. Bang. Bang.

It had been going on all morning. Banging, often followed by cursing. I glared at the door to the garage. What the *hell* was he doing out there? Better question: why wasn't he in here doing *me*?

Bang! Bang! 'Stupid fucking car!' *Bang!*

I couldn't take it any more. My head was starting to throb in time to the banging he was doing – which was a far cry from the banging I wanted to be doing. I opened the door and tried to keep my voice even and serene. 'You OK out here, sweetheart?'

Mark glanced around the hood of his jet-black '69 Mustang. Actually, *glowered* was a better word to describe what he was doing. 'Does it *sound* like I'm doing

56

OK? This piece of shit engine is giving me fits. It used to purr like a kitten and now it rattles like an old man on a respirator. I'm a shit mechanic if I can't make this baby run.'

I bit my tongue to keep from stating the obvious solution. It was a familiar argument. Every time I suggested buying a new car – even a new Mustang – Mark went postal. He was a mechanic by trade and would not hear of parting with his 'baby' no matter how many dollars – or hours – he ended up dedicating to the cause of keeping her running. Or how many hours it cost us in matrimonial togetherness, apparently.

Not that I hadn't known what I was getting into when I married him. Mark had been recommended to me by my friend Hannah when my Mini Cooper had needed some serious work. He'd been so sweet and charming, I hadn't minded the grease under his nails or the fact that he always smelled faintly of gas, oil and that harsh cleaner all men keep in the garage. I had even enjoyed hanging out and watching him work – watching the easy way he moved around a car, admiring his ass when he had his head under a hood. Mark was a manly-man and that had an appeal a girly-girl like myself couldn't resist, even if he did take his work home with him. Or, in this case, *drive* his work home. I was trying to be patient, I swear I was, but a girl can only take so much.

The Mustang had belonged to his father and I knew there was no way he would part with it. And I wouldn't ask him to. But we could afford another car so that the Mustang wasn't his primary means of transportation. Mark wouldn't hear of it. 'A car is meant to be driven, not kept in a garage,' he would say, repeating something his father had said back in the day when money was tight and there were five kids to feed. I tried to remind Mark that our financial situation was far better than his dad's had been – and we didn't even have kids yet to worry about – but my argument was as ridiculous to him as an automatic transmission in a sports car. It was enough to have me banging my head against a wall in frustration.

'Well, why don't you take a break and have lunch with me?'

Mark's head had disappeared under the hood again. 'Maybe in a few minutes,' he mumbled. 'Thanks, babe.'

Bang! Bang! 'You stupid fucking –'

'Right,' I said, slamming the door on the cacophony of noise.

An hour later, when Mark was still a no-show for lunch, I gave up and ate my soup and sandwich alone at the kitchen table. Every weekend, Mark promised he'd give the car repairs a rest and every weekend, there he was, greasy and sweaty and cursing until all hours while I waited for him to return to the land of the living. It hadn't always been like this. He used to put in a couple of hours on the car on Saturday morning and be done with it so that the weekends were our own. But since his father died a couple of years ago Mark seemed to spend more and more time on the car. At first I thought it was just his way of staying close to his dad, some sort of testosterone-fuelled grief process, but it was starting to feel like he was avoiding me.

Enough was enough. Either I needed an all-consuming hobby of my own or I needed to remind Mark that there was another kitten in his life in need of some attention. I didn't want a hobby, though. I wanted my husband back. I decided it was time to bring out the big guns and stop waiting around for what I wanted.

Twenty minutes later, after some primping and a wardrobe change, I carried a sandwich and glass of iced tea out to the garage. Mark didn't notice, of course, because his head was where it always was – buried under the car hood. I smiled, watching his bent head, blond hair tousled and a streak of grease along the back of his neck. His head would be buried some place else momentarily if I had anything to say about it. My confidence wavered for a moment. It's not as if we'd just met and I could lure him with my pussy. Marriage had the effect of softening the edges of our lust. On the other hand, it had been a long time since I'd put this kind of effort into enticing him.

'I brought lunch to you,' I said sweetly. 'Since you're so busy.'

Bang! Bang! Bang! 'Fuck!'

'Honey?'

'Thanks, babe,' he said, not even looking up.

Not easily deterred, I put the sandwich plate and glass on his workbench and leaned against the car. 'You really should eat something. It's after three and I'm not making dinner.'

I didn't know if it was the tone in my voice or the fact that I was in the garage for more than thirty seconds, but Mark finally looked up. Looked up and did a long, slow double take. Then he straightened to his full six-foot-two height and gave me a long, slow smile that made my toes curl in my four-inch shiny patent-leather fuck-me pumps. Even with the shoes, I was still several inches shorter than him. I felt a shiver of desire looking up at Mark, his broad shoulders straining the seams of his old white T-shirt. We'd been together since high school, but he still took my breath away.

I returned his smile and crossed my arms under my breasts, accentuating the low, low cut of my wispy white blouse and the fact that I was not wearing a bra. While his gaze hovered at my cleavage, I spread my legs slightly and watched the marionette-like shift of his eyes downward, to the denim skirt cut so short I was practically flashing him and the red heels that were a remnant from an ill-fated pole-dancing class I'd taken three years ago.

'Going somewhere?' Mark asked, though it took him three tries to get the words out.

'Coming, not going.' I licked my bottom lip, glistening with a lipstick appropriately called *Sexy Harlot*, and smiled. 'I hope.'

I'm pretty sure he wouldn't have heard a 747 landing in the backyard at that moment. 'Uh-huh.'

'What's the matter, sweetheart?'

He was trying hard to focus on my face and failing miserably. 'Did I miss a holiday or something?'

I walked around him – enjoying the way he pivoted to watch me – and slammed the hood of the Mustang. I slid up on the car, feeling the cold metal against the back of my bare thighs. 'Nope. No holiday that I know of.'

To his credit, he didn't comment on how hard I closed the hood or on the fact that I was sitting on his 'baby'. Maybe there was hope for him after all. The good thing about being together so long was that I knew exactly which buttons to push – and how far to push them – to get what I wanted. I might have gotten a little complacent with familiarity and my skills might have been a little rusty, but it was all coming back to me now. And I intended to make the most of every trick I had up my sleeve – or up my skirt, as the case may be.

Mark visibly swallowed when I braced my heels on the bumper of the Mustang. I wiggled on the hood, making a show of tugging at the frayed hem of my impossibly short skirt that I wouldn't wear outside this garage. Normally, Mark would have gone nuts at the possibility of me scratching his precious paint job, but he didn't so much as grunt a protest. I actually believe he might have forgotten about the car altogether. I bit my lip seductively and smiled. Chalk one up for feminine wiles and a neglected libido.

'Do you think this skirt is too short?'

Mark's gaze was riveted between my legs. He stared as if all the answers of the universe were contained in that shadowy space. 'Too short? Um, I guess it depends on what you're looking for.'

'I'm looking for a little attention,' I said, running a finger along my bare thigh.

At that, Mark puffed out his chest like a rooster, all gruff, masculine possessiveness. 'From *who*?'

I lowered my eyelashes. 'Hmm. Well, not you. You're too *busy* for me lately.'

'I see,' Mark said. 'This is a ploy to get me away from the car.'

'Do you think that's even possible?' I crossed my legs, rotated my ankle and swung my red pump back and forth in front of him. 'Can I distract you from your precious Mustang for a little while?'

'I think I can spare a few minutes.'

Mark started toward me, his gaze fixed on the hem of my skirt and the sweetness it hid, but I wagged a discouraging finger at him. 'Hold it one minute there, big boy. I don't want a few *minutes* of your time.'

'Huh?'

I tried not to roll my eyes. 'Focus, baby.'

He finally glanced up at my face. 'What's up, Cat?'

'You've been distant,' I said, trying to keep the levity in my voice and still convey how concerned I was. 'I miss you.'

Despite my tone, his expression closed down. 'Sorry, I just need to get this car running –'

'It's not going to bring him back,' I said gently.

He jerked like I'd slapped him. 'That's not why –'

'Yeah, it is, honey. You miss him, I know you do. And you love this car almost as much as you loved him.' I stretched out my hand to rub my thumb across the grease spot on his bicep. 'I know that.'

He sighed, covering my hand with his own. 'I can't get rid of the car, Cat.'

'I never want you to. But maybe it's time to consider getting another car, huh?' I shifted on the hood, the skirt sliding up another inch. 'Take a break from the constant maintenance so we can enjoy the weekends together?'

He nodded. 'Yeah, maybe it's time.'

'I miss you, baby,' I said, putting all my longing and

lust into the words. I was already wet, creaming at just the thought of him being inside me.

'Your legs look a mile long in that skirt.'

And just like that, we shifted from serious conversation to full-on seduction. I was more than ready for it, and for him. But that didn't mean I wasn't planning on making him work for it.

I lay back on the hood of the car, braced myself on my elbows and placed my foot in the centre of his chest. 'You're not getting anywhere near me until you promise me some time.'

'How much time do you want?'

Tugging at my skirt – up rather than down – I revealed a tiny, lacy navy-blue thong. 'How much time have you got?'

I didn't give him a chance to respond. He opened his mouth to say something and I hooked two fingers in my thong and pulled it aside. I watched his expression turn from amusement to lust. *Bam*. Just like that. Amazing what a glimpse of pussy will do to a man.

'Damn. When did you do that?' he asked, referring to my fresh Brazilian wax.

I teased him by running my fingers over my bare skin. 'Two days ago. You might have noticed if you'd come to bed last night instead of staying out here with your car until I was asleep.'

I might as well have been speaking Latin. He could

not take his eyes off my hand playing between my legs. Slowly, so he wouldn't miss a thing, I slid one finger between the lips of my bare pussy. The purpose of this little exhibitionistic show was to get Mark hot and bothered, but I was so hot and wet I forgot about him for a moment and focused on pleasuring myself.

Dragging some of my moisture up over my clit, I gasped. 'I've been doing this three or four times every weekend because you're too busy lately. See what you miss when you're working on your car?'

'I'm seeing that.' Mark wrapped his hand around my ankle and moved my foot from his chest. 'But I'm not working on my car now.'

I kicked off my pumps and braced my heels against the hood of the car. 'No, you're not.

It's nice to have your undivided attention for a change.'

'You definitely have my attention,' he said roughly. 'I just wish you'd said something a hell of a lot sooner if this was the end result.'

'Me, too.'

'Damn, Catherine, I'm about to burst through my pants, you've got me so worked up.'

I smiled, noting his sizeable erection in his grease-stained jeans. 'I see that. It's about damn time.'

'Yeah, it is, isn't it?'

Mark moved closer, running his hands up my shins to my knees as I masturbated. He gently pressed my legs apart, until I was splayed across the hood of the car. Fully exposed to his view, I paused in stroking my clit to hold my labia open with two fingers.

'Like what you see?'

Mark nodded, gaze riveted.

'Want a lick?'

Again, he nodded.

'Lick it,' I demanded in a voice that didn't sound at all like me but was, suddenly and passionately, *all* me. 'Now.'

Mark wasted no time in leaning between my spread thighs and running his tongue slowly up the length of my pussy. He held my legs apart, pushing them up and back until my knees nearly touched the hood of the car. I was fully exposed to his gaze – and his questing mouth – but I needed more. I felt open, empty ... and I wanted to be filled.

'Push your tongue inside me,' I whispered.

I was never this demanding. I was the quiet type in bed, moving him where I wanted with a sigh or a moan or my hands. But we weren't in bed – and the combination of my slutty outfit and being spread out on Mark's car like some kind of porn star was making me bold. I felt as if I was waking up from a very long sleep, all these months of waiting for Mark to snap out of his grief, trying to be patient but just becoming more and more resentful.

I knew we still had some work to do and that it wasn't all better just because I'd concocted a silly plan to seduce him. But maybe this wake up call of what we had – what we'd always had in good times and bad – was a much-needed reminder for both of us. I hoped so. And, judging by the way Mark was staring at me, teasing me by making me wait, I think he was hoping for the same thing.

I sighed as he finally fulfilled my command. His tongue was velvety soft between my juicy slit as he nudged the opening of my pussy before circling around my clit. He made figure eights along the thick lips of my labia, tormenting me mercilessly before dipping back into my wetness. I squirmed against his tongue, but had nowhere to go as he held me pinned to the hood. Not that I wanted to go anywhere. I was exactly where I wanted to be, even if it wasn't the most comfortable place to be.

My smell – the sweet and salty scent of my wet pussy and the hint of floral perfume I'd dabbed on my thighs – aroused my senses as it blended with the musky garage smells of oil, rubber and sweat. I was out of my element amongst all this testosterone and grease, but I suddenly felt like I was the one with the power. I reached down and gripped Mark's head between my thighs, pressing him into me as I ground against his mouth. The combination of the hard metal car beneath me and Mark's silky tongue on my pussy was driving me closer and closer to release. I moaned, on the brink of orgasm, and heard my voice echoing off the concrete walls and floor.

Rocking my pelvis against Mark's mouth, whimpering and gasping, so close to release, balancing on a razor's edge between pleasure and tension. Then Mark slid two fingers into me as his tongue nursed my clit and I nearly levitated off the car as my orgasm spiralled through me. A gush of liquid heat trickled down my ass as Mark stroked my pussy, every nerve ending throbbing as I clamped my thighs around his head. I clung to him, hands and legs, until I thought I couldn't take another second of contact. But he kept stroking me, licking me, drawing every last sensation from my sweat-slick body.

'Enough, enough,' I wailed, pulling his hair hard to get him to release me. 'I can't take any more. I'm too sensitive.'

Mark pulled back, an amused grin on his glistening mouth. 'Enough? Are you sure? I thought you wanted more than a few minutes?'

Still trembling through the aftershocks, I pulled my knees together and put my hand low on my stomach. 'I do. I do. I just need a minute.'

I closed my eyes, my thighs quivering from the exertion of being held apart. I heard the rasp of Mark's zipper and a soft moan escaped my lips. Eyes still closed, I felt him anchor my legs around his hips and pull the crotch of my panties aside again. I felt like I was falling, sliding, helpless. I reached out for him and my hands caught in his T-shirt. Then the head of his cock was nudging my pussy, opening me to him. He slid up and dragged his cock over my still-sensitive clit, my thighs quivering anew as I went rigid beneath his silky soft touch.

'Oh, God,' I moaned. 'Oh, God. That's – I don't know if I can take it.'

'Relax,' he soothed. 'You're so wet. I want to be inside you. I *need* to be inside you.'

And then he slowly pushed into me until he was buried inside me, filling me up in a way his tongue could only hint at. I moaned as I hooked my legs around him and pulled him down on top of me. I slid down the hood and was impaled further on his erection. Metal and flesh, hardness and softness, my body was ricocheting from one sensation to the next, need overruling everything. The need to be filled, to be fucked, to be held. I was so needy. And Mark was there to give me everything I asked for – and everything I didn't.

He took his sweet time with me, as if he wasn't as needy as I was, sliding out to the tip of his cock before pushing back inside me. The squishy sounds of my pussy seemed incongruous in the garage – illicit, naughty. Dirty. I clung to him, not caring if he got grease on my skin or sweat all over my delicate white blouse, caring only about how it felt to have him inside of me like this. I raked my nails roughly down the back of his T-shirt, rending the thin fabric as I urged him on. I wanted everything he could give me, as hard as he could give it to me.

'More, baby, please,' I gasped. 'More. Harder.'

Mark thrust inside of me, again and again, the car's shock absorbers setting me in motion as we bounced. I cried out again, not caring that my voice echoed off the walls and that the neighbours could likely hear. The thought turned me on even more. I was aroused again, as if I hadn't just had a full-body orgasm. My pussy, swollen and wet, gripped Mark's cock the way I held onto him with my body. Maybe it was because we were fucking in the garage or maybe it was the fact that I'd taken the initiative, but I couldn't remember being this turned on in a long, long time. I could feel the promise of another orgasm building inside me and I rocked up to meet his thrusts, my clit rubbing roughly against his pelvic bone on every upstroke.

He slid his hand under my ass, giving me something softer to push against than the car hood. He raised me up as he fucked me, pulling me on and off his cock so hard I whimpered. The barest hint of pain only fuelled my passion and drove me higher. I arched my back, every muscle quivering in anticipation as he drove into me. So ready, so hot and wet ... I felt as if I was coming apart when another orgasm crashed over me. He kept fucking me hard and fast, not giving me a moment's rest from the unrelenting sensation of fullness.

Then he went still, buried inside me as far as he could go. I was still floating in a haze of orgasmic release, so it took me a moment to realise he was coming, too. But then I heard the telltale catch in his breath and felt the shift from need to release in the way he moved inside me. He pulled me up off the car then, his hands supporting me under my thighs, his cock so deep inside me I whimpered, both of us trembling as his cock pulsed inside my quivering cunt. I wrapped my arms around him for support and bit his neck hard, screaming against his salty skin. Rocking ever so slightly against him, I was rewarded with his guttural moan.

Slowly, he lowered me back onto the car and I wrinkled my nose at the cold wetness that assaulted the backs of my thighs. I squirmed to the edge of the hood to avoid it, smearing my juices as I went. He noticed and I expected him to be horrified. Instead, he threw back his head and laughed, the deep, satisfied laugh of a man well loved and well fucked.

'I'm sorry, baby,' he said. 'I've had my head someplace else and I didn't realise how far away I'd gotten until you showed me.'

'I think I showed us both.' I shifted uncomfortably. 'And this has been fun, but maybe we should take it inside?'

He caught my wrist in his hand as I sat up. 'I don't know,' he said. 'We haven't even tried out the back seat yet.'

71

I laughed, enjoying the look of possession in his eyes as he pulled me toward him. 'Are you kidding? Really?'

'Sure, why not?'

I eyed the car with new appreciation. 'And the front seat, maybe?'

'Sure, why not?' he echoed me. 'If I can't get her running right, I can think of a few other good uses for her. And they all involve you, naked.'

That's all it took. I scrambled off the hood and was indeed sprawled naked in the back seat before he could get his pants the rest of the way off. I opened my arms to him as he folded his big frame into the car and pressed his body on top of me.

He sighed, sounding utterly content. 'You know I'm never going to be able to look at this car again without getting a hard on, right? Maybe it's better she doesn't run any more – wouldn't want to risk an accident because my dick is draining the blood from my brain.'

'I'm sorry about the car, but you definitely know how to make *me* purr,' I whispered, and nipped at his shoulder with renewed desire.

'Good.' He moved against me, rubbing against my wetness until I moaned against his shoulder, his cock slowly thickening against me. 'Because that's all that matters.'

Love and Lust

I had been in a few relationships, but never one like this. Never with someone who had broken down every wall that I attempted to build, who left me feeling raw and exposed and vulnerable. *Vulnerable.* Me. I was the one that had ended every relationship I had ever been in, but the idea of leaving Christopher was incomprehensible. It was love, I guess. Maybe I had never really been in love before. Maybe you can't really know what it means to be in love until you meet someone who gets into your head and knows you better than yourself. It's a scary thing, having no secrets, no way to protect yourself. You have to trust that the one you love also loves you back – and I wasn't so sure Christopher did. That, more than the vulnerability, scared me. Not that he might not love

me – I could live with that – but that he might be the
one to leave me. I was the one who escaped from relationships first. I was the one to say enough was enough.
But with Christopher there was no such thing as enough.
I wanted more. And I wanted him to *want* to give it to
me.

The doorbell rang and I responded like Pavlov's dog.
My breath caught in my throat, my nipples tightened
and I felt a spasm low in my belly. It annoyed me, and
to give him so much power over me seemed dangerous,
but I had no real control over it. I didn't *give* him anything
– my body simply responded to what I felt whether I
wanted it to or not. I was in love, damn it all to hell,
and there was nothing I could do about it. And now my
thoughts scattered to the wind because Christopher was
here.

'Hello, Laura.' He dropped a kiss on my upturned lips
as I opened the door. 'How are you?'

'I'm good. It's nice to see you.'

We sounded like strangers at a cocktail party, but I
knew I was only responding to his stiffness and formality.
Despite the affectation that made him seem distant, it
was almost too easy to imagine myself as his wife,
welcoming home my tired spouse. That image gave way
to a more likely one of the bewitching mistress, desired,
yet disposable when the time came. Mistress wasn't right,
either, because it suggested a relationship we didn't have.

There was no wife waiting at home for Christopher. He was all mine. Except he wasn't. The barriers he had broken down in me were always in place for him. He probed my vulnerabilities and urged me to let go, something he could never bring himself to do. At least not with me.

'You look pretty this evening. I like your hair down like this. You look very different, relaxed.' His voice dropped to a husky drawl as he pulled me close and tangled his fingers in my long brown hair. 'I can see your breasts through your shirt, bad girl.'

I didn't bother telling him that I had chosen the sheer blouse and forgone a bra for just that reason. He already knew. 'Thank you, Christopher,' I murmured, pulling away and reaching for the glass of wine on the table. 'Do you want some wine?'

'Of course.'

I felt like the exhausted prey at the end of a long cat-and-mouse chase. Except the evening had only begun. My hand trembled slightly and the wine sloshed up the side of the glass as I handed it to him.

I watched him while he drank his wine. He wasn't a handsome man, not in the conventional sense. He was tall enough that he attracted attention wherever we went, but his face was angular, his nose prominent, and his often serious expression rendered him harsh and hawk-like. But he had the lean body of a runner and everything

75

about him suggested movement even when he sat still. Watching his long tapered fingers manipulate the stem of the wine glass made me shiver. He was energy and power in one tightly controlled package and I longed to be the one to snap his control and experience that energy and power in its purest form. Or so I fantasised.

His gaze never left my face as he pressed the glass to my lips. 'Have a sip, love.'

I drank and his cool fingertips stroked my throat as I swallowed. It was an oddly intimate sensation and I fought to control my throat muscles. Then he poured too quickly and I couldn't swallow it all. The wine trickled from the corner of my mouth and I reached for it, but he quickly caught the drop of crimson on his fingertip. He stared through me with his ice-blue gaze as he sucked the liquid from his finger. I shivered. I knew that look and what it promised.

'Come,' he said, taking my hand and leading me towards the bedroom. The word was more than a command, it was a prophecy of the evening ahead of us.

I followed him down the short hall.

Standing in front of me in the doorway, he sighed. 'It's ridiculous to become attached to a piece of furniture, but I really do love this bed.'

The bed had belonged to my mother and my grandmother before her. It was too big for a cramped one-bedroom apartment, taking up most of the floor and giving me mere inches of space all the way around, but it was a small sacrifice to make and I made it willingly. I loved the bed and everything it represented – peaceful slumber, a respite from reality, uninhibited passion. It was adorned with white sheets and a white down comforter and a dozen pillows in white and beige, all on top of a ridiculously thick pillow-top mattress. All of that white offset the ornate bronze frame that gleamed in the light of the dozen or so candles I'd lit before he arrived. I felt like a princess in that bed, but there was nothing virginal and innocent about it. It was the essence of seduction and I was the wicked princess filled with carnal desires. And that made Christopher my handsome prince, right? Or was he the evil sorcerer, intent on enslaving me, body and soul? The latter seemed more accurate.

He pulled me towards the bed and reached for the buttons of my gauzy blouse. He peeled the cloth away slowly, kissing my exposed skin here and there as he went. I felt like I was shedding the skin that the rest of the world saw and revealing my true self for him only.

'I've missed you,' he murmured.

His confession left me breathless.

I was his graduate assistant and saw him three days a week at the university, but I knew what he meant.

'I missed you, too,' I breathed against his mouth as his hard, warm lips slid against mine. I caught my breath as he moved down the hollow of my throat. 'I – I love you.'

He pressed his cool fingertips against my lips. 'Shh. Get on the bed now.'

He helped me climb onto the tall bed and I knelt before him, wearing only a pair of faded denim jeans, the knees torn out and worn spots on the insides of my thighs. He stood in front of me, stroking the swell of my breasts until my skin dimpled with gooseflesh.

'I love your breasts, they're so beautiful,' he murmured, taking my small tight nipples between his fingers and tugging. 'So responsive.'

I moaned low in my throat at the slight hint of pain, my hands automatically coming up to cover his.

'Put your hands behind your back,' he said softly, but the words were very much a command.

I eagerly complied, anticipating what my obedience would bring. 'Yes, Christopher.'

The barest hint of a smile came to his lips. 'You must have missed me very much to be so agreeable.'

I could only nod. I hated that I was so transparent in my need for him. That he seemed so cool and controlled in the face of my runaway heart. But as I knelt there, my taut nipples between his fingertips and wetness gathering between my thighs, I didn't care. This was an addiction I had no interest in curing.

My hips moved imperceptibly, or so I thought, as I

rubbed my clit against the unyielding seam of my jeans. The relief was bittersweet – enough to take the edge off, but not nearly enough to give me the release I wanted. Only he could do that, and he was in no hurry to offer me anything but this slow, sweet torment.

'I didn't tell you to move.' He slapped the side of my bare breast with the palm of his hand hard enough to make my breast sway. 'Stay still.'

It didn't hurt, but the sharp sound made me gasp. I dropped my chin to my chest, properly chastised and loving every second of it.

His slid his hand down my belly and over my jeans. I tried so hard not to arch my hips towards him, but I couldn't help myself. I could never help myself with him. He brought out impulses that were impossible to control. Lust, I told myself, my brain fuzzy from the endorphin rush he was already raising in me. Just lust. But I knew it was more than that. I could walk away from lust. I couldn't walk away from this.

He cupped my denim-covered crotch in the palm of his large hand and squeezed hard. 'You are so hot down here,' he murmured, alternately squeezing and releasing. 'So hot and needy.'

'If you keep that up,' I gasped as his middle finger rode the seam of my jeans, 'I will come.'

'We can't have that, can we?' He removed his hand and I bit back a groan. 'Undress me, Laura.'

I blinked, his words barely registering in my lust-addled brain. Then I realised what he had said and reached for his tie. In a haze that felt as if I was moving in slow motion through molasses, I removed the crisp burgundy tie, then his shirt, my fingers fumbling with the buttons. He helped me by slipping off his shoes and socks while I worked at his belt. It was an expensive piece of stiff dark leather that I had known intimately on other occasions. I shivered, wondering what he had in mind for me tonight. Whatever it was, I would spend many hours masturbating shamelessly to the memory of it, as I did with all of our erotic encounters. However fleeting the experiences, the memories lingered on and on, tormenting me with their sweetness and making me long for more – more pain, more pleasure, more Christopher.

I unfastened his trousers and guided the zipper down over his semi-hard penis, my fingers brushing along his length. He was as large there as everywhere else and my cunt throbbed in remembrance. His trousers dropped to the ground and he stepped out of them. I reached for the waistband of his boxers then, but he caught both of my wrists in his hands, pressing his fingers into their boniness hard enough to leave marks.

'No. I want you to use your mouth on me.'

I whimpered in anticipation as I bent over, still on my knees, and pressed my lips to his cloth-covered cock. It twitched against my mouth, hardening, lengthening, as

I traced the outline of his arousal with my tongue. Finally, I zeroed in on the swollen head, sucking the engorged tip between my lips. He stood there, hands at his sides, silently observing me. I sucked him until the cloth of his shorts was soaked through and I could see hard, dark pink flesh beneath the pale blue cotton.

'Enough,' he ordered, pulling me away by my hair. 'Are you hungry for me, Laura?'

I nodded, licking my lips and imagining I could taste him. 'Oh, yes,' I breathed, my hips moving in a natural rhythm again.

'Let me feel you.'

I sat up and his hand went back between my legs. My cunt felt swollen, almost uncomfortably so, against the tight denim. He squeezed my flesh hard until I made a noise that was somewhere between a moan and a plea. It felt as if he was wringing the wetness out of me.

He pulled his hand away and showed it to me. His palm glistened. 'You wet straight through your jeans,' he said, sounding pleased with his discovery. 'Taste yourself.'

He held his hand to my mouth and I licked his palm, tasting my essence. Then I sucked his fingers into my mouth one at a time, teasing him until he pulled away and stripped off his boxers. His cock jutted out at me, thick and heavily veined. He slowly ran his hand up the length of his shaft to the swollen red knob, taunting me the way I'd taunted him. I felt myself leaning towards him, nearly losing my balance in an effort to be closer to his hard body.

'This is what you want, isn't it? This is what you need.'

A crystal-clear drop of arousal appeared at the tip, a reminder that I wasn't the only one who was in need right now, no matter how controlled he might be. That thought made me smile. He wasn't the only one with power.

I licked my lips and leaned forward to suck him into my mouth, but he stepped back from the bed, as far as the dresser behind him would allow. I made a sound of disappointment low in my throat. My hips were swaying to a rhythm all their own as I rubbed my cunt against the soaked crotch of my jeans. 'Please, Christopher. I want you. I can't take any more.'

That wasn't true, of course, and he called me on it. Christopher had tested my limits many times over and I would have been disappointed if he had given in to my request so quickly. Maybe that's why I loved him so much. Where other men were easily manipulated, Christopher maintained self-control even when he was hard and wanting. He not only played the game, he played it even better than I did.

He laughed. 'I'm going to push you as far as you can go, Laura. And then I'm going to push you some more.'

'I know,' I whispered.

A smile still lingered on his lips. 'Show me how much you want me.'

I tugged at my jeans, but they were so tight they clung to my damp skin. I lost my balance and tumbled sideways on the bed before I got them down around my knees. I plunged my hand between my thighs, dipping my fingers into my wetness. I moaned in relief, but also in frustration because I wanted him inside me.

'Greedy, greedy,' Christopher reprimanded me. He grabbed the waistband of my jeans and jerked them the rest of the way off, turning them inside out in the process. Then he wrapped his arm around my waist and flipped me over onto my stomach as if I weighed nothing. 'Show me your ass, love.'

I did as he said, my back arched, my bare ass stuck in the air before him. My fingers never stopped working between my spread thighs. I knew he'd make me stop soon enough, knew I'd never reach orgasm before he did, but I couldn't stop. My need was too great.

His hands spanned my narrow hips and he pulled me back against his cock. He didn't go into me, not yet. He held me there, quivering against his hardened shaft, both of us breathing roughly. He hadn't even told me he wanted me yet, but I knew it in the hardness of his cock and the roughness of his hands. He wanted me as much as I wanted him. I marvelled over that truth every time we were together – how did I ever forget it? Why did I ever question it? His every action and every word showed me how much he wanted me, even if he didn't say it. I was as much his drug as he was mine.

Then he uttered one word. 'Beg.'

My mind was reeling with thoughts but my mouth couldn't form a coherent response. I whimpered. I felt a primal need to scream, to cry out in longing. Finally, in a voice I didn't recognise, I gasped, 'Please, Christopher. Please, fuck me. Please.'

He thrust into me then, that one powerful stroke driving me nearly halfway across the wide expanse of the bed. 'Yes!'

'Please, please, please,' I continued to plead even though he was giving me what I wanted, for fear he would stop if I stopped begging.

He drove himself into me, over and over, driving all reason out of my mind in the process. I could feel his emotions in his thrusts, there was nothing aloof or distant in the way he fucked me, no walls between us. He was raw with lust and need that were as real and as strong as mine. I took what he gave, but I gave in return – thrusting back against him, clenching my muscles tightly around him, working my hand down between my legs to rub his balls and stroke his wet shaft as he slid out of me.

We were equals here in this mind-space of emotional desire and physical release, equals and halves, completing each other in a way no other could. At least in a way no one else could for me. The idea that Christopher might feel this connection with anyone else was enough to stop my heart in my chest, but I knew, I felt, that there could be no other. Between the narrow space of his true self and the wall he kept up so much of the time, there was no room for anyone except me. Only me.

It was only in moments like this, only when he was lost inside me, that I truly felt like he was mine, that I had all of him, including his heart. I was torn between needing to come and wanting to make it last as long as I could. My need, denied too long, won out. Orgasm washed over me, tingling up from my belly and spreading along my skin, making my cunt wetter and my nipples harder, making my muscles go rigid and my neck arch.

I screamed his name as I came, panting raggedly like a woman in labour. He let me come alone and I knew he was listening to me, watching me, memorising every detail of my physical response. Noting the way I gasped when he slid halfway out of my clenching cunt, the way I arched my back even harder and pushed against him to keep him inside of me. The way I whimpered and trembled like a newborn pup when he shoved his cock into me again, filling the space he had left.

When my orgasm had faded to the faintest of ripples, he gave three short, deep thrusts and came with a guttural moan. His cock swelled and throbbed inside me as his breath quickened and his hands tightened on my hips, enough to leave bruises in their wake. I felt him go still and tense behind me, his chest draped over my lower back as he came down from the rush of release.

At last he pulled away from my damp body and I collapsed on my stomach. After such a feeling of fullness, I felt bereft at his absence. No amount of time was ever enough to feel him inside of me. At least, I hadn't experienced it yet.

He stretched out on the bed and I rolled towards him, a hand still clenched between my damp thighs. I watched the gentle rise and fall of his chest as his breathing evened out. I reached out to lay a hand on his chest, over his heart, but I pulled away.

'Christopher, do you love me?'

He glanced at me the way a man might glance at another passenger on a bus, as if suddenly realising he's not alone. 'Why do you ask? Are you feeling all romantic in your big bed?'

'It's a simple question.' I felt my own protective emotional barrier go up, the intimacy of a moment before drying like sweat on my damp skin. 'It's OK if you don't,' I said, sounding as pathetic as I felt. 'I just wondered, since you've never said it.'

'Do you think I love you?'

How could I answer that question and not sound needy or conceited? I shook my head, something hard and cold settling behind my breastbone like a rock. 'I don't know. Why can't you just answer the question and tell me?'

'What do you think this is between us?'

He was like that, always responding to my questions with questions of his own. Forcing me to analyse my motives for even asking in the first place. Why did I want to know? What did it matter? I was finishing my PhD and would go wherever I could find an academic job. I couldn't stay where I was just because of Christopher.

Unless he loved me, too.

The thought, the faintest whisper in my heart of hearts, is why I asked. Why I needed to know.

'Do you love me?' I asked again, on a rush of breath that left me feeling as if I would suffocate if he didn't say what I needed to hear.

'I love your body and how it responds to my words and my touch. I love your clever, inquisitive, sexy mind,' he said, reaching to tug at my bottom lip, which I realised was quivering, the only hint that I was feeling any emotion at all. 'I love the way you whisper my name – and scream it. The way you grow your hair long just for me even though you'd rather keep it short and simple.

'I love that you know my favourite wine and how to touch me to get me instantly hard,' he continued. 'I love how we fuck – and how we make love, because there is very much a difference between the two and you fulfil me in both ways. In all ways.'

He paused, and in that space I asked, 'Is that all?'

'Isn't that enough?' he asked, his eyes impossible to read. 'What more do you want?'

'Your heart.' I whispered it so softly, I wasn't sure he heard. I wasn't sure I even wanted him to hear. I had my answer in the words he did not say and the rest, lovely, beautiful, sexy compliments all, didn't matter a whit to me.

He closed his eyes and I thought he was going to sleep. Then he turned to me and gathered me in his arms, roughly yet somehow tenderly, and pressed a kiss to my lips that was enough to spark my arousal all over again.

'I love you, Laura. Of course I love you. It's in every word, every look, every action,' he said, sounding slightly exasperated, as if I'd asked for the combination to a lock and he couldn't remember the digits. 'You have my heart and I love you with all of it, almost to the point of anything else. And it scares the hell out of me.'

'It scares me, too,' I whispered, tucking my head against his shoulder.

'Then let's be scared together,' he said, giving me a little shake. 'Love me and I will love you and we'll be scared together.'

It was me that was falling asleep, every need I had satiated by this man whose kisses were rough and sweet and whose touch left bruises on my body. I had his heart and he was as terrified of that as I was.

'Yes,' I said. 'Yes. Let's be scared together.'

Healing the Wounds

The clock hanging on the wall behind me ticked loudly. I dug my fingers into the arms of the leather chair and studied the man behind the big desk. Jason looked older than I remembered. He still had the same square jaw and blue eyes, but the face had more lines, the hair more silver. There was a sag in his shoulders that had never been there before. That shouldn't be there now.

It had been nine months – no, ten, I amended – but he looked like he had aged ten years. I was one to talk, of course. I resisted the urge to brush a tendril of hair from my cheek, certain that my severely cut short hair made me look like a matronly grandmother. It had been a dramatic move, cutting off my shoulder-length hair, but I didn't regret it. I had needed a change – a change

I could control. I had lost my husband. Cutting my hair off the day after his funeral, the thick wavy curls he had adored so much falling like black feathers to the white bathroom floor, had seemed a fitting tribute. And I had maintained the short length and natural colour, despite the silver that increasingly threaded through the cropped curlicues.

'I never thought I'd see you sitting behind a desk.'

It was true. Jason wasn't the sedentary type any more than Randy had been. The two of them were like thoroughbreds in a race for the triple crown – powerful and fast and meant to run until their hearts stopped.

He shrugged, a smudge of colour coming into his ruddy cheeks as if I'd accused him of looking at porn at work. 'I was too old to stay on active duty, and defence contracting pays the bills. It's not so bad.'

'No?' One word, but that's all it took to make his cheeks redden even more.

I knew the age comment was a lie. I knew why he was no longer a SEAL. I glanced at the photo on the file cabinet behind him – a picture of Randy and him in sand-coloured fatigues, standing in some desert somewhere in the mid-90s. The years had been kind to Jason and he was in as good shape now as he had been then. Age had nothing to do with him leaving the military. It was the man next to him in the picture that was the reason for the suit and tie and mahogany desk in a nondescript office building amid a landscape of concrete and asphalt.

'I'm surprised to see you,' he said. 'You look ... good.'

The hesitation intrigued me. I laughed. 'What were you really going to say? I want to know.'

He hesitated a moment longer, as if gauging what my reaction to the truth would be. He knew me well enough to know I'd settle for nothing less than his honesty. It was ironic, considering the secret I had kept for so long. 'I was going to say you look older, but that seemed rude.'

'I was just thinking the same thing about you,' I said. 'And I *am* older. Forty in August. I was twenty-five when we ... met.'

It was his turn to laugh, though it was more of a bark than a chuckle. 'We're both getting old, aren't we?'

'In some ways. In other ways, it seems like I'm still that girl.'

I didn't have to specify *what* girl. He knew. We both knew. But neither of us was going to say it out loud. The elephant in the room would have to wait patiently for a while longer. We had another dance to do first.

'So why did you come, Cele?'

His abbreviation of my name – he was the only person to call me anything other than Cecelia – gave me a jolt. I had a flash of a memory, passing in a moment, of him cupping my face in his hands and saying, 'I need you, Cele.'

I shook my head to clear the cobwebs and bring me back to the present. Front and centre to the last man who had seen my husband alive.

'I want to know what happened that day.'

His expression didn't change. 'Why?'

'You were his best friend. You were there,' I said. 'I need to know –'

'No, you don't,' he interrupted. 'You need closure and I can't give it to you.'

I clenched my hands into fists. 'Stubborn as always, Jason? Still?'

He smiled and it was as if the years melted away. 'Me? Cele, you're the most tenacious woman I've ever met. How many times did you call me? Office, home, cell. Hell, you even called my ex-wife.'

I could feel heat suffusing my cheeks. 'I didn't know you'd gotten divorced.'

'Of course not,' he said gruffly. 'I didn't even tell Randy we'd separated. By the time it was finalised –'

'I'm sorry,' I said softly. I was sorry for so much.

His easy shrug belied his grief at all the losses he'd suffered. 'Life goes on.'

'For some of us.'

It was his turn to look pained. 'Sorry. I'm – sorry.'

'Life goes on,' I said. 'Right?'

'Jesus, Cele.' He smacked his hand on the desktop, the vibration causing a ceramic mug to fall off the edge and crash on the floor, shattering into a hundred jagged fragments. 'I don't know how to talk to you. I don't know what to say to you.'

'Tell me what happened. I've turned it over and over in my mind and I just need to hear it from you. I trust you.' Another irony. There were so many.

His expression was stark and angry. 'No, you don't need to hear it from me. Because you won't like it. You want to hear something that I can't say.'

'No, I don't. I just want you to be honest with me.'

'I can't say what you want to hear, Cele. Trust me.'

I stared at him, focused on his eyes, because they were the one thing that hadn't changed, and the years slipped away before me. He used to laugh so much, Jason. He wasn't like Randy. Randy was serious, always so serious. Everything was life and death to him, everything was personal. Randy couldn't do anything halfway. He lived by the motto 'Go big or go home' long before it became popular. It wasn't just work that drove him. It was his need for excellence. To be the best at everything, no matter what the consequences. Randy ran full tilt into danger like a kid running after an ice-cream truck. I had spent two decades holding my breath with him, waiting for something bad to happen. And then it finally did. I was still holding my breath, waiting for answers only Jason could give me.

'He was a SEAL,' I said evenly, not betraying the

tempest going on inside of me. 'I know his work was dangerous, but he was on the downhill slide to retirement and shouldn't have been on the front lines of anything.'

The information had been vague. Randy was dead, that much they would tell me for certain. But that was *all* they would tell me. Everything else had been couched in shadowy terms. He'd been caught in some crossfire in a hostile situation somewhere. I wasn't even sure where he'd been. Iraq? Afghanistan? He'd been everywhere, twice. Broken every bone in his body, twice. Received more blood transfusions than a vampire. Had bullet wounds and knife wounds that he couldn't – wouldn't – tell me about. And now he was dead. And the only person I trusted to tell me the truth was sitting across from me.

'I need to know, Jason. Please.'

Jason was different than Randy. Jason had a soft spot. *Me.* And I knew it. I had only ever taken advantage of it once before and I was doing it again. Shamelessly.

He let out a weary sigh. 'Fine. But not here.'

I wondered if it was paranoia left over from his SEAL days or something else. 'OK, where? Do you want to meet for dinner?'

'Nowhere public,' he said. 'This isn't something I'm supposed to be talking about.'

Ah, paranoia. I was all too familiar with it. Taking

different routes to and from a restaurant. Checking the perimeter of the house before letting me go inside. Booby-trapping the lawn with household items. Just in case. Always being careful. I'd never so much as broken a toe, but Randy was convinced something bad was going to happen to me because of him. And because of him, we didn't have children.

'OK. Come to the house. I'll make dinner,' I said. It sounded like an invitation to a date. I could feel the heat suffusing my cheeks. 'I didn't mean that to sound like it did.'

Jason smiled. One minute he was glowering at me like I was the enemy, and the next he was the boy I remembered, fresh-faced and eager to serve his country. 'You don't have to apologise to me, Cele. I'd love a home-cooked dinner.'

And that was that. After months of tormenting myself with doubts and questions, wondering if I could have said or done something to keep Randy from that last assignment, Jason was going to tell me the truth. Dread crept along my skin. Could I handle what he told me? He said he couldn't tell me what I wanted to hear. I had no expectations – I only wanted to know how Randy had spent his last weeks, his last day. To know what, exactly, had happened to him. I suspected Jason was right – he wouldn't be able to tell me what I wanted to hear. Because I wanted to hear that Randy hadn't been planning to divorce me when he came home from his last mission.

* * *

I was nervous as a high school girl on her first date when Jason rang the doorbell at six o'clock on the dot. Military men, always so precise. Even in retirement, I thought as I took the steaks off the broiler and answered the door.

My first thought was that I was grateful I'd seen Jason at his office first. I was already nervous, but breaking the ice across a desk had been easier than having him up close and personal like this. My second thought was he looked a hell of a lot better in a polo shirt and khakis than he did in a suit. He looked … free. Unconstrained.

I ushered him into the house and took the bottle of wine he offered with a shrug. 'I felt like I should bring something.'

I laughed, leading him into the kitchen. 'Always the gentleman.'

I flashed back to the night I had met him, Randy's best friend since boot camp, the three of us going out to dinner before they shipped out on their first mission together. He'd opened my car door for me and I'd laughed and called him a gentleman then, too.

'Smells delicious,' he said, pulling me from my reverie.

'Just steaks under the broiler. Caramelised onions and

baked potatoes on the side.' I opened the wine to let it breathe and then faced him for the first time, my arms out in an awkward appeal for a hug. 'It's good to see you, Jason.'

He took me in his arms, the two of us standing there in the kitchen, holding each other like strangers instead of the longtime friends we were. And the lovers we had been, once.

I pulled away first, my thoughts going down a path that was better left unexplored. I laughed. 'Well, that was weird.'

He didn't share my amusement. 'I didn't say it earlier, but it's good to see you, too. I just wish –'

I laid my fingers across his lips. 'Don't say it.'

A moment ago, it had seemed strange to hug him. Foreign. Now, I touched his lips like we'd been intimate for ever. Granted, it was to still him, to keep the words he was thinking – I was thinking – from being spoken. As if that would keep them from being true.

My fingers lingered on his lips too long. Long enough for me to feel the soft heat of his skin. Long enough for him to smell my hand lotion, his nostrils flaring as if it was the most erotic scent he'd ever encountered. Long enough to bring it all back in vivid detail. A young, sad, drunk couple missing a friend, a husband, needing comfort and empathy, needing human touch and love, falling into an unmade bed, stripping off clothes as they went, loving and touching and whispering words of longing that could never, would never, be repeated in the light of day.

I had slipped out of Jason's bed the morning after our indiscretion and I didn't see him again for five years. When I did, I kept my distance. Which was easy enough, since it was his wedding. At that point, I'd been married for six years and was chasing after two toddlers. And he only had eyes for his bride and his best friend, who was none the wiser. We both pretended it had never happened, but I had never forgotten – and I had never forgiven myself until a few months before Randy's death.

I felt Jason's lips moving over my fingers, the softest of kisses, the barest touch of his skin on mine. And that was all it took to have me instantly, immediately aroused. It had always been this way between us, this chemistry that burned hot and bright under my skin like an electrical fire racing through the walls of a house, unseen until it was too late to do anything about it.

I knew he was going to kiss me before he even took me in his arms. I could see the promise of it in his steady, steely grey eyes. He was a man who made quick, life-changing decisions. This wasn't war, this wasn't a mission, but he was making that decision even as his lips descended over mine. And I was letting him. Again.

The last time he had kissed me, he hadn't had all the details about why I was letting him. This time, there was information he still didn't have – and information I needed. Which is why, after only a moment of the warm press of his mouth against mine and the telltale press of his erection against my belly, I pulled away. It wasn't because I didn't want him – God help me, but I had wanted him and fantasised about him for fifteen years – but it was time to set the record straight. On both sides.

'I'm sorry, God, Cele, I'm sorry,' he said, backing away from me as far as the kitchen counter would allow. 'I don't know why I did that.'

'I do.' I reached out to him and took his hands in mine. 'We both know why, then and now. But we need to talk. There are things I need to know.' I hesitated. 'There are things *you* need to know.'

He was a man of action. I knew that about him. I also knew he didn't do anything without being one hundred per cent committed. In that way, he was just like Randy. He squeezed my hands, calluses still rough on the balls of his fingers despite his office job. 'OK, let's talk. Let's eat, let's talk, let's make this right.'

And we did. I served him dinner in front of the big bay window that looked out over the wide leafy oaks I loved so much. As the sun went down, we ate steak and potatoes and drank a fine red wine that made it easier to say the things I did and to hear the things he said.

'It was ugly, Cele,' he said. He was staring at his plate,

but he was thousands of miles away. 'Randy wasn't even supposed to be there, in Kabul, did you know that?'

I shook my head. 'No, I – we – hadn't talked much before he left. I didn't even know where he was. I never did, sometimes not even after he got back.'

He glanced up at me then, but he didn't ask why we hadn't been talking. 'He wouldn't. But we had lost a unit in that helicopter crash –'

'I remember,' I said. It had been all over the news.

'– and Randy insisted he wanted to go. I was fine sitting back and running intel, but he wanted me with him. "One last hurrah," he called it. Fuck, I wish I'd talked him out of it.'

He ran a hand through his hair, hair that was longer than I had ever seen it. Thick, wavy, silver at the temples. My fingers clenched into my palms with a desire to push my hands through his hair the way he was doing, to soothe him, to comfort him.

'No one could talk Randy out of anything, you know that,' I said, words the only comfort I could offer for now. 'He was doing what he wanted to do.'

'That's just it, Cele. He was doing what *he* wanted to do. He changed things up on us at the last moment, ignored intel, decided to go in four hours early to take out the key players, when there were two sets of body-guards on duty, when there were civilians crawling all over the place.'

'Why?'

He shook his head. 'Hell if I know. He had a fucking death wish, is what it seemed like. Pardon my language.'

I waved him off and poured myself the last glass of wine. 'Please. I lived with a SEAL for a long time. There isn't anything you could say to shock me.'

'Sorry, yeah, I guess you've heard it all.'

I hadn't, not yet, but I would before this dinner was over. 'So why did y'all follow him?'

'Your southern drawl comes out when you're drinking,' he said, ignoring my question. 'It's cute.'

I could feel the heat rising in my cheeks. 'And you get more personal when you're drinking,' I said. 'It's sexy.'

Hell. I hadn't meant to say it, but the words just slipped out.

He laughed. 'Uh huh. I guess I'll have to take a page from your book about remaining *impersonal*.'

'Sorry,' I muttered. 'I really do need to know the rest.'

He sobered immediately. 'It was rough. We fought over it, Randy and I. We'd lost radio communications with HQ and our people back here. It was our call and Randy took the lead. And I let him.'

'You were a good friend.'

'No, I was too fucking weary to fight him on it. He said it was easy, we'd done it before. In and out, before they knew what hit 'em.' He swallowed the last of his wine and eyeballed the bottle. 'I'm going to need more alcohol to get through this.'

It was an admission of weakness and I wondered what it cost him in pride, but I didn't ask. I had another bottle of wine on the counter and motioned for him to continue as I poured it.

'I believed him, Cele. Honest to God, I believed his bravado. He seemed so cocksure that he knew every inch of the compound, that he'd combed over the intel and was certain the bodyguards would be clustered in the front and leave their back wall exposed ...'

His words trailed off and I could see in his drawn expression that he was reliving it. I was making him relive it. I hated myself for that, but I needed to know.

'Fortification,' I said, raising my glass in a toast. 'To the difficult stories, may they be told quickly so the happy memories can begin.'

I don't know where it had come from, but it eased the tension between us. Jason came back to me then, away from the haunting memories of that day in Kabul, and told the rest of the story in as quick and dispassionate a tone as he could. Randy's insistence that he knew what to do, the SEAL team's belief in their captain, Jason's support of his friend. The ambush by the guards, the civilians caught in the crossfire, the four wounded and two dead and one dying – Randy – as they hauled ass to the chopper.

'I thought he was going to make it,' Jason said as he filled in the details the officials hadn't told me. 'But a bullet nicked his aorta. He probably wouldn't have had a chance even if he'd been in a hospital when it happened.'

'Was he in pain?' It was the first time I'd spoken in a while and my throat felt rough and dry, despite the wine. 'Was he conscious?'

'In and out. I know he was hurting, but I've seen him in worse pain. He was relaxed when he finally went. Even smiled at me and shrugged, like he knew he'd fucked it up.'

'Thank you,' I said. 'For telling me. I know it isn't easy.'

Randy shook his head. 'I'm a bastard for saying this, but the hard part then was knowing that someday I'd have to tell you and that I'd have to say I failed to save him.'

'It wasn't your job to save him. And he sure as hell didn't want to be saved,' I said. I reached across the table and ran my fingertips over the back of his hand, stroking the knuckles, scarred from who knew what battles. 'Trust me, I know what you were dealing with.'

He turned his hand palm up and caught my fingers. 'Yeah, you do. Now you tell me what it is I need to know.'

I took a deep breath. 'It's not as dramatic as yours,' I said. 'Randy was cheating on me. He asked for a divorce about two months before he left for that mission.'

Jason's sharp intake of breath answered the one question I couldn't ask him. He hadn't known. He squeezed my hand tightly, shaking his head as if to negate my words.

'Randy was cheating? Are you sure?'

'Yes, I'm sure. He admitted it when he asked for the divorce. He was leaving me for someone else.'

'Damn,' he said. 'Damn him.'

'Damn me. I knew it. Had always known it. I knew it when I married him.'

Jason didn't react this time. I hadn't expected he would. 'I'm sorry, Cele.'

'Why didn't you tell me?' It was a ridiculous question – I had always known Randy was a womaniser and he didn't cover his tracks well. But the root of the question was why Jason hadn't ever told me he knew about Randy so I could confide in him.

He shook his head again. 'I don't know. I wanted to, but then that seemed like a betrayal to him.'

'He was betraying me.'

'And you – we – betrayed him. I felt like a jackass for justifying it like that, but I did.'

I swallowed hard past the bitterness lumped in my throat. It was an emotion I'd fought long and hard against in the past year, the past sixteen years, but it still tinged my feelings toward Randy. And Jason. 'I justified it the same way. Only I had more of a conscience than he did and I guess you did, too, or you would have come after me for more.'

'He told me he was done,' Jason said. 'Every time I caught him talking up some chick in a bar or getting a phone number from some file clerk, he said that was the last one.'

I nodded. 'I know.'

'And how was I supposed to come to you, after what I'd done, and tell you what he was doing?'

'You should have.'

He pushed back his chair, the legs scraping loudly on the tile floor. 'Why didn't you tell me you knew?' he asked. 'I felt like shit for not telling you, for taking advantage of you that night, for not being fully committed to my marriage because –' He broke off there, shaking his head the whole time.

'Because?' I asked softly, knowing the answer to this question too. 'Because you were in love with me, the way I was in love with you, the way we were both in love with Randy. And he could hurt me, and he could hurt you, but we couldn't hurt him. So we pretended it never happened, but you could never fully commit to your marriage because you were in love with me and I could never leave Randy because I did love him despite his flaws, but also because the only man I truly wanted was married to someone else.'

He stared at me. Just stared. 'Yeah. That.'

'I love you, Jason. I always have. I married the wrong man.'

He'd already pushed his chair away from the table, so it was one quick move for him to stand and pull me from my chair. There was nothing awkward about the way I fitted into his arms this time, maybe because there was nothing between us now. Not regrets, not questions, not the past, not Randy. It was just us now. The way it always should have been.

He kissed me hard this time, his lips angling across mine like they were meant to be there, nothing soft and tentative about him. He was the SEAL he was trained to be – no, *born* to be – and he knew all the intel about what I was offering and how to meet my needs.

I kissed him back the way I'd been fantasising for the past fifteen years. Not the way I had that one fateful night when we'd gotten drunk on much cheaper wine and tumbled into his bed in a crappy little apartment in San Diego. Not tentative and nervous, not guilty or lonely. No, I kissed him back like a woman who has tasted the world and knows what she wants. This time I was going to get it, come high or hell water. I kissed him with years of pent-up passion and hundreds of unrealised sexual fantasies pent up in a body that had gotten softer with age, but not less passionate. I kissed him like a woman who was available, attainable and willing, because I was all of those things. For him and only him.

We made out like teenagers in the middle of the kitchen floor. I braced my hand against his chest and pushed him back, giggling. 'We need to take this elsewhere. My neighbours can see in my kitchen windows.'

'So? They won't be watching.'

I thought about looking out that very same window just the night before and catching a glimpse of Rachel and Nathan going at it on the counter in their kitchen. The fact that they're about ten years older than me wasn't the shocking part – the shocking part was they had just gotten divorced and were in the process of moving out. Lust and love are a powerful thing when they collide – earth-shattering and all-encompassing. Unforgettable.

'Let's go to the bedroom anyway,' I said, my cheeks flushing hotly at the idea of being watched by anyone. My passion was for Jason only.

'Whatever the lady wants,' he said as he started walking me backwards into the foyer and toward the stairs. 'Bedroom upstairs?' he mumbled against my lips.

'Yes,' I gasped back as his hands found my breasts and tweaked my nipples through my blouse. 'Upstairs, end of the hall.'

'This house is too damned big and I've waited too damned long,' he said, pushing me up against the wall in the narrow front hall. 'I need you now.'

I didn't argue. There was no reason to. No one to come home and catch me doing something wicked right there in the front entrance. No one to judge me or criticise me. For the first time in my adult life, I could do exactly what I wanted to do with exactly the person I wanted to do it with and I was going to enjoy every minute of it.

'Yes,' I said again. 'Yes, *now*, here.'

He already had his hand up under my skirt and was tugging my simple cotton panties down and out of the way. They slipped to my knees and I used my foot to push them down the rest of the way and step out of them. His fingers slipped inside my wetness, his thumb on my clit. I didn't need any more than that, a few strokes of his callused thumb on my clit and two fingers gently massaging my pussy and I came, braced between the wall and his hard body, my voice echoing up to the vaulted ceiling and falling back on me. A woman in the throes of passion. I wondered if the neighbours could hear me. Suddenly, I didn't care who could hear or who might see. I just wanted Jason. *Now.*

'I need you inside me,' I said, reaching for his belt.

Impatient, he pushed my hands out of the way. 'I can do this quicker.'

'As long as that's the only thing you're quick at,' I teased, tugging my blouse out of the waistband of my skirt and unbuttoning it.

He paused long enough to watch me shrug out of my blouse, release the clasp on my bra and let both fall to the floor. I stood there in only my skirt, my heavy breasts swaying, watching him drop his pants. He slipped out of his shoes, stripped off his socks and pushed his pants and briefs off in one smooth stroke, his eyes never leaving my near-nakedness.

'You are so fucking beautiful,' he said, taking me in his arms again, the thick hair on his chest rubbing sensuously against my sensitive nipples. 'I have wanted you ever day. Every single fucking day.'

'You can have me. Here. Now. Upstairs. Anywhere you want.'

'Good,' he said. 'We'll start here and work our way through the rest of the house.'

What would have sounded like bluster from any other man sounded like a promise from Jason. A promise I desperately wanted him to keep.

'We have all night.'

'I hope we have every night for a very long time.'

I shivered, my longing for him so overwhelming I could barely stand still. 'We do. Oh, *God*, we do.'

I hooked one leg around his hip and reached between us to take his cock in my hand. I moaned at the thickness of it – how could I have forgotten? – and rose on tiptoe to guide him into me. Even as hot and wet as I was, it was a tight fit. I hadn't had sex in … I couldn't remember when. Well over a year, and then it had been by rote, married sex with Randy because he felt the need to keep up the pretence he was a faithful husband. At that point I had known he was cheating again and he'd already known he was going to leave me, so neither of us enjoyed it much. And neither of us had said a word.

This time, *this* time, I had a lot of words to say. A lot of sounds to make. A lot of positions and tricks and techniques to try. This time, I was with the man I loved. Had always loved. And I told him so as I slowly lowered myself onto his erection, taking the full length and breadth of him inside me, filling me. We stood like that for a long moment, simply absorbing the reality of it. We were *together*. He was inside me. Nothing had ever felt so right in the world.

'I love you, Cele,' he said, cupping my ass in his hands and pulling me up against him, sinking deeper into my wetness. 'I love you.'

I echoed his love, and his lust, crying out as he drove into me with increasingly hard thrusts. I loved it. I loved his rough hands on my bottom, his hard cock buried inside me, the low moans that sounded like growls in the back of his throat, the way my breasts rubbed against his muscular chest. I loved it all.

I arched my back against the wall and clung to his shoulders, careful not to dig my nails into his flesh, until he growled, 'Don't hold back. Never hold back with me. I want all of you.'

And I gave it to him as he thrust into me. I dug my

nails into his shoulders, crying out as I felt myself on the verge of another orgasm. He sensed it too, dropping his mouth to nip at my neck, whispering in my ear, 'I can feel you, so tight and wet around me before, but even tighter now. You're going to come for me, aren't you, Cele?'

I nodded, unable to string words together. It didn't matter, I was right there already and I could tell by the way he went rigid against me that he was close, too. My pussy rippled around him, tightening as my orgasm rocked us both. He pulled me up off the ground then and pressed me against the wall. I wrapped my legs around his waist and hooked my ankles, just holding on for the ride of my life. I screamed out my second orgasm, more powerful than the first, almost painful with how full I felt and how hard the thrust, and heard his responding moan, softer and deeper, the sexiest thing I'd ever heard in my life.

I clung to him, resting my head against his shoulder as he slowly lowered me to the ground, worn out from my release, both physical and emotional. He cradled me against his chest, so strong and yet so gentle that I felt tears slipping down my cheeks.

'What is it?' he asked, taking my chin in his hands and tilting my head up so he could see my face. He wiped my tears away with his thumb. 'Cele, did I hurt you?'

I shook my head and smiled. 'No, sweetheart, you didn't hurt me. You healed me.'

111

Coming Home

I knew I shouldn't be there. I mean, hell, it wasn't like I had even been invited. I'd broken in, for God's sake. I'd broken the law – and for what? To sit in the dark and wait for Quentin to come home so he could throw my ass out. Not for the first time, I wondered if he even would come home. It was 3 a.m. and I'd been sitting at his kitchen table for two hours already, running my fingers over the scarred surface and planning what I was going to say to him. Two hours in – make that two *months* – and I still wasn't sure what words were going to come out of my mouth when I saw him. For the hundredth time, I reflexively pressed the keypad on my phone and watched it light up with the time. 3:17.

Quentin and I were a lot alike. Both of us slung drinks for a living – alcohol for him and coffee for me – and we were both quiet and introspective, which made us good listeners for other people's issues but not too good at sharing our own problems with each other. Quentin was stoic in dealing with life's curveballs, whether it was his father's unexpected death or a tree falling on his truck, and he could get focused on work or helping his brother rebuild that old Mustang of their dad's, or repairing the fence on that piece of property out in the country, until the crisis passed.

Me, I was more inclined to run away from anything I couldn't face head on – and sometimes that meant skipping town for a few days. Or a few weeks, in this case. I'd told my boss I had a personal crisis and needed to take as much of my vacation time as he could give me. He said my job would be waiting when I got back. All I could do was hope he was telling the truth. I was going to need a steady paycheck. Especially if Quentin bailed on me.

I knew he was still bartending at Kayla's – but this wasn't a city where bars stayed open until dawn. One or two, maybe, but it was getting on to the time when I needed to pack it in and go – that, or plan to make a night of it and hope he didn't call the police when he found me on his couch in the morning.

I was still debating my limited options when I heard

the distinct *snick* of a key in the front door lock. I threw a quick prayer up to the patron saint of stupid, lovelorn women that he hadn't brought some chick home from the bar, and waited.

I hadn't wanted him to call the police as soon as he pulled up, so I'd left the place dark when I'd helped myself to the spare key I knew he always kept tucked under the mat. He didn't turn on any lights either, so he was just a shadowy figure standing in the doorway. Could've been anyone, I guess, except I knew it was Quentin. Five years with a man will make you remember the tilt of his frame and the cant of his walk. And a whole lot of other things I didn't want to be thinking about just yet. It was Quentin all right, and by the tight way he carried himself he had either jacked up his back again or he knew I was here.

'Little late for a visit, ain't it, Rebecca?'

He knew it was me. 'Hey, Quentin.'

Two months of trying to sort through the mess that was my life and two hours sitting at his kitchen table and that's the best I could come up with.

He flipped the light switch by the door and I blinked in the glare. He looked tired. And pissed off. Not much had changed. 'What are you doing here?'

Any hope I had of a warm reception evaporated. I could freeze water in his glare. I dropped my eyes and shrugged, spinning my cell phone around on the table.

'You disappeared. I asked around and found out you were living here.'

He took two long steps and slammed his hand down on my phone to stop it spinning. 'First of all, *you* are the one who disappeared. Second of all, you could've just come by the bar instead of breaking into my house.'

'I came back in two weeks. You were gone,' I said, daring to meet his stony face again. 'No note, no forwarding address, not even money to cover the rent. Just gone. I waited, but you didn't come back.'

'You left first,' he said.

'You left *for ever*!'

He sighed heavily. 'I moved one town over to be closer to work and put some miles between us.'

'I came back,' I said again, sounding as miserable and lost as I felt. 'I was afraid to show my face at Kayla's, I didn't know what you'd told her and the rest of the guys. You changed your phone number so I couldn't even call you. What else was I supposed to do?'

'Get on with your life like you obviously wanted to do when you decided to leave me.'

Dammit, I was crying already. I scrubbed at my eyes, determined I wasn't going to let him get to me, but I knew it was already too late. He'd gotten to me the minute I'd fallen for that crooked smile of his almost seven years ago.

He sat down in the chair opposite me, crossed his

115

arms and dropped his head down to the table. When I finally dared to look at him, the anger was gone. He looked as weary as I felt.

'Why'd you leave? Where'd you go?' he asked quietly.

'Does it matter?'

'Yeah, Becca, it matters. You might've left a note, but it wasn't much comfort to read, "I need to think about things." You didn't answer your phone, you didn't respond to texts. After a week I was freaking out, thinking you were dead by the side of the road, so I called the coffee shop. They said you were taking a leave of absence, but no one could tell me how long that might be. After two weeks, I figured you weren't coming back.' His voice had started as a whisper and finished on a growl. 'You broke my fucking heart.'

'I came *back*,' I said. 'I was gone sixteen fucking days, Quentin. I left most of my clothes, all of my furniture and everything else. You had to know I was coming back.'

'Maybe I did. Was I supposed to wait around and see how long it took? Or see if you only came back to pack your stuff and go for good? Or hear about how you found someone else who was better for you?'

And there it was. His masculine pride. I might have broken his heart, but first I had hurt his pride.

'So you packed up your stuff and left for good before I could do it to you,' I said. I resumed spinning my cell phone on the table and he didn't stop me this time. 'How do you think that felt, coming home to a half-empty closet and your phone number disconnected?'

I could hear the bitterness in my voice, but seeing his face close up drove it home that two months had passed and we were still two very broken people. What the *hell* was I doing here?

'Probably the same way I felt. Shitty, I'm guessing.'

I deserved it. I knew I did. But it still stung. 'I'm sorry, Quentin.'

He spread his hands out in an expansive gesture. 'For what? For leaving? For not coming back until I'd given up? For not talking to me?'

'For all of it. I didn't know what else to do.'

'Where did you go?' he asked again.

'I went to Florida to see my sister.'

'Why?'

I hesitated. I knew I had to tell him. I had come here for that very reason. He had a right to know, after all. 'I'm pregnant.'

Whatever he'd expected, it hadn't been that. I could practically see the wheels turning in his brain and then grinding to a halt. He blinked at me. I stared back, giving him time to process it. He ran a hand over his jaw, scratching at the stubble there. He was impossible to read. I didn't realise I had been holding my breath until he finally spoke.

'Why didn't you tell me?'

Quiet, no anger. No happiness, either. I felt something inside me collapse in on itself, my hope snuffed out. 'You've been saying since the day we met that you didn't want kids. I didn't want any either. I was careful – *we* were careful – but accidents happen.'

He nodded. 'Yeah, they do. And then the two people involved talk about it and decide together how to handle it.'

I shook my head. 'Why? What was the point?'

Something fluttered behind his eyes. 'The point is I love you,' he said softly. 'The point is you shouldn't have had to deal with this alone.'

'I needed to figure out what I wanted to do. I never planned on having kids, much less being a single mother.'

The tears started again. You'd think I wouldn't have any left at this point, given how many I had shed in the past two months. I brushed them away, the cuffs of my shirt already damp. Quentin got up and left the room. He came back with a wad of tissues and handed them to me without a word. He returned to his chair, watching me with that steady look of his.

I did my best to clean myself up, but I knew I looked like a mess. 'I'm sorry. I really am. I should've found some other way to tell you. Or not tell you at all, maybe. But I thought you had a right to know and I couldn't show up at Kayla's and have everyone watching while I broke down –'

'What did you decide?' He interrupted my near-hysterical ramble. 'What do you want to do?'

My laugh sounded maniacal even to my own ears. 'I'm going to have a baby, Quentin. I'm going to be someone's mother.'

'Then I'm going to be someone's father. We are going to be parents.'

It wasn't a question. It was a statement of fact. Quentin had a way of saying things that gave them weight and meaning. I knew I was pregnant, had seen the positive signs and smiley faces and the word 'Pregnant' on three different brands of home pregnancy tests. I had even seen the flutter of a heartbeat on an ultrasound monitor at the gynaecologist's office. But until Quentin said it, it hadn't seemed real. Now the truth of it hit me square in the chest and I gasped as if the wind had been knocked out of me. The tears started fresh, accompanied by great wailing sobs.

I held my face in my hands, as if I could contain the waterworks with the press of my palms, and heard rather than saw Quentin slide out of his chair. I felt his hands on my shoulders, squeezing, kneading, working out the tension that was knotted so tight even as I kept crying. He didn't say anything. That was Quentin's way. A bartender to the core, letting people work through their problems without interfering. It was a good thing – except when it wasn't. Like now. I needed to know what was going on in his mind, and in his heart.

I covered his hands with mine. I hadn't seen him in two months, hadn't touched him. It felt good. But I needed to talk. No, I needed to listen.

'How do you feel about this?'

He threaded his fingers through mine, still standing behind me so that I couldn't see his expression. 'How do you feel about it?'

I squeezed his hands. 'Don't twist it around, Quentin. I need to know what you're thinking.'

'I'm thinking I've missed you,' he said in that low growl I knew so well. I felt the knot of tension in my belly tighten, but in a different way. A familiar way. A way I longed for.

'I've missed you too.'

His kneading fingers turned softer, as if his longing could reach through skin and bone and touch the part of me that longed for him too. I sat there, waiting. Waiting. Two months. *Waiting*. Not knowing what he'd say or do or how he'd feel, but showing up here anyway, waiting.

I was tired of waiting.

He pulled me out of the chair, his big arms around me even as my legs gave out from sitting in the same place for so long. He scooped me up like I was no heavier than a tray of glasses at the bar. I was still catching my breath at the suddenness of it when he strode down the narrow hall and into his bedroom. I must have made a sound because he paused at the bed and looked down at me.

'We're still together, right? You didn't leave me, you just went away to get your head straight?'

I nodded. 'But you left me.'

'Like hell I did,' he snarled, and it would've sounded mean if not for the smile that transformed his expression into one of joy. Weary joy.

He deposited me on the bed carefully, as if I were the most fragile piece of bar glass he'd ever handled. Then he set to undressing me. Slowly.

He unbuttoned my long-sleeved shirt, his big hands making easy work of the small buttons. He kissed the beauty mark on my neck as he leaned in to strip the shirt down my shoulders. Then he went to my waist, hesitating at the stretchy waistband of my newly purchased maternity pants. I was afraid he was taken aback by the swell of my belly – still small at fourteen weeks, but a lot bigger than it had been when we'd last been together. He put my concerns to rest with his words.

'Talk about easy access. I think I like your new wardrobe.'

I laughed as he stripped my pants down in one smooth move only to tumble me back on the bed when they wouldn't come free of the boots I still wore. He unlaced my boots and took them off along with my socks and then finished the job with my pants. I lay there watching him in just my plain beige bra and panties that curved under the swell of my belly.

He sat down next to me, his hip touching mine. He stared at me long enough to make me blush. He brushed his hand along my shoulder, pushing my hair up and back so that I was exposed to his steady gaze.

'I guess I should ask if you want this. Are ready for it,' he said. 'I mean, I don't know how you're feeling or what you need. I don't know about this stuff. You'll have to teach me.'

'I need you,' I said. And it was true.

'Good.'

He took his time removing my bra, reaching under me to release the clasp, then sliding the cotton cups over my breasts. He stared at me, a smile tipping the corners of his mouth as he ran his hands over my breasts, fuller now and with darker nipples than when he last saw them. He circled each nipple slowly with just the pads of his thumbs. They pebbled under his gentle touch, aching for more. Aching for him. I squirmed on the bed, pressing my thighs together.

He tucked his fingers in the sides of my panties and slipped them down over my hips. I knew they were already damp, I could feel the moisture growing at the juncture of my thighs. He'd hardly done more than undress me and I was already wet for him. Not much had changed in two months, pregnant or not.

I was completely naked under his scrutinising gaze, feeling alternately shy and wanton, while he was still fully clothed. I let him look his fill. My body was rounder and lusher now and I waited to see what he would say.

His words, when he finally spoke, sounded faint and rough. 'You are so beautiful.'

The tears came again and rolled down my cheeks.

'What's wrong, baby?' he asked, gathering me up in his arms. 'What?

I couldn't explain it all to him. The weeks of wondering how I was going to do this, alone or with him. The fear of his rejection, of me and the baby I was having. The roller-coaster ride of pregnancy hormones combined with self-doubts and insecurities over everything from my new body to how I was going to support a baby on a barista's salary.

I shook my head, tucked my face into the curve of his shoulder and inhaled his unique scent. His T-shirt smelled like beer, but under that was the scent I'd missed. I had taken his Virginia Tech sweatshirt with me to Florida, as a promise to myself that I'd be back. Every night I'd curled up with that shirt and cried, wishing I could just call him and have him make everything be OK. After two months, his scent had faded – a faint memory of the real thing. Here, now, in Quentin's bed, I was reminded of everything I loved about him.

'I was an idiot for leaving,' I said between sniffles. 'I should've just told you. But we'd never even talked about having kids and neither of us really wanted them anyway and our schedules are so crazy and we already hardly see each other and –'

He laughed, a deep rumbling laugh I could feel as well as hear. 'Is this some kind of pregnancy thing, all this crying and babbling?'

I hiccupped and swallowed and nodded. 'Yes.'

'It's cute. I like it. I love you.'

'Are you going to get naked?' I blurted, grabbing his T-shirt in my fist and tugging. 'This is kind of embarrassing.'

'Why? You're gorgeous and pregnant. I'm a grubby bartender who just pulled a twelve-hour shift and smells like it.'

'You smell like home,' I whispered into the curve of his shoulder, feeling suddenly exhausted. It was as much emotional as physical, I knew.

'Aw, baby, you're about to fall asleep on me,' he said.

I shook my head. 'No, I'm not. I want you.' I attempted to wriggle seductively against him, feeling the press of his erection against my naked ass. 'And you want me.'

'Very much,' he said. 'But maybe we should just sleep and talk more in the morning. Or later, since it's after four already.'

'Quentin, if you don't fuck me right now I'm going back to Florida.' He wasn't the only one who could growl, I decided.

He laughed again. 'Oh, so it's going to be like that, huh?' He jerked his hips, pressing his cock against me. 'You want me?'

'I do,' I said, scooting out of his lap and reaching for his belt. 'Now.'

'Yes, ma'am.'

He let me unfasten his belt and the button on his jeans before he stood up and stripped off his clothes. T-shirt, sneakers, socks, jeans, boxer briefs, all in a pile on the floor before I could even catch my breath. He had lied, though. He wasn't a grubby bartender, he was beautiful. His body was well-muscled, from years of hauling cases of bottles back and forth from the basement of the bar, and lean, because he liked to go for a run when he got off work, to wind down so he could sleep.

I reached for him, wanting to feel the warm press of his body against mine. He eased down on the bed, keeping his weight off me. I grunted a protest, pulling him closer.

'I don't want to hurt you,' he whispered, arching up over me.

'You're not going to hurt me. I promise.'

He searched my face, his brown eyes serious and maybe a little scared. 'Are you sure?'

'Yes! Please, Quentin,' I said, my need raw and immediate. The surge of pregnancy hormones intensified everything, I was discovering.

He didn't argue with me again. He lowered himself

on top of me, his cock pressed firmly against my rounded stomach. I reached between us, stroking him, feeling the weight of them there, too. He dropped his head to my shoulder, trailing kisses along the curve of my neck, down my throat and to my breasts. I trembled as his mouth encircled first one nipple, then the other, leaving them wet and tingly.

'Do they … hurt?' he asked. 'They're bigger, darker.'

'More sensitive,' I gasped, as he flicked his tongue along one swollen ridge. 'I don't know how much of that I can take.'

'I guess we'll have to figure it out,' he murmured, rubbing his stubbled face between my breasts. 'I want you to tell me if it's too much.'

I nodded, unable to speak. My skin felt sunburned, my sensitivity heightened. I fisted my hands in his hair, thinking I would pull him away in a moment because I couldn't take any more, only to hug him to me when he moved to slide lower.

'Let me go,' he whispered. 'I need to see how sensitive you are … everywhere.'

I whimpered as he slid down the bed to the V of my legs, where his mouth hovered above my pussy. I resisted the urge to pull his face into me, knowing he would make me feel good when he was ready.

He inhaled deeply and I squirmed in embarrassment at his appreciative moan. I couldn't keep my fingers out of his hair – the only part of him I could reach now – tousling the brown locks as he gently parted me with his fingers. My body trembled with anticipation, waiting for that first touch of his tongue.

When I didn't think I could stand it any longer and would be reduced to begging, he put me out of my misery with one long stroke of his tongue between my lips and over my clit. It was so startling, I felt like I'd gotten a dose of static shock. I shrieked, nearly coming up off the bed.

He chuckled and raised his head from between my thighs to look at me. 'My neighbours get up early, so you might want to keep it down if you don't want them knocking on the door wondering if I'm killing you.'

I gasped as he tongued me again. 'I'll try, but you're not making it easy.'

'I don't want it to be easy,' he mumbled, his mouth full of my wetness. 'I want it to be hard. Very, very hard.'

'Oh, God,' I groaned, probably loud enough for his early neighbours to hear.

After that, I was reduced to incoherent whimpers and moans as he devoured me with his mouth. Pregnancy had brought on a new sensitivity there, too, and I revelled in every exquisite sensation of his mouth and tongue and teeth and beard stubble. It was all too much – and still not enough.

My body quivered on the edge of release, Quentin's

mouth working my swollen pussy to a sopping wet frenzy as he lapped at me and suckled my engorged clit. I dug my nails into my thighs, spreading myself for him, urging him onward with every lift of my hips. I was right there, so close I could taste it on my tongue. But I needed more.

'I need you inside me,' I gasped, clutching at his hair as desperately as I had clutched my own flesh. 'I need to feel you.'

A few years of sharing a bed with me meant that he didn't question my need. One minute his mouth was on my pussy and the next he was surging up over me, pressing the head of his cock between my swollen, sensitive lips.

I gasped, 'Oh yes!' and wrapped my legs around his muscled back as his cock found my opening and slid home.

It took no more than a few quick, shallow thrusts and I was going over the edge into a spiralling orgasm that had me clinging to him and screaming out my release. The neighbours would just have to deal with it, I thought hazily as I arched up to meet him.

His strokes turned longer and deeper as he sought his own release. I worked my hands down to the small of his back, then over the curve of his ass, pulling him into me, coaxing him deeper. Feeling the subtle changes in my body that made it difficult for him to go as deep as he once had. Wondering, again somewhat hazily because I was still in the thrall of my own orgasm, if I felt different or better or worse. There was no anxiety in my thoughts. I could tell how much he wanted me, needed me, by the way his body moved, the way he wrapped his arms around me and pulled me up to meet him, the way his breathing turned harsh and ragged as his desire exploded in a rush of heat and wetness. I held him to me, soothing the muscles in his back with my fingers, feeling the tension ease out of his body.

He rolled us on our sides, afraid I guess of hurting me despite my assurances that he wouldn't. I hooked a leg over his hip to keep him inside me for as long as possible. I curled my fingers at the base of his neck and pulled him down to me for a long, lingering kiss. I laughed into his mouth, realising we'd hardly kissed at all.

He smiled. 'What's so funny?'

'All these years together and we don't even need to make out before we're going at it like rabbits,' I said.

His smile faded. 'I'm sorry. I guess I should've taken my time and done it proper.'

I tugged a lock of hair that was in need of a trim. 'I didn't mind at all,' I said. 'Not at all. You're my home, Quentin.'

'And you're back home where you're meant to be.' He reached between us, palming my expanding stomach with a protective hand. 'You both are.'

I closed my eyes. We were going to be OK. All three of us.

The Art of Desire

They say life imitates art. More often I've found that art imitates life imitates art. Or something like that. I'd never had much interest in art – or painting, at least. I didn't really understand it. Oh, I could appreciate it, stand still long enough to admire the brush strokes on a painting or the contrast and complement of colours, but I've always liked photography more. In photography, what you see is what you get. Photography is reality, painting is fantasy. Or so I thought. Until I met an artist who created reality from fantasy and captured truth and beauty in the strokes of paint on a canvas and the strokes of his fingers on my body.

What first caught my attention were his hands. His hands, with their long bronzed fingers and short buffed nails that often had half-moons of paint under them when he was painting. His hands stroked me and with his touch he memorised me with his fingertips. With his hands he turned me on, got me wet, got me off. Antonio's hands. His strong, beautiful hands teased my fevered imagination long before he even touched me for real, after his scent faded from the air around me and his laughter was just a memory of the day before. His hands were as much a work of art as anything he painted on canvas.

Antonio was an artist struggling to put together a gallery show while teaching art classes to students with a fraction of his talent. I met him through a life drawing class at the college. I'm not an artist, I'm an actress. Correction: I'm an actress who doesn't work enough to support herself, so I wait tables and do some modelling for extra cash. Modelling for an art class means stripping down to my birthday suit. There are worse ways to earn money and I didn't have to worry about the art students pawing me because they're too busy trying to capture the creases in my thighs and the dimples in my ass in their careful, self-conscious way.

It's a good gig, being an art model. Good pay, good atmosphere. I'm a big girl, but I'm not particularly modest, so it doesn't faze me to be the only naked body in the room. Granted, it can get a little tedious sometimes having to hold the same pose for an hour or more, but I have an active imagination. I keep myself entertained by practising my monologue for auditions or, when I'm lucky, running lines for whatever theatre production I'm currently in. Sometimes I spin stories to myself – ideas for screenplays I want to write.

Antonio's class was composed of about a dozen students of varying ages, most of them edging closer to the retirement home than the club scene. They were all respectful of and almost deferential to Antonio, with his dark Mediterranean good looks and soft voice that would whisper, 'Yes, very nice' in their ear as they dragged their charcoal across the sketchpad in front of them. On the other hand, they seemed positively terrified of me, as if I had an explosive device strapped to my thigh. They spoke to me haltingly when I was naked and they weren't much more comfortable with me when I was clothed. That was more than OK with me. I preferred the solitude of coming and going from the studio without having to make small talk.

The only one who would meet my eyes when I was naked was Antonio, but that had as much to do with his own self-confidence as it did with his familiarity with models. He didn't acknowledge my nudity except to point out certain features to his students and then it was as non-sexual as if he was talking about the table in the corner – if the table had breasts and hips. But while he shifted his attention from my body to his students' sketches, I would spend my time studying him. His body was angular and graceful – much like his hands. From his longish dark hair to his nearly flawless olive skin, he was beautiful. He wasn't the type of guy I was normally attracted to, actually. I tended to go for the rough-around-the-edges guys, the ones with big bodies and big hands that made me feel petite in their arms. Antonio had a more slender build than most of the men I dated and wasn't much taller than me. But it wasn't his looks that kept me from approaching him outside of class. He seemed aloof, untouchable. Too striking for an actress-slash-waitress. I was the one who was uncomfortable around him, especially when I was naked.

I'd sat for three of his classes over the summer term and we were well into fall when he asked me to stay after class one evening.

'Valerie, could I speak to you?' he asked softly as the students filed out of the studio and headed for the coffee shop on the corner.

Idly, I wondered if he raised his voice when he argued or when he was happy – or in bed. I stifled a yawn and smiled at him. The ninety-minute art lesson had left me exhausted and stiff and I longed for a hot bath and my warm bed. But Antonio's request felt more like a command and I nodded tiredly in agreement because I had nowhere to go but home and no one waiting for me there except my cat, who was probably sleeping on my pillow anyway.

'Just let me get dressed,' I said, tying the belt of my robe as I padded toward the workroom where I stored my clothes during class.

'Could you wait?' he asked. 'It won't take long. I want to show you something.'

He sounded almost anxious, which piqued my curiosity. I sighed, too tired to be self-conscious at this point. 'Sure. What's up?'

'Wait here.'

I sat on one of the stools, twisting my neck to crack it and release some of the tension in my tight shoulders. It was late September and the room was cooler than usual, probably because no one had thought yet to turn on the heat. We had been in the grip of a very pleasant Indian summer for weeks and no one was in a hurry to welcome winter. Still, I would have to make a point of saying something to Antonio so I wouldn't have to suffer through the next class session. My nipples were like rocks, poking through my thin pink robe like some 1950s pinup and aching like they'd been pinched and twisted all night. Like the natural redhead I was, I blushed hotly at the thought of Antonio's capable hands on my breasts.

Thankfully, before my thoughts could go too far down that dirty path, he returned carrying a medium-sized canvas. He had it facing his body, so I couldn't see the painting. Despite my exhaustion, I was more than a little curious. I assumed it was the work of one of his students, but I wasn't sure why he'd be showing it to me privately. I knew nothing about art. He put the canvas on one of the students' easels, but it wasn't until he stepped to the side that I could get a good look at it.

'No one has seen this yet,' he said, his voice sounding hesitant. 'I wanted you to be the first. What do you think?'

It was a painting of me, though it took me a moment to even realise that it was me. Seeing a painting is a visceral experience, much more so than seeing a photograph. I responded to the art first, not to the subject. What I saw were the soft, rounded curves of a woman, her pale body stretched out on an ornate purple couch, her long red hair trailing down one shoulder, a playful smile teasing her lips in a way that made me want to smile too. The light of the painting was ethereal, as if the woman – who I finally realised was me – cast the glow that lit the space around her. It wasn't quite an angelic effect, because the woman so obviously revelled in the sensuality of her nakedness, but it was other-worldly. I realised the luminosity was not light at all but eroticism, as if all her passion was bottled up, trapped beneath the surface of her skin, illuminating her and the room around her. It was, to say the least, a breathtaking effect and nothing like any of the other work Antonio had done.

It wasn't until I took a deep breath that I realised I'd

been holding it in since Antonio revealed the painting to me.

'Well?' he asked, sounding wholly unlike himself. 'What do you think?'

I was moved by his art, but I was even more touched by the tentativeness in his voice, the realisation that he was nervous about my reaction and eager for my approval making me forget how beautiful and aloof he was. This was not the Antonio I knew, but I liked him and was even more attracted to him for this show of vulnerability.

'It's incredible, Antonio. I'm honoured,' I said. 'I hope it doesn't sound vain to say that it's one of your most beautiful paintings.'

He laughed, regaining some of his confidence, though I think it was more masculine than artistic pride. 'It is vain, but that's all right. You inspire beautiful art.'

I couldn't stop looking at the painting, at myself. Was that how he saw me? Was I that beautiful, erotic creature on the canvas? I didn't feel like that. While I recognised myself in the features, I didn't think I looked like that, either. I had taken enough classes with bitter, brutal acting coaches to know I would never pass for the ingénue or even the leading lady. I was a character actress, the full-figured best friend, the comedic relief in a drama, the secondary character who added colour and dimension to the plot – and I was fine with that. But Antonio had made me into – *painted* me into – a seductress, an erotic beauty.

'Why –' I couldn't quite figure out how to phrase the question. I didn't know if he would understand. I tried again. 'Why did you paint me like *that*? So ... exotic?'

He looked from me to the painting and then back to me. 'Because you are so incredibly beautiful and you don't even know it.'

It was trite, clichéd. Simple. Yet I believed he felt that way. 'Thank you.'

I took a step towards him, wanting somehow to let him know how grateful I was that he would not only paint me but let me be the first to see it. I put my hand on his shoulder, felt the fine bones shift beneath my hand as I leaned forward and kissed his smooth cheek.

'Thank you so much for showing it to me, Antonio.'

'Valerie –'

When I started to move away, he put his hand on my waist, stilling me. He leaned in, as if to kiss my cheek, but his lips settled against mine. They were cold, from the air or from nervousness, I couldn't be sure. Our lips and his hand on my waist were the only parts of our bodies that touched. As I relaxed into the kiss and felt his lips part and his tongue tentatively lick my bottom lip, I realised I wanted to touch more of him. I put my arms around his narrow waist and pulled him closer, feeling soft and feminine and desirable in his arms.

He let out a soft sigh against my mouth as if, finally, he could relax. 'I have wanted to kiss you like that since that first night in the summer class,' he confessed. 'I've been a man obsessed.'

'Why didn't you?' I murmured against his open mouth.

'I didn't know how to approach you.'

His confession, his raw vulnerability, made me ache with need. I kissed him again, taking his bottom lip into my mouth and sucking it with gentle persistence. He pulled me closer, moulding his angular body against my rounded one, stroking my hip with one hand while he twisted my long hair up in the other, his fingers tangling in the wavy strands.

'So beautiful,' he murmured against my mouth. 'So luscious.'

No one had ever called me luscious before. I felt myself responding to his words as much as to his gentle caresses.

I whimpered as he trailed feather-light kisses across my jaw and down my neck. I clung to him, not sure who was supporting whom, as we sunk to the hardwood floor in one slow, fluid motion. He was stretched out on top of me, his warm body between my legs, the cold, hard floor against my back. I hardly noticed any discomfort as he looked into my eyes and smiled.

'Is this OK?'

'More than OK,' I breathed. 'It's wonderful.'

He knelt up between my spread thighs and undid the

belt of my robe. I trembled as he parted it, feeling shy and vulnerable, as if he had never seen me naked before. In a way, Antonio had seen more of me than anyone ever had. And yet, this was different. This was ... intimate. I resisted the urge to cover myself with my hands and lay there, letting him study my body in a way that had nothing at all to do with art.

He leaned forward and ran his hands down my body, pausing to stroke my plump breasts and hard nipples before running the flat of his hand over my rounded stomach, down farther over my bare mound. I spread my legs wider, opening myself fully to him as he touched me. I could feel the wetness growing between my thighs, could almost imagine my pussy swelling and opening for him, an exotic pink flower tipped with dew.

'You are stunning,' he said, his gaze between my legs. He slid a finger gently inside me, then pulled it out and over my clit. I gasped and he chuckled. 'I can't believe you're here, like this.'

He stretched out on top of me again, shifting his weight so that his legs were spread on either side of my right leg while his hand worked between my thighs. He wore a white linen shirt and dark trousers and his body was warm, far warmer than the room warranted. I was making him hot. I was arousing him the way he was arousing me. I put my hands on the back of his head and pulled him down so I could kiss his mouth while he slid his finger back inside of me. He caressed me lightly, as if learning my internal curves the same way he had memorised my external ones.

I thrust my hips up to meet that one slender finger, longing for more. Needing more. Needing everything he could give me. He gasped as my thigh pressed up hard between his legs. I held onto his waist as he rocked against me, pressing his impressive erection against my thigh. I gasped when he added a second finger inside my wetness, imagining how good his cock would feel.

'Oh, God. You're driving me crazy, Antonio.' I pressed my mouth against his neck and bit down, gently at first and then harder as his fingers became more insistent. 'I want you.'

He didn't answer, but only continued to press his fingers deep into my pussy and then withdraw them before pushing them into me once more. Fucking me slowly with those long, graceful fingers. I braced my feet against the floor to keep us from sliding, my robe riding up underneath me. Reaching between his legs, I rubbed his erection through his pants, trying to give him just a taste of the pleasure he was giving me. I felt myself grow even wetter as I touched him and felt his cock jump against my hand.

He kept fucking me, slowly, steadily, those two fingers making me throb inside for something else. Something bigger.

'More, Antonio,' I whimpered. 'More, please.'

He added a third finger, slowly twisting them inside me like a corkscrew in a wine bottle, capturing me on his hand. He pinned my shoulder to the floor, his fingers hard on my tender flesh. I writhed against him as I cried out my pleasure, my voice echoing in the empty studio. I knew I would be bruised from the experience, but it didn't matter. If anything, it only aroused me more to think of having Antonio's mark on my body like a smudge of paint on a canvas. I fondled him roughly, impatient to feel him buried inside of me.

'Fuck me,' I cried, my voice a plaintive plea.

I ground my clit against the palm of his hand, whimpering as he fucked me. Shifting his weight, he braced himself on his knees so I could work his zipper down over his swollen cock. I reached into his pants, pulled his erection free, ran my fingers along the glistening tip and then stroked the length of him roughly. He moaned in response and pinched and rolled one of my nipples between his fingers.

'Do you want me?' he asked, barely a whisper.

I nodded.

'Yes?'

'Please, Antonio, yes.' He was playing with me, making me want him more, teasing me with his fingers and his dark eyes heavy-lidded with his desire, my pale body reflected in their depths.

141

He pulled his fingers from my pussy and I cried out at the sudden emptiness. He dragged his trousers down to his hips, freeing himself just enough to take his cock in his hand and press it to my pussy.

'Yes?' he asked again, rubbing the head along my slit, teasing me, making me squirm.

I groaned in anticipation and longing, shaking my head back and forth on the floor, my long hair making a swishing sound on the hardwood.

'No?' He made as if to pull away.

I reached down and gripped his wrist. 'Yes!' I moaned through gritted teeth. 'Yes! Now!'

He let me guide his hand, pressing the wide tip of his cock to my opening stretched from his fingers. I blinked away tears of intense emotion as he carefully slid into me and the softness of my body enveloped the hardness of his.

'Fuck me, Antonio,' I whispered. 'Please.'

He did. He pushed into me, rocking his entire body on me, hitching my hips up around his waist so he could go deeper. Slowly, slowly, so slow I thought I would die from the excruciating need, he fucked me. I tilted my hips, felt the slightest twinge of pain as he went as deep as he could and then we were pressed together hipbone to hipbone, rocking on the floor in a slow, sinuous motion that pressed my clit against his pubic bone. I shivered, quaking against him with the need of my release. We were barely moving, but the combination of fullness and friction brought me to orgasm in a gush of wetness that surrounded him.

I felt him tense, felt the quiver in his taut thigh muscles as I came, my muscles tightening down on his thick length. He went rigid above me as I rolled my hips down and back and then up and forward, letting him feel every wet inch of my pussy. He came with a deep inhalation of breath, his cock swelling and releasing inside of me, my thighs damp from both of us.

He shifted off me and moved his hand between my legs, pressing the tips of his fingers against my pussy, making slow circular motions over my engorged labia. I felt swollen and sensitive and moved to stop him, but he resisted.

'Let me,' he whispered. 'Please trust me.'

I relaxed my hold on his slender wrist, whimpering at the intensity of the sensations as I went limp on the floor. His fingers stroked me harder, bringing me to the edge all over again, and I bit my lip to keep from screaming.

'Look up, Valerie' he said. 'Look at how beautiful you are.'

I couldn't speak, could barely breathe. I was nearly incoherent, so close to another orgasm I felt as if my muscles had turned to liquid and were leaking out from between my legs. I did as he said, looked up and over his shoulder. I saw myself looking down from his painting, saw the knowing smile, the light illuminating not just the painting but our bodies on the floor. I saw myself the way Antonio saw me, I saw the passion, the eroticism. And then I came again.

I arched my hips off the floor until the only things supporting my and Antonio's weight were my shoulders and feet pressed to the floor. I came with his fingers pressed to my vulva as he painted my wetness over swollen, tender flesh. I came, screaming his name over and over in a litany of desire even while I stared into my own eyes in the painting he had created of me. *For* me.

'Beautiful girl,' he murmured, his fingers still pressed against me, my thighs clamped tightly around his wrist. 'My beautiful, beautiful muse.'

Above us, I smiled wickedly.

More Than Friends

The rain beat at the windows as if it intended to get in.
I stared out the windshield and concentrated on driving.
The car was silent except for the sound of the unrelenting
rain and the soft snores from my three passengers.
Damned men. They could sleep through anything.

Somehow, I'd gotten suckered into going on this trip.
I couldn't remember exactly how it had happened. One
minute I'd been sitting in the office listening to the guys
talk about their fishing trip and the next thing I knew I
was nodding my head and agreeing how great it would
be to get away from it all for a spell in the woods, with
a room to myself and all the fresh air and sunshine I
could stand. Fast forward a month, and here I was driving
Landon's truck through a pounding rainstorm during an

unseasonably cold April in Virginia, while Landon, Brian and Greg slept like the proverbial three bears. Which I guess made me Goldilocks in search of a soft place of my own to sleep.

'Hey,' I whispered to Landon, who was snoring away in the passenger seat. He didn't stir. 'Landon, wake up,' I said a little louder, punctuating my words with a poke to his ribs.

'Huh? What?' He sat up and yawned. 'Still fucking raining?'

I ignored the obvious. 'I'm tired. Want to drive for an hour?'

He yawned again and ran a hand through his tousled brown hair. 'Not really. Why don't you get one of them to drive?'

I jerked my thumb toward the snores coming from the back seat. 'Listen to them. They're not going to want to drive, either.'

Landon sighed. 'All right. Lift up and I'll slide over.' He scooted closer to me. 'C'mon, move.'

I looked at him. 'Don't be stupid. Let me pull over somewhere.'

'Don't be such a girl. It'll only take a second,' he argued. 'Besides, if you pull over, they're going to wake up and we're going to be stuck at a truck stop somewhere while Greg hunts for something fried and Brian calls Jules for the tenth time since we left.'

He had a point. 'Fine,' I sighed. 'But hurry up. I don't want to wreck your truck.'

'Do and die,' he growled as he slid under me.

Thankfully, the truck had a bench seat instead of bucket seats, so it was just a matter of raising up and scooting over in synchronicity with Landon sliding under me. I let go of the wheel when he slipped under me, and our hands grappled with each other as I wriggled across his lap and plopped into the passenger seat. It wasn't the most graceful move, but it worked and Landon was safely driving within moments. He had left a nice warm spot for me to settle into but I was having a hard time appreciating it. The warmth registered fuzzily in my brain only as a secondary thought because, in our quick exchange, I'd felt Landon's very noticeable erection against my bottom.

The thing about having so many guy friends is that, after awhile, I stop noticing their gender. Well, for the most part. I'd never slept with the three guys I called my best friends, not that Brian and Greg hadn't tried. But that was before Brian met Jules and before Greg realised I really wasn't his type because I'd want a commitment. They were good guys and I would do just about anything for them, including trying to find someone who could reel Greg in once and for all, but I had never really been physically attracted to either of them. Not even after several shots of tequila and a lot of weepy hugging and proclamations of undying devotion.

Landon was another story. I had been attracted to him since he'd first flashed his Tom Cruise smile at me. But for as long as I had known him, going on five years now, he'd had the same girlfriend. Candace was a statuesque blonde with pouty lips, a perpetual French manicure and a taste for trendy restaurants and expensive shoe boutiques. I had never quite understood what Landon – sports-watching, fly-fishing, environmentally conscientious outdoorsy guy that he was – had ever seen in her. Or her in him, for that matter. He was a creative director for an advertising agency, hardly wealthy and hardly her type. But for some reason the relationship worked and I wasn't a home-wrecker. Not that Landon had ever given me a reason to attempt a little discreet wreckage. In comparison to Greg, he was positively eunuch-like around me. Even Brian still threw me a little flirtation once in a while, sometimes while his girlfriend was around.

But it seemed like the eunuch was no more. Having felt Landon's rather impressive erection, I was suddenly seeing him in a whole new light. Of course, he still had a girlfriend and I still wasn't a home-wrecker, but just knowing he was *interested* was promising.

I fastened my seatbelt and tried very hard not to think about him. I was obviously suffering from sleep deprivation and caffeine withdrawal. Still, it was hard to ignore him considering he was less than two feet away from me and I'd just felt his hard on. In addition to needing sleep and caffeine, I obviously needed to get laid, but Landon wasn't going to be the man to do the job.

Why not? a little voice in my head asked. I didn't bother responding. There were a half a dozen reasons why not. A full dozen, if I tried hard.

Logic did very little to quell the heat rising in my cheeks. I squirmed in my seat, trying to get as far away from him as possible.

'You OK?'

I refused to look at him, staring out the window at the grey morning sky. 'Yeah, great.'

'You don't sound great. Are you mad at me about something?'

I gritted my teeth and refused to speak. Stupid, oblivious man.

With a big, hard cock. I wanted to slap that little voice in my head.

'Katie? What's up?'

'I'm just tired,' I lied. 'It's been a long drive.'

'Uh huh.' His scepticism was about as deep as the puddles in the potholes of the road. 'What's going on?'

I sighed. 'Let it go, Landon. It's nothing. It's stupid.'

Most men would have taken me at my word and let it go. Not Landon. Landon is that rare combination of sensitive and analytical. Which meant, of course, that he was going to pester me until I told him the truth – like a dog worrying a bone for the last bit of meat.

Mmm … meat. I knew I was blushing and there wasn't a damned thing I could do about it.

'C'mon, tell me.'

I sighed. Heat rose in my cheeks. This was Landon, I reminded myself. I could tell him anything. Then we'd get a good laugh and all would be well again. It felt weird to keep a secret from him.

'When we swapped places?' I had made it a question, like some teenager unable to complete a sentence without affirmation.

'Um – yeah? I was there. What about it?'

I licked my dry lips. That conjured up a mental picture of Landon naked. I had seen him a couple of times, by accident, of course. Once, in the shower at my apartment when his water had been turned off for maintenance. After living alone for so long, I'm not used to having other people around and had just burst in on him. The other time, when he'd been changing beside the car after we'd gone surfing. He had a towel wrapped around his waist as he stripped off his suit, but the towel slipped and I got a full frontal view. Of course, he hadn't been aroused either time, so I could only imagine how much more impressive his assets were when he was turned on. Like now.

I thought back to those instances and giggled nervously. Landon was cute – and hung – but for some reason, this was the first time I had really considered him as anything more than a friend or contemplated those fleeting accidental moments as opportunities rather than accidental eye candy.

'Well?'

I glanced sideways at him. What was wrong with me? I shook my head. *Just tell him.*

'I felt you,' I said.

'OK?' He drew the word out into a long sigh. 'So?'

'I mean, I *felt* you. You had an erection.'

'Oh.'

That was it. He kept his eyes on the road, his expression blank. I squinted at him, willing him to say something, to acknowledge the moment with more than an 'Oh'. With a start, I realised it wasn't just embarrassment that made me say something to him – it was ego. I thought Landon was cute. Didn't he think I was cute?

'Well?' I asked this time.

'Well, what?'

He was deliberately playing dumb. At least, I hoped he was. 'Isn't that kind of ... weird?'

His expression was still impassive. 'Why would it be weird? I'm a man, I have a penis, it occasionally gets hard.'

My face had to be tomato-red by now. 'OK, stop, stop,' I said, holding up my hands as if to ward him off. 'I know you're a man. It just seemed weird that you'd be excited now, like this, with me.'

151

'You mean, after I was woken up from a sound sleep?' He slid a sideways glance at me. 'You've heard of morning wood, right?'

'What? Morning ...'

I felt like an idiot. I wanted to slither out of the car and spend the rest of my life living in a roadside puddle. Landon wasn't turned on by *me*. He was just a typical, healthy, red-blooded male who got a little *engorged* while sleeping. I'd spent the night with enough men to know the truth of his words.

'Sorry,' Landon said. 'I didn't mean to embarrass you.'

I turned my head to the window. 'I'm not embarrassed,' I mumbled into my fleece collar. 'I just thought, well, figured I should, um ...'

I shut up, lest I put both feet in my mouth. But while my mind was horrified at the conversation, my body was still tingling from the very masculine contact. I squirmed in my seat, pressing my thighs together in an effort to quell the ache. It didn't help.

'You OK?'

'Sure, I'm great,' I said, a little too shrilly.

'Did you think –' Landon broke off and I could almost see the wheels turning. 'Oh, you thought –'

'Stop. Don't say it. Please.'

He didn't stop.

'You thought I was hard for you.'

I groaned. It sounded sexual and he was hammering

home the point that it hadn't been a sex thing at all. 'You can let me out here,' I said. 'I'll just hitchhike home.'

Landon laughed, but it wasn't mean-spirited. 'Oh, Katie, you're cute.'

'Cute, great,' I muttered. 'Can we drop it?'

'OK.'

We rode in silence for a few minutes, Landon watching the road, me alternately watching the road and watching Landon. He was cute. Cute because he was unattainable, maybe? I let myself drift into a little fantasy of what it would be like if Landon wasn't so damned committed to his high-maintenance girlfriend. This weekend in the woods might take on a whole new meaning. And why stop at Landon? Even if Brian was off the market now, Greg was still a good-looking guy, too, and he wasn't looking for a relationship. I was in the middle of a female fantasy and I wasn't taking advantage of it. Maybe I needed to rethink my priorities. Friendship with the opposite sex was great, but the potential of two men and a lady seemed pretty great, too. Especially considering how long it had been since I'd had sex ...

'Stop staring at me.'

'What?' I swear, I squeaked. 'I'm not staring –'

'Yes, you are.'

'Sorry.'

I could practically peel the tension off the dashboard. I had managed to curl up so tight I was almost taking up negative space. And yet my mind kept whirring. Why had I never taken advantage of the benefits of being 'one of the boys'? Why had I been the designated driver instead of the girl stripping on the bar and being carried to bed by one or more strapping fellows? I felt like I was experiencing an epiphany and I hadn't even gotten to the woods yet.

Landon cleared his throat. 'Kate?'

'Mmm?' I was envisioning being between two of the boys, it didn't really matter which two – though I decided Landon needed to be part of any equation – getting happily serviced.

'Do you think of me like that?'

I could have played it coy, but coy wasn't going to get me anywhere. 'I didn't use to, but now I do.'

If he was taken aback by my bluntness, he didn't reveal it. 'That's cool. Why didn't you ever say anything?'

'Candace.'

'Oh.'

I felt like I had a wool sock in my throat, but I had to ask. 'Do you – have you – ever thought of me like that?'

'Sure.'

Whoa. That caught me by surprise. Landon thought of fucking me?

'So why didn't you ever say anything?'

He shrugged, waiting to answer until he passed a

slow-moving truck. A spray of water flooded the windshield for a second before the wipers cleared it away.

'Candace. And, you know, you're my best friend.'

I snorted. I couldn't help it. 'Right now I'd trade a best friend for a hard dick.'

It was such a surreal situation that I didn't quite realise I had said those words out loud until I heard Landon practically choking on his tongue.

'What?'

'God, would you just pull over and leave me by the side of the road, please?' I tucked my head deeper into my hoodie. 'I don't know what's wrong with me.'

We rode in awkward silence for a few minutes. I squirmed in my seat, as much from arousal as embarrassment. Heaven help me, but I was still turned on at the thought of fucking Landon. I think all those years of platonic friendship had been masking some sort of hidden desire I had for one of my best friends. That, or I really had gone too long without getting laid.

I was musing over my miserable situation when Landon pulled off the highway at one of the 'scenic overlook' exits. I glanced at him curiously as he slowed the Explorer to a stop next to the guardrail. The view beyond the windshield was lush evergreen-covered mountains.

'What are you doing?' I asked.

'The cabin is another two and a half hours and we

need to talk. *Now.*' With that, he shut off the ignition and opened his door. 'Come on.'

I gestured to Brian and Greg, still asleep in the back-seat. 'What about them?'

'Let 'em sleep.'

I would have argued with him, but Landon closed the door and started walking away. With a worried glance at the boys in the backseat, I climbed out and went after Landon. A primitive set of wooden stairs had been built into the steep incline down to the creek that flowed through the foothills. I followed Landon down, though it was slower going for me. The rain had trickled down to a steady mist and the steps were treacherously wet, but Landon acted as if we were taking the escalator at the mall.

'I'm going to fall and kill myself,' I grumbled above him.

'No, you won't. I won't let you.'

I don't know why, but I believed him.

Landon was waiting for me at the bottom, looking like a real mountain man in his red flannel shirt and two-day scruff of beard. I stared at him, feeling like I had never really seen him before.

'What?'

I shook my head. 'Nothing. This is just all too weird.'

As if wanting to add to the weirdness, he took my hand. My heart nearly jumped out of my chest at the feeling of his strong, warm fingers threaded through mine. I looked up at him, my breath caught in my throat.

He laughed when he saw the look on my face. 'Will you relax? I don't want you to slip while we're walking.'

'Oh. Right.'

I felt like an idiot, but I didn't want to fall on my ass in front of him, so I clung to his hand as we walked. There was an overhang carved into the hill about twenty yards from the stairs and he headed for it. A wide wooden bench had been placed there, ostensibly for tourists who wanted to stop and admire the view. I shivered, a combination of the cool, damp air and nerves. Safely at our destination, I pulled my hand from his and tucked it in my pocket.

'This had better be good.' I sounded pissed off and I couldn't have even told him why because I didn't know myself.

'It will be,' he said. Then cupped my face in his hands and kissed me hard.

His lips were cool at first, but they quickly warmed against mine. His tongue glided across my bottom lip before teasing the crease of my mouth and slipping inside. I caught my breath as he deepened the kiss, holding me still with his hands on my face, our noses bumping awkwardly in that way of first kisses.

When he pulled away, my hands were still tucked in my pockets but I was a hell of a lot warmer than I had been. He smiled.

'Get it now?'

'Um, I thought I got it before, when I felt you. Maybe you should explain.'

'Candace and I broke up a month ago.'

I blinked at him. I hadn't expected that. He didn't sound broken up about it and I wasn't really sorry, so I just said, 'OK.'

'Don't you want to know why?'

What I wanted was for him to kiss me again, hard. But I played along. 'Why?'

'Because we'd been together six years and I still hadn't asked her to marry me.'

'OK.'

He raked a hand through his damp hair. 'You're not making this easy for me.'

'Funny, I was just about to say the same thing to you.'

I sat down on the bench, feeling the moisture instantly soak the seat of my jeans. I was beyond caring. This day couldn't get any more surreal. And then it did.

'She gave me an ultimatum. She wanted us to set a date or she was gone. I tried, Katie, I tried.' He sighed. 'I couldn't do it. I couldn't look into my future and see myself with her. But I could see myself with you.'

I was still caught up in the idea that she'd actually given him an ultimatum that I missed the last part. Did women really *do* that kind of thing? And did men really cave in to that kind of emotional blackmail? Then I realised what he'd said.

'Me?' It came out sounding like a croak.

He dropped down on the bench next to me before I could warn him that it was wet. He made a face. 'Well, I guess I deserved that.'

I laughed. 'Yeah, you did. But I got wet too.'

We sat there watching the slow-moving water in the creek. I glanced over at his profile. He looked irritated. At me? I wasn't sure.

'So, you couldn't marry Candace, but you could see yourself with me,' I prodded him. 'Care to expand on that thought?'

'I'm in love with you,' he blurted out, a proclamation made to the rocks and trees and the running water. 'I couldn't marry her because I'm in love with you. It's not a crush or because I want to have sex with you – which I do, don't get me wrong – but this is the real deal. I love you.'

Whoa. That was a lot to take in all at once, especially since I'd only just found out he'd broken up with Candace. I held my hands up to stop his confession, but it was too late.

'Dude, you can't just blurt out that you love me when up until thirty seconds ago I still thought you had a girlfriend. Damn, what am I supposed to say to that?'

He gave me a sidelong glance. 'Ideally, you'd tell me you were in love with me, too.'

'Are you *kidding* me?' I didn't just sound angry,

I *was* angry. 'I've walked around for the past five years pretending you didn't *have* a penis because I didn't want to wreck our friendship and biting my tongue whenever that harpy snapped her fingers and you jumped – and you want me to tell you I'm in love with you?'

'So you're not?'

His voice sounded strangled and for a minute I felt bad. It didn't last. 'No, I'm not in love with you. I don't run around coveting other women's men. *Or* my friends.'

He leaned over, his shoulders shaking. I stared at him. I'd made him *cry*? Holy hell, what alternative world had I slipped into? I was ready to bolt back to the truck and rally the troops for help when I realised Landon wasn't crying, he was laughing. Great guffaws shook his shoulders, startling the birds that were sheltering themselves in the trees.

I punched him in the arm. Hard. 'What is *wrong* with you? I thought you were crying.'

'I am.' And he did have tears in his eyes, but he was still laughing. 'You just sound so furious at the idea, it's funny.'

I punched him again. 'So you're not upset I'm not flinging myself at you with proclamations of love?'

He wasn't laughing any more, just staring at me with a goofy smile. 'Upset? No. I didn't expect it. Would've been nice, but we haven't really gotten to know each other like that. I just figured, since you were talking about my dick, that maybe ...'

I blushed. My comments took on a whole new meaning in this context. 'Sorry about that,' I muttered. 'I do think you're hot. Always have. And you're a great guy, my best friend.'

'Are you building a case for falling in love with me?'

I leaned my head on his shoulder. 'Maybe.'

'Can I kiss you again?'

I felt like I was in high school. 'Yeah.'

He turned toward me, cupped my face in his hands again and kissed me just as hard and seriously as he had before. Except now I knew what was behind it. I knew he was single. I knew it was more than just sex. And where it had just been a sleepy fantasy before, I felt my desire shift from purely physical to something with some roots. I kissed him back, wrapping my arms around his neck and shifting until I was practically sitting on his lap. And this time when I felt his erection it didn't seem weird at all.

I pulled back and searched his face. 'When you were hard earlier, was that really because you just woke up or because of me?'

'You,' he said simply, going back to kissing me.

I don't know how long we sat like that, making out in the still-drizzling rain, but I wasn't chilled any more. He ran his hands up under my hoodie and along my bare back and I pressed against him. It wasn't love, not yet, but it sure as hell was desire driving me when I tugged his shirt up and tucked my fingers in the waistband of his jeans, feeling his warm belly against the backs of my hands.

'What are you doing?' he murmured against my mouth as I slipped off his lap and worked his zipper down.

His cock popped free of the confines of his jeans and I sighed at the sight. Leaning over his lap, I said, 'What I've been wanting to do all morning.'

And then he was in my mouth, his hand sliding up my back to the hood of my sweatshirt, pulling it free so that he could stroke my hair. 'Damn, Katie. Damn,' he said, as if he couldn't catch his breath.

I took him as far as I could, which still left several inches of him to go, and wrapped my hand around the base of his cock. Up and down, mouth and hand working in tandem, stroking the length of him to the back of my throat and back out, his sighs and gasps in my ears, along with the rain and the birds. Breathing in the scent of this man I knew so well, and yet was just starting to learn. I sucked him slowly, drawing out the pleasure for both of us, my pussy creaming through my own jeans as I pressed my thighs together. Landon. I still couldn't believe it, even as I caressed the head of his cock with my tongue and tasted his sweetness.

'I can't take much more,' he said, and that was my cue to take him to the back of my throat and swallow, the ripples massaging his erection. 'No, God. Stop before I explode.'

He pulled me up, his cock popping out of my mouth and bobbing in the air. 'Not like this,' he said. 'I want to be inside you the first time.'

I wasn't going to argue with him. Between us, we got my jeans down over my hips, and he turned me so that my back was to his chest and I was once again sitting on his lap, his cock pressing up between my thighs. I shifted my knees apart and rose up, taking his cock in my hand to guide it into me. He slipped his hands under my hoodie, cupping my bare breasts as I lowered myself onto his erection.

We both let out a long sigh as he filled me, my wetness slicking his length as I lowered myself back to his lap. We sat like that, looking out over the forest and the creek running below us, with his cock buried inside of me and his hands cupping my breasts while his thumbs massaged my nipples. If anyone had glanced over the barricade above, we would've looked like a couple in love, two tourists taking in the view. I imagined we weren't the first couple to take advantage of the overhang and the bench and I sat there enjoying the feel of Landon inside of me in a way I'd hardly even let myself fantasise about.

I tried, but I couldn't stay still, couldn't resist rising up so that his cock slid out until only the head remained pressed between the lips of my pussy, then sinking back down until he was fully inside of me. Up and down, slowly, feeling every inch of his erection. He let me control it, for a while, and then his hands on my breasts became more insistent, tweaking my nipples hard, tugging on them until I moved quicker, harder, riding him. I leaned forward, bracing my hands on his knees, tilting my hips back to him for my pleasure, but hearing his corresponding groan to let me know it felt pretty damned good to him, too. I rode him hard, slamming down on him, crying out as he raised his hips to meet me halfway.

I was right there, clinging to the edge of control, no longer even trying to be quiet because it felt too damned good. I moved one hand between my legs, rubbed my swollen clit, stroked Landon's cock where it went into me, the combination of internal and external sensations pushing me higher until I was coming and coming. He groaned as I tightened on him, my hips rolling with the force of my orgasm, driving him up deep into my clenching pussy. I reached lower and fondled his balls, rolling them in my hand and tugging on them gently. That was all it took and he was coming, surging up into me until I was nearly unseated. I didn't worry about tumbling headlong into the creek – I knew Landon wouldn't let go.

Blood pounded in my ears as my voice echoed off the overhang, along with the sounds of the birds going wild. Only birds didn't clap. As I caught my breath, I realised we had an audience. Above us, half-hanging over the guardrail, were Brian and Greg, applauding wildly and acting like jackasses with their hoots and hollers.

'Hell, if I'd known there was going to be a free show, I would've made popcorn,' Greg called.

'Get back in the truck, you jerks,' Landon yelled, turning away from them to shield my half-nakedness. 'Show's over.'

Their laughter faded as they walked away, but I wasn't embarrassed. Much. Somehow, what I'd just shared with Landon made up for any ribbing I'd get over the next couple of days. He held me cradled to his chest, his heart thudding against my back, his hands still under my hoodie, cupping my breasts. He nuzzled my neck and I leaned back against him. I struggled to pull my damp jeans up over my hips.

'I guess we have to go,' he said, sounding genuinely disappointed. 'They're never going to let us live this down.'

I climbed off his lap so he could get dressed. 'So? I can live with it if you can.'

He smiled. 'The hard part is going to be explaining to them why I don't want to do any fishing this weekend.'

'Sounds good to me,' I said.

I took his hand as we walked back up the stairs. Love? Nah, not yet. But I could see myself with Landon. For now, that was enough.

Their Lover

I was riding Eric slowly, angling my hips so his cock hit my sweet spot in that way that makes me never want to stop, my pussy gushing with every short, quick stroke. It was then, when I was reaching the point of no return, that he said, 'Would you like to try a threesome?'

My orgasm, which had been right there a minute ago, decided to leave the room. Or maybe the planet. I stopped mid-motion like a car that has just run out of gas on the freeway and looked down at him, my long hair swinging in his face.

'Now? You ask me that *now*?'

I might have lost my concentration, but Eric's cock was still in the game. He thrust up into me, his face contorting in a way that let me know he was getting close to his own release. 'Why not now? Seems like a good time to talk about sex while we're having sex.'

In spite of myself, I swivelled my hips and moaned. 'Fine,' I gasped, 'If you can keep talking through me riding you, let's talk about having a threesome.'

Eric braced his hands on my hips, guiding me up and down on his erection. 'I didn't say we had to talk about it. It was just a question, Nina.' He thrust up into me hard enough to make me cry out. 'A yes or no question.'

And just like that, I was right back in the game myself, my orgasm not only back in the room, but front and centre and demanding attention. Eric's words repeated in my head as the whole world started spinning and I started coming.

Would you like to try a threesome?

'Yes, yes, yes!' I cried out, and it was as much in response to his question as it was to the pleasure he was giving me. 'Yes!'

Eric was right there with me, coming with a primal groan. 'Yes,' he echoed me. 'Yes.'

* * *

And that, more or less, is how I came to find myself sitting in a hotel lounge, sipping a watered-down cranberry and vodka, waiting for our 'date' to arrive. I nursed my drink and watched Eric, wondering if he was nervous, too. He didn't look nervous. Of course, Eric *never* looked nervous. About anything. He was fearless, an adrenalin junkie. A scuba instructor, skydiver, white water rafter and rock climber, among other equally dangerous pursuits. Eric organised extreme adventures for tourists who had office jobs and lots of discretionary income even in a lousy economy. People whose most extreme act in their day-to-day lives was switching to non-dairy creamer would find themselves praying to a God they didn't think they believed in within twenty-four hours of one of Eric's trips. At the end of the trip, they'd be tanner, leaner and braver than they ever imagined and would have the pictures to prove it. He was so good at what he did – giving people a taste of something they'd never had, that pure adrenalin terror he called freedom – that most of his trips were with repeat customers

Even though we'd been together for six years and married for two, I still had no idea why Eric was attracted to me. I didn't share his interest in dangerous pursuits. I was the office manager for an advertising agency, my most adventurous vacations included room service and massages, and the idea of jumping out of a plane or diving with sharks gave me hives. But I loved Eric and his crazy energy and he loved me and my predictable ways, so I bit my lip over his interests and he didn't make fun of mine. And never the twain shall meet ... until now.

Not that a threesome was particularly dangerous, but it did have my adrenalin up. I took another long sip of my drink and tried to breathe.

'Are you nervous?'

I stared at him over the rim of my glass. 'What do you think?'

He laughed and leaned into me, our shoulders brushing. Bolstering me. 'We don't have to do this.'

My lips twitched. 'Want to back out, huh?'

His expression turned serious, his brown eyes searching my face. 'Seriously, Nina. I know I kind of ambushed you with this idea, I just thought –'

I bumped him with my shoulder. 'Hey, I'm here because I want to be here.' I shifted on my bar stool. 'The idea kind of turns me on.'

A hand rubbed up my arm, along my shoulder and settled on the back of my neck. 'Just "kind of", huh? I hope that changes before the night is over.'

Joe had arrived and, just like that, my nervousness was gone. I was ready for whatever would happen.

* * *

My threesome conversation with Eric had ended abruptly with our orgasms, but continued the next morning when I decided to revisit the idea. 'So you really want to have a threesome?' was how I phrased it. Not exactly delicate.

We were sitting in the kitchen, digging into Eric's egg and potato casserole and swapping sections of the Sunday *Times*, and the topic of sex with another person seemed a little more incongruous – and therefore less intimidating – by the light of day.

Eric shrugged. His bare shoulders carried just a hint of sunburn. He spent so much time outside that he had a perpetual tan, but it varied in degree depending on the season. It was still early in the rafting season and I knew by September he'd be bronzed and beautiful. I felt such a tug of desire for this man I loved, I wanted to walk around the table and straddle him like I had the night before.

'It might be fun,' he said. 'But not if you're not comfortable.'

'I wouldn't know if I was comfortable unless I did it.'

He looked up at me. 'So you want to?'

'I don't know. Maybe. Yes. Maybe.'

He shook his head and smiled. 'I know that answer. It means you want to, but you're scared. Don't be scared, baby. It can be anything you want it to be.'

Eric was forever saying things like that. 'Life can be anything you want it to be.' 'You make the rules.' 'Be your truest self.' It was all very Zen and beautiful and most of the time I liked it, liked what it represented. Other times, I resented his cavalier attitude. Not all of us could run around playing games all day. Of course, whenever I said something to that effect, Eric would grin and ask, 'Why not?'

I didn't know why I was seriously considering his suggestion. Or question. Whatever it had been. Something brought up in the middle of sex was just fantasy, right? Yet I found myself watching the sunlight stream across the kitchen table and wondering what it would be like to be with someone else. To share Eric with another woman, to explore another woman's body. I wondered if I could go through with it, if Eric would be disappointed if I didn't, or what it would do to our relationship if we did. Eric is the one who throws caution to the wind while I analyse everything in excruciating detail. For whatever reason, or for no reason at all except I wanted to do this strange and exciting thing, I decided to stop thinking.

'Let's do it,' I said.

He looked up, fork halfway to his mouth. 'Yeah?'

I nodded. 'Yeah.'

'Cool.'

Of course, having decided to have a threesome, I now had a million questions. I didn't even know the logistics of finding someone to have sex with us. Did we just ask a friend? Put an ad on an adult website? Hit on someone at a bar?

'Why don't you ask Joe?

I blinked at Eric. 'Joe? My friend, Joe?'

'Sure, why not? You're always saying what a player he is and how open-minded he is and that you're pretty sure he's done everything, so this won't faze him in the least. Why *not* Joe?'

It had never even crossed my mind that Eric meant a threesome with a man. I had visions of a leggy blonde prancing through our bedroom or a redheaded vixen doing wicked things to me or a raven-haired beauty doing kinky things to both of us ... but a guy? And Joe, at that?

'Wow. Joe. Huh.' I considered it.

I'd known Joe since I was a freshman and he had been working three jobs to put himself through college. He tutored me in Spanish. He'd been cute and funny and the most open person I'd ever met when it came to talking about politics, religion and sex. But we'd never slept together. He'd been out of my league, or so I thought. We'd stayed friends though and gotten closer over the years. He was single and, according to him, kinky, with a high sex drive. I felt something like excitement stirring at the thought. Arousal? Over Joe? Maybe. Or over the idea that Eric had thought about me having sex with Joe. In either case, it didn't seem all that strange any more to consider my friend in that particular light.

'Why not Joe?' I said, marvelling at Eric's suggestion. 'But I figured you had a girl in mind.'

Eric smiled. 'Would you prefer another woman?'

Despite a little making out at college parties and a couple of really serious girl crushes, I had never been with another woman. And while I technically didn't *have* to do anything with another woman in a threesome, I figured that was the only reason men ever suggested it – to watch the two women together.

I tried to look as casual as he did. 'The threesome was your idea. What do you want?'

'I want to do something we've never done before and I want to do it together. Doesn't matter who's there or what parts they have, it's about you and me doing something new,' he said. 'I figured you'd be more comfortable with another guy, but if you'd prefer finding a woman I might know a couple.'

Something I hadn't felt in a very long time stabbed me in the heart. Jealousy. Pure, cold, irrational jealousy. 'No, I think a guy would be fine.'

He laughed. 'OK.'

Curious, I asked, 'You won't be jealous? I mean, there will be ... things going on, right?'

'You mean you'll be having sex with Joe.'

I cringed at the way it sounded. 'It was your idea!'

'Oh, baby, you're so cute,' he said. 'Yes, it was my idea. And I've thought about it a lot. There might be some jealousy, but I think it will be outweighed by happiness to watch you being pleasured by two men and one of them will be me.'

173

Eric was good at making things sound more enticing than they really were. I was trying to sort the fantasy from the reality. 'So you admit you'll be jealous but not so much you won't be able to enjoy it.'

He shook his head. 'Nope.'

'OK. This whole thing is blowing my mind, but I think I'm in,' I said.

Knowing I would be the centre of attention made me incredibly nervous, but I wasn't sure why. Performance anxiety? I had seen enough porn to know that a woman in a threesome doesn't get to just lie back and enjoy – she has twice the men to pleasure. But I reminded myself that we could make the rules up as we went along. Maybe I would just lie back and enjoy. Maybe that's all that Eric expected of me and Joe wouldn't mind. My tension eased a little. This was my husband and one of my best friends. It would be OK. But I was getting ahead of myself and the situation at hand.

'Now how to I bring it up to Joe?'

'Just ask him,' was Eric's ever-simple response.

And so I did.

* * *

Joe dropped a brotherly kiss on the top of my head. 'What's up, lovers?'

I laughed, not nearly as uncomfortable as I might have

been before my drink. 'Just waiting for you. Late as always.'

Joe checked his watch. 'I'm two minutes late, love. Anxious to see me? Or anxious to see me naked?'

I blushed and Eric laughed. Nothing was different about this exchange than it ever had been. Joe had always been touchy and flirty, even in front of Eric. I didn't know why I hadn't noticed it before, but this easy camaraderie had always been there. Maybe it was the vodka, but this whole threesome idea was making more and more sense to me. Why *not* Joe, I had been asking myself since I sent that two-line email asking him if he wanted to have drinks and maybe go to bed with us. Ha ha. Joe's response, 'Yes and definitely,' had been so quick and easy, I wondered if the two of them hadn't been plotting this behind my back. But I watched them now, shaking hands, joking about Joe's cerebral legal career and Eric's death-defying hobbies, and realised no, this was new to both of them, too. They were just that comfortable with each other. And with me.

'Are you in there?' Eric asked, as he left a twenty on the bar to cover our drinks. 'Joe asked if we were ready to take the party elsewhere.'

'Oh, yeah, let's,' I said, sounding as enthusiastic as both my husband and my friend. And I guess I was. I felt as if a door had opened inside me, brought on by their enthusiasm and how comfortable we all seemed together.

It had been Joe's idea to get a room at the hotel downtown. 'Neutral territory,' he called it. 'Keeps the marital bed sacred. My house is off limits because I don't want you having any weird association when you come over for my dinner parties.'

Apparently, Joe had been the third party in a lot of threesomes. I was fine with letting him take the lead and Eric, having put the idea out into the ether and gotten the ball rolling, was content with whatever made me happy. Could it be this easy? I wondered as I took Eric's arm on my right and Joe's arm on my left and let them lead me to the bank of elevators in the lobby. Joe's longer, leaner body was an interesting contrast to Eric's muscular, stocky frame. I felt like I was getting the best of all possible worlds. I giggled.

'Why the hell not?' I asked out loud.

They both laughed, as if knowing exactly what I was thinking. Joe had chosen the hotel and booked the room, and it was gorgeous. There was a bottle of champagne and three glasses chilling on the bar and the bed was already turned down. I felt like a princess who didn't have to choose between her princes, for tonight at least.

I'd spent about two hours getting ready for tonight, choosing my outfit with the kind of careful attention I usually reserved for formal events. Even more. Eric had laughed as he watched me go from closet to bathroom mirror, back to closet, rejecting each outfit as too revealing (I didn't want to look like a hooker in the hotel bar), too tight (unsightly lines from clothing would be a turnoff), too frumpy (I had two men to arouse) or because it just didn't feel like *me*. I wanted everything to be perfect, whatever that meant, since I wasn't sure this would ever happen again.

'You're just going to end up naked, anyway,' Eric had called to me as I made wardrobe change number three.

I'd ended up in a slinky black wrap dress that was cut to flatter my curves without showing too much skin. I might end up naked, but I wanted to start with a good foundation. To that end, my underwear was new and sexy as hell. I was actually looking forward to revealing it to the two most important men in my life. My lovers. The words sent a shiver up my spine.

Joe rested his hands on my shoulders as he semi-steered me toward the bed. 'Are you cold? I think we can warm you up.'

The cliché made me laugh, but his big hands on my shoulders were doing funny things to my insides. 'I think we'll all be warm before the night is over, right?'

'Indeed.' Serious Joe, a lusty libertine in an attorney's body. 'Warm, hot, sweaty, flushed ...'

He left me to sit on the edge of the bed while he popped the cork on the champagne. Eric had been quiet since we got to the room and I watched him move around, closing curtains and adjusting lights. He was more serious than I thought he'd be under the circumstances – I'd expected a lot of levity from him. Despite the alcohol and my newfound sexy persona, I felt my nervousness return.

'Everything OK?' I murmured, as Eric moved past me to the bathroom.

He flashed me his biggest grin. 'Oh, yeah, baby. I just want to make sure once we hit the sheets we don't have to get up for anything.'

I shook my head. I should have known. Eric is an adrenalin junkie, but he isn't reckless. He is prepared for anything he does, whether it's cave diving or mountain biking – or a threesome, apparently. I smiled to myself. This was going to be OK.

Of course, there are no books about the etiquette of a threesome. Or, if there are, I haven't read them. Somebody had to break the ice and Joe was busy pouring champagne and Eric was pulling a strip of condoms and a bottle of lube out of our overnight bag, so I figured it was up to me.

Neither man was looking at me as I stood up and unfastened the buttons on my dress. I slipped it from my shoulders and felt the silky fabric slide down my body to puddle on the floor. The move had been silent, but it caught the attention of my two men. They both pivoted to look at me standing there in my underwear and heels – a lacy pushup bra to accent my full breasts and a hip-riding lacy thong. I'd forgone stockings – too many porn movies featured actresses whose stockings had rolled down or gotten runs – because I didn't want to attempt to remove them gracefully.

I took a deep breath, which served to push my breasts even more up and out over the cups of my bra. And that was the last breath I really remember taking. Both of them were on me before I could exhale, Eric pushing me down on the bed and Joe kissing the side of my neck. Joe had never touched me intimately before, but my body didn't seem to resent the new guy. My nipples tightened and I arched my neck to give him better access while Eric parted my thighs.

I was hazily aware of my already damp thong being stripped away by one set of hands while my bra clasp was released and the cups of my bra peeled from my sensitive breasts by another pair of hands. I had the sudden urge to giggle because I was, in fact, lying back and being pleasured, in-between them stripping off their own clothes. I thought I'd enjoy being the recipient of their attentions a bit longer before I took a more active role.

Joe eased me back on the bed, his long, graceful fingers cupping and stroking my breasts while Eric knelt between my thighs. The clash of familiar and foreign touches, the combination of so many hands on my body and the sheer decadence of being the centre of attention had me writing on the bed before Eric even put his mouth on me. He anchored my hips to the bed with his hands, rougher and bigger than Joe's, and dipped his head between my spread thighs. The first feather-light touch of his tongue on my engorged clit was enough to have me clawing at the pillow above my head, a banshee wail rising up from deep within me.

Both men chuckled, sounding relaxed and pleased by their efforts. Embarrassed by my outburst, I grabbed the pillow and pulled it over my head to stifle my cries as Eric began to eat me out in earnest.

'Oh, no, you don't,' Joe said, pulling the pillow from my face. 'I want to hear every whimper and squeak. I've been waiting for this for a long time.'

I wanted to ask him what he meant when he said he'd been waiting, but I couldn't catch my breath. Eric was devouring my pussy, licking and sucking at my labia like he was starving and I was dinner. I pressed my hand over my mouth despite Joe's protests, and cried out. I wouldn't last long at this rate.

Joe, determined to stay in the game, began nibbling his way from my neck down to my breasts. When his mouth closed around my nipple at the exact moment Eric's lips began sucking at my clit, I thought I was going to levitate off the bed. The dual sensations were too much for my already heightened senses and I could feel my stomach clenching as I began to come. I grasped the backs of both their heads and held them in place as I rode out the most exquisite orgasm I had ever experienced. Everything tingled, every nerve ending responding to their mouths, the sensations travelling along my skin, my body going rigid as I clung to them and rode out my orgasm.

Eric spoke first, after what seemed like several long minutes of only my heavy breathing filling the air.

'Well, that was quick.'

We all laughed, whatever tension there might have been dissolved like my inhibitions.

'Had to get the first one out of the way,' Joe said, stretching out on the bed next to me. 'Now we can take our time.'

I found myself glancing at his erection, then looking quickly away in embarrassment, only to sneak another look when I stretched and sat up. I had no idea why I was feeling so shy

'Sweetheart, you can do more than look.' Joe's dry wit came from years of dealing with the law. I had no idea where his hedonistic ways came from.

I looked at Eric, who was grinning the way I'd seen him grin before he went off on one of his adventures. There was no sense of regret or hesitancy in his expression. Joe looked equally eager to get on with things. Now that I was coming down from my orgasmic rush, I searched my emotions for some sign that I might want to back out of this and be the tease in this three-way

181

party. But I felt nothing but love and anticipation – and a growing sense of renewed arousal as I watched Joe's cock jump under my steady gaze.

'Seriously, Nina, you're torturing me here,' he said, and he did actually sound like he was in pain. 'If you want to back out, I'll understand, but if you don't –'

I leaned over and took him in my mouth. I think it was the first time ever that Joe hadn't completed a sentence. I giggled around the head of his cock, which was both familiar and strange after so many years with Eric. But it was strange in that exciting way something new seems strange – the strangeness quickly fading to be replaced by curiosity and a need to rise to the challenge of pleasing him. Wondering how he would respond if I flicked my tongue this way or that, feeling the urge to bit down in that way Eric liked, but doing it carefully to see if it was something Joe would appreciate. He did, groaning as he pushed his hips up and drove his cock another inch into my mouth. I stretched my mouth to accommodate him, making an appreciative sound that vibrated around him and made him gasp.

My eyes were closed, so I didn't know what Eric was up to until I felt his hands on my hips, raising me on my hands and knees. I groaned around Joe's cock again, amused by the way he gasped and tugged my hair.

'You're driving me mad, woman,' he said. 'I can't take much more.'

'We have all night,' Eric reminded him, nudging the head of his cock between my thighs.

I felt him at my entrance and I widened my stance while keeping Joe entertained. I couldn't voice my desire, but I needed to be filled. Now.

Eric granted my silent wish, pushing ever so slowly into my wetness. I groaned, my throat muscles vibrating around Joe's cock. He had given up all attempts at composure and was driving his cock into my mouth almost to the point of making me gag. I wrapped one hand around his shaft to control his motions while Eric shoved his entire length into me. It was an amazing sensation, taking Joe to the back of my throat while feeling Eric so deep inside me. Why had I never tried this before?

There was no time to consider my future threesome plans because the men had found a rhythm between them. Eric's strokes pushed me to take Joe's cock deeper in my throat, while Joe's tugs on my hair to keep my strokes going served to make me move back on Eric's cock. Back and forth, they seesawed me for the purposes of their pleasure – but I was the one enjoying it the most. Pleasuring two men this way, satisfying them both while enjoying myself, was more than I could take. I could feel another orgasm rising in me, making me breathe harder and take my mouth off Joe's cock.

Joe groaned at the sudden lack of friction and I stroked him with my hand, looking up into his face as I came on Eric's cock. I was slipping into some other mental space, feeling wild and wanton in a way I never had before. Completely out of my mind with lust, I pushed back on Eric's cock, seeking to maximise every sensation my body was feeling.

Eric drove into me hard, rough in his own lustful need. My knees went out from under me, my upper body collapsing across Joe, his cock rubbing erotically against my breasts. He moaned, Eric moaned, I screamed, every muscle in my body going tense as I strained for release.

Eric pulled my hair up in his hand, murmuring, 'Take him in your mouth again.'

Still caught up in my own need, I could only whimper. Then he did something that only served to send me hurtling into an orgasm as intense as the first one – he leaned over me, grasped Joe's cock in his hand and guided my mouth down over the head. I gasped in shock and arousal, watching Eric's big hand around Joe's thick cock. And then, as Joe slipped to the back of my throat once more and my lips brushed Eric's hand holding the base of his cock on the down strokes, I started to come.

Eric released my hair, but kept his hand around Joe's shaft, whispering in my ear, 'I'm going to come so deep inside you, baby. You look so sexy.'

I went as far down on Joe's cock as I could and felt Eric slip a finger inside my mouth alongside Joe's shaft.

I groaned as Joe tensed, then released a hot thick

shower of come across my tongue. Eric resumed thrusting into me, clearly not wanting to be left behind, and within moments was joining Joe in flooding my body with semen. I whimpered and groaned between them, my poor body wrung out from the multitude of sensations.

I was still stretched across Joe and now Eric was stretched across me. As the high from my orgasm started to subside, I started to be uncomfortable in the middle of this man sandwich.

'You can release your death grip on my wang now,' Joe said, his sense of humour still firmly in place despite our amorous adventures.

'Sorry,' Eric said. 'I got caught up in things.'

'No worries.' Joe stroked my hair. 'I rather enjoyed the entire experience. Who knows what might have happened if this one hadn't practically swallowed me whole. A man can only take so much.'

Eric laughed. 'Don't I know it.'

I listened to their conversation without comment, my imagination whirring over Joe's offhanded 'Who knows what might have happened.' I found myself wanting to explore exactly what he meant – and just how far both of them were willing to go. I squirmed from between them and looked at them lying side by side on the bed, Eric's body at right angles to Joe's, still close to Joe's crotch. The thought – the possibilities – stirred something in me. It wasn't arousal, not yet anyway, but it was getting there.

Eric laughed. 'You look like the cat that just ate the canary, babe.'

'You have no idea,' I said, smiling wider. 'But you might, before the night is over.'

Joe shook his head. 'You're going to break us both, aren't you?'

'No doubt.' I ran a fingertip along his limp cock, watching it twitch under my light touch. 'And you're going to thoroughly ravish me, too.'

They both reached for me at the same time and tumbled me down across their supine bodies in a tangle of limbs and sheets and pillows tossed every which way. We laughed for a long time. And then we explored all the things three people can do in a bed.

Learning Curve

I think it took me twenty minutes to get out of the car and make my way up the stairs to the second floor, occasionally squinting at the apartment number I had scribbled on my notebook. I found it, at the end overlooking the rear parking lot, and spent what seemed like another twenty minutes looking at the door in front of me. Three stickers with the names of rock bands I vaguely recognised – though I wasn't entirely sure they *were* rock bands – and the mangled cord of a pair of ear buds hanging from the doorknob were the only clues that this was a college kid's apartment. I decided that this must be the low point of my life.

The problem with returning to college at the age of thirty-five is that everywhere I look on the expansive campus, I see someone who could be my kid. OK, maybe not my kid – but almost. This is not a good thing. I don't know when or how thirty-five snuck up on me, but it did. Everyone says I don't look thirty-five, but more importantly, I don't *feel* thirty-five. It doesn't matter, though. I'm thirty-five and that means half of the students on campus are about half my age. It was demoralising to even contemplate, but if the campus were to be quarantined in the event of a zombie apocalypse, everyone would be looking to me for mature, maternal leadership. *Damn*.

Being a graduate student only helps a little. It's true that a lot of people in graduate school programmes are older – there are even a few students who are older than me – but with the new accelerated programmes, there are plenty of kids in my classes. Kids who just started drinking legally and who think the 90s are cool because they're retro. Truth is, I don't usually mind being the oldest chick in the room. I get along better with people who are younger than me, but it's hard to keep up with the slang, never mind the technology, and sometimes I feel my age.

It was a computer project that was kicking my ass. I can write a twenty-page paper, no problem, but tell me to do something with computer-based presentation and I'm like a deer in headlights. My brother Charlie is always after me to take a class at the local library, but I'm getting my M.A. in English, not engineering, so I figured I could muddle through with the basics of word-processing. That was until I got an English professor who wanted us to 'think outside the box' and create a multimedia presentation for our semester project.

I'd gotten married right out of undergrad, young and idealistic and thinking there would be plenty of time to start a real career. I was in love and content with receptionist jobs – about the only thing I was good at – until my ex took off five years ago and I realised I had essentially been making the same amount of money for eight years while he'd worked his way up the corporate ladder. I couldn't even afford to pay the mortgage on the house we owned, so he'd bought out my half and promptly moved his twenty-two-year-old girlfriend in with him. I'd decided I needed to do something meaningful with my life and put my half of the house money towards getting a Master's degree. Now, facing the complications of computer software, I was thinking I should've just bought myself a little condo and kept answering phones until I retired.

Dr Davis – who told us to call him Nathan and was sexy as sin but reconciling with his ex, if the rumours were true – had given me the number of his teaching assistant. Matthew Wheaton was apparently not only an excellent English Literature student, he was also a whiz with computers. He probably looked like a baby-faced sixteen-year-old kid, but on the phone he sounded like an adult. He had a deep, soothing voice, the kind that wouldn't be out of place in a radio announcer, and was good-humoured as I stumbled my way through what I needed.

'Sure, I can help you. No problem,' he had said and those few words had been enough to ease the tension my shoulders. Until I actually had to meet with him, of course.

I had suggested he come over to the house, but either he was one of those super eco-friendly types or he'd already acquired enough DUIs to get his licence revoked because he'd politely nixed the idea. 'I don't have a car. But I live right off campus if you want to come by after class.'

So there I was nervously knocking on the door of Matthew's right-off-campus apartment, vowing to take a computer class over the summer and never, ever feel this helpless again, when someone spoke behind me.

'Sorry, I ran out for some stuff and it took longer than I thought.'

I jumped and spun, nearly stumbling. Though I hadn't spoken to him before, I recognised Matthew from around campus. He had the boyish good looks of a college nerd who didn't realise his potent charm, with caramel-coloured hair that needed a trim, black-framed glasses and piercing green eyes that crinkled in the corners when he smiled. He wore dark jeans, a T-shirt of one of the bands on the door, and brown sandals, the early fall weather still nice enough for summer outfits. He smiled crookedly and my heart started hammering in my chest like some adolescent girl with a crush. I pulled myself together and tried to act my age.

'Hey,' I said, sounding like a croaking frog.

'You're Andrea, right?'

'Oh, right. Sorry.' This geeky college guy had me stumbling over myself and we weren't even in his apartment yet. 'Dr Davis – Nathan – said you'd be able to help me with this presentation.'

'I have all sorts of skills,' he said with a wink that was more playful than lascivious. For some reason, I didn't think he even knew *how* to leer at a woman.

I found myself wondering what his other skill sets might encompass, but I didn't ask.

He manoeuvred past me, opened the door to his apartment and tossed the tangled ear buds onto a kitchen table, followed by the bag of groceries he had been carrying. 'I was wondering where those went to. Come on in.'

I'd seen my share of college apartments when I was an undergrad, so I was expecting the worst, but Matthew's apartment wasn't so bad. It was small but tidy and, judging by the laundry basket by the door with women's underwear folded neatly on top, he had a girlfriend. The place smelled like pizza and pot and the furniture was old and worn, but for the most part it looked sanitary.

Matthew went into the kitchen, which was little more than an alcove with the basics, while I stood awkwardly by the door, waiting for him to put away his groceries. Unlike most college-age guys I had once known, his purchases consisted of wheat bread, some kind of cheese, a few apples and a box of granola cereal. Times really had changed since I went to college, apparently. He kept glancing up at me and smiling from under his mop of hair, like I amused him. I fidgeted nervously, contemplating taking an incomplete in the English class just so I could get out of there.

He wadded up his shopping bag and shoved it into a paper bag by the refrigerator. When he bent over, I could see the white band of his underwear above his low-slung jeans. 'OK. Now we can get to work.'

I looked around the apartment, spotting a television, stereo and gaming system, but not seeing a computer. 'Um, sure … where?'

After I declined his offer of a beverage, Matthew grabbed a bottle of juice from the refrigerator and headed down the hall. 'My room.'

I'm glad he wasn't looking at me, because I was pretty sure my eyes were bugging out of my head. I had no idea what the hell was wrong with me and as I followed Matthew down the short hall, trying not to notice his cute ass in his jeans, I chastised myself. Good grief, I needed to find a guy my age and just get laid. I had no business swooning over some geeky college boy.

Unfortunately, whatever mechanism controls the libido wasn't buying the old-lady lecture. I felt young and horny, ready to do nasty things to the innocent young man who only wanted to help me with my project. I did some mental math and figured out it had been nine months since I'd gotten laid, so it was no wonder I was thinking about Matthew's bedroom in other than academic terms. But still, this was definitely the wrong place and the wrong time to be thinking like this. Wasn't it?

'Crash anywhere you want and I'll boot up my computer,' he said, dropping into his desk chair, which happened to be the only chair in the room.

I looked around with a growing sense of dread because there was only one place for me to sit. The bed. I perched on the edge, nearly falling off in the process, more than a little self-conscious. At least the bed was made, I thought, as I watched Matthew sitting close enough to touch. Granted, he was hunched over his computer and not flinging me down on the mattress, but I have a good imagination. Too good, maybe.

I fixated on the way his jeans rode down when he leaned forward, revealing the top of his underwear again. Something about that line of white above the rugged blue of his jeans made me squirm in my own jeans. It was, quite possibly, the sexiest thing I'd seen in a very long time. I didn't know what was wrong with me, why I was even thinking like this, but I was wildly attracted to this guy in a way I hadn't felt attracted to anyone in a long time.

'So, where do we need to start?'

I was so lost in my fantasy of slowly stripping sweet Matthew and discovering whether his underwear was boxers or briefs that I hadn't really been listening. 'Huh?'

He looked at me over his shoulder. 'Where do you want me to start?'

I could think of a few places, but I refrained from offering those suggestions. 'Well, I know how to use a mouse and I know how to turn on the monitor, but beyond word-processing, I'm clueless.'

Matthew made a little grunting noise and nodded. 'OK. Don't worry, I'll get you up to speed. You should really invest in a laptop. I could help you find one that will suit your needs.'

I bit my tongue on the words 'I want to be on top of your lap so you can suit my needs,' and simply nodded instead.

Over the course of the next two hours, a bottle of juice and then three beers (one for him, two for me), Matthew was true to his word and brought me into the twenty-first century. I not only knew how to put together a computer-based multimedia presentation, I had a pretty good start on my*Frankenstein: Monster or Man* project. I also had a pretty good buzz. That's another thing about getting older: I couldn't hold my alcohol any more.

I giggled and didn't even care that it didn't sound very adult-like.

Matthew gave me a sidelong glance. 'Um, you OK?'

'Sure? Why?' I giggled again.

He smiled benevolently, slow-blinking like a wise owl. 'Oh? 'Cause you sound a little drunk.'

Oops. I'd been caught. I felt warm, but I couldn't tell if I was blushing or if it was just the beer raising my temperature. 'I don't usually drink that much.'

'You only had two beers.'

'Exactly,' I said.

He laughed. 'I like you. You're funny.'

'I like you, too. You're cute.'

He studied me like he'd been staring at his computer screen, sizing me up. I winked at him. It might have been a leer.

In truth, I wasn't drunk. I knew exactly where I was and exactly who I was with. And exactly what I wanted to do with him. *To* him. I was just nervous as hell about making my desires known. And even more nervous that he'd laugh at me. It wasn't the age difference – I was guessing it couldn't be more than ten or twelve years – it was my lack of experience. I'd married the first guy I'd slept with and in the five years since my divorce there had only been three other guys. None were anything to write home about. Matthew was cute and smart and the first guy I'd ever felt instantly attracted to.

'Come here, Matthew.'

He continued to stare at him.

I patted the bed. His bed. 'C'mon, I'm not drunk and I won't bite.' I gave him my best 'come hither' glance, hoping it wasn't too dusty from lack of use to be effective.

Confusion turned to understanding. Apparently some things didn't change from one college experience to the next. One minute Matthew was sitting at his desk and the next minute he was sitting next to me. 'OK, I'm here.'

'Is this crazy?' I was having doubts. Not doubts about what I wanted to do, but doubts about whether it was a wise choice.

Matthew shrugged. 'It's all good.'

'Yeah?'

'Yeah.'

'What about your ... girlfriend?' I gestured vaguely towards the living room, indicating the panties in the laundry basket.

He looked confused for a minute. 'Oh – I don't have a girlfriend. My roommate's a girl, but she's not my girlfriend.'

So he was OK with me making the first move, OK

with the age difference and he didn't have a girlfriend. I couldn't think of any other reason to delay what I wanted to do. Well, I probably could have thought of a dozen reasons – but I decided not to dwell on them.

I smiled. Matthew smiled. I'd love to say it was the alcohol buzz that made me lean forward and kiss him, but it wasn't. It was lust. His mouth tasted like beer, and mine probably did too. His lips were warm and firm and he definitely knew how to kiss as well as he knew how to make computers do his bidding.

At some point, Matthew decided I was wearing too many clothes and I felt him unbuttoning my shirt. I appreciated his attention – I didn't think I had it in me to do more than make the initial first move. I moaned when he fondled my tits, my nipples standing at attention and probably wondering what the hell was going on, they had been neglected for so long. He got my shirt off easily enough, but I had to help him with the bra when he couldn't locate the clasp because it was in the front. I giggled and fell back on the bed, pulling him down with me.

'This is crazy,' he mumbled as he kissed and nibbled his way down my neck and across my collarbone.

'I thought you said it wasn't crazy,' I said, going suddenly still.

He didn't stop nibbling. 'A different kind of crazy.'

At least he hadn't said 'weird'. 'Crazy good or crazy

bad?' I asked breathlessly when he latched onto one swollen nipple.

'Good,' he said, his mouth full.

'Right answer,' I breathed, happily letting him suck and nibble his way to the other nipple.

After a few minutes, I was anxious to get things moving past second base so I nudged his shoulder. 'Hey, Matthew?'

He looked up, his eyes heavy-lidded with his own growing lust. 'What? Did I do something wrong?'

Younger men are just so damned adorable. 'No, I just wanted to know what you're wearing under your jeans.' To accentuate my point, I ran my finger along the elastic of his underwear.

He looked at me as if I'd asked him who his long-distance provider was. 'Huh?'

'Boxers? Briefs? Oh, never mind, I'll find out for myself.' I reached for the waistband of his jeans and got them unfastened. The rasp of the zipper made my clit tingle. 'Oh,' I sighed, tugging his jeans down to his thighs. 'Boxer briefs.'

Matthew raised his hips so I could get his jeans off and reached for the waistband of his underwear.

I put my hands over his. 'Wait,' I whispered.

'Why?'

I spoke to his impressive erection. 'Because I really like your underwear. It's sexy as hell.'

Matthew's boxer briefs fit him like a second skin, hugging the bulge of his swollen cock. I licked my lips. I was looking forward to seeing him naked, but I was teasing myself – and him.

'You're driving me crazy,' he whispered, reaching for me.

'It was already crazy, remember?'

'Crazier. Craziest.' His hands were all over my body, caressing, fondling, trying to get my pants off.

I pulled back. 'Wait.' With a few awkward moves, I got my jeans and panties off and stretched out on top of him. 'Mmm, that feels nice.'

I wiggled on him, feeling the press of his cock between my legs.

'C'mon, baby,' he said.

It had been a long, long time since I'd heard someone call me baby. I rather liked it.

'Not yet. No need to rush. I want to enjoy this.'

I kept rubbing against him. The friction of the cotton of his underwear against my clit was nearly enough to make me come. I knew I was leaving a wet spot on his underwear, but I didn't care. I kept rubbing. He pressed his hips up to meet my downward movements, anchoring his hands on my hips as I rubbed against him.

As if sensing my approaching orgasm, he started thrusting against me harder. I whimpered, burying my face in his neck as my orgasm slammed into me. He kept

199

sliding me up and down his crotch as I clung to him. I felt like I'd never stop coming and I ground myself against him, wanting something inside my throbbing cunt. Finally, my orgasm subsided and my breathing returned to normal.

'Wow,' I said.

'Hell, yeah.' He laughed.

I pulled away, leaned over his body and pressed my lips to his cloth-covered cock. His underwear tasted like me. His cock twitched against my mouth and seemed to swell even more, if that was possible. I traced the outline of his arousal with my tongue. Finally, I zeroed in on the head of his cock, sucking the engorged tip between my lips. He lay there, arms at his sides, eyes closed, content to let me have my way with him. Despite my orgasm, I had never felt so aroused – I marvelled at how responsive my body was to this guy I'd just met and how right it felt.

Slowly, ever so slowly, I dragged his underwear down until his cock popped free. It was so hard and beautiful, I ached to feel it inside me. I hesitated.

Reading my mind, he pointed to the table beside the bed. 'In the drawer.'

I found a box of condoms and fumbled with one until I got it open. I rolled it over the tip of his cock and down the thick shaft. Lying there, with his boxer briefs pushed down to just below his ass, his heavy cock lying against his thigh, Matthew looked at me and said one word.

'Please.'

I straddled his hips and guided his thick cock inside me inch by excruciating inch until we were both panting with need. Finally, I slid all the way down on his erection and felt the slightest twinge of discomfort before raising myself up and sliding back down again. Up and down, I rode Matthew's cock until he couldn't take any more of my slow movements and quickened my pace with his hands on my hips.

'Oh, God, fuck me,' he groaned. And I did.

I arched my back, reaching behind me to twist my hands in his boxer briefs that were still around his thighs. He slid his hands inwards across my hipbones, zoning in on where his cock went into me, his thumbs settling on my swollen clit. With every downward thrust, he rewarded me by rubbing my clit until I was riding him as hard and fast as I needed to come again.

'Yeah, that's it,' he gasped.

I started coming as he thrust up into me, a combination of his cock hitting my G-spot just right and his thumbs working their magic on my clit. He threw his head back and moaned, the tendons in his neck bulging with exertion as I rode him. He tried to hold me still but I kept grinding on his erection as he came. Finally, when his moans tapered off to heavy breathing, I let him pull me down, my body as limp and damp as he was. He stroked my back slowly, soothing me.

I kissed the pulse in his neck and sighed. 'Thanks. That was incredible.'

'Yeah, it was.'

I waited for the awkward after-sex moment to come, but it never did. He kind of nestled me against him and we lay there for a long time, catching our breath.

'Still crazy?' I asked.

'Yeah. The best kind.'

I nodded. 'Yeah. So, can I come back tomorrow for another computer lesson?'

He laughed. 'I was thinking more like I'd make you dinner and then we'd try another lesson. And maybe another one after breakfast in the morning.'

By the time we got out of bed, it was a very late dinner. And, thanks to Matthew, I got an A in Dr Davis's class.

Remember When

I strained against the bonds that held me to the bed. The well-worn and carefully knotted ropes at my wrists and ankles had just enough play to let me stretch and arch. The illusion of bodily control until I literally reached the end of my rope and realised I couldn't escape. Face down on the bed, my ass already stinging from seven – or was it eight? – lashes of the belt, my pussy trickling wetness down onto the sheets as I screamed and squirmed. A steady *beep-beep-beep* broke through the haze of pleasure and pain and I twisted my head to hear it better. What was that noise?

'How many was that?' Aidan asked, trailing the end of the belt between my cheeks.

The beeping had distracted me. I had lost count. I bit the inside of my mouth to keep from groaning. 'Eight?'

'Are you asking me or telling me?'

'It was eight,' I breathed into my shoulder. 'I'm sure of it.'

The belt whistled through the air and I cried out even before the leather cracked on my already fevered skin. I jerked against my bonds, fingers tightening in the ropes, grateful for something to hang onto even while I strained to break free. *Beep-beep-beep.*

'*Now* it's eight,' he said. 'Ready for nine?'

'Yes, sir, but could you make that beeping stop?'

'What beeping?'

'Don't you hear it?' *Beep-beep-beep.* 'Turn it off, please.'

'What, baby?'

'Make it stop. Turn it off, please,' I mumbled into my shoulder. 'Please make it stop.'

Aidan caressed my back. When had he gotten on the bed with me?

'Honey? You have to get up. The twins are awake and I have to get to work.'

He smacked my ass, pulling me from the sweet torment of my dream. Not just a dream, a memory. A distant memory, BB, Before Babies. The twins were two and a half. Which meant I was dreaming about something that had last happened ... nearly three and a half years ago. BP, Before Pregnancy. Before the ultrasound showed two heartbeats, before my doctor put me on bed rest, before the emergency Caesarean section, before postpartum depression. Before. Just *before*. Back when I was me.

I sighed, the remnants of the dream fading away as reality took over. Aidan turned off the alarm and kissed me goodbye.

'I gave them breakfast,' he said, giving me the rundown of what I was in for. 'Tyler wanted Froot Loops, Zach wanted Cheerios. Somewhere between serving and eating, they decided to swap bowls. Then they decided they would share. Which involved pouring all the cereal on the floor and mixing it up before putting it back into bowls.'

I groaned. 'Did you clean up the mess?'

'Yeah, but they're probably into something else so you'd better get your tail in gear if you're going to make it to school on time.'

He gave me another swat. It was affectionate and nonsexual, but it stirred something in me. I caught his wrist as he pulled back. 'I could use more of that,' I said.

He looked like he was going to say something, but then one of the twins let out a banshee wail, followed immediately by the other one screaming, 'I didn't do it!'

'Gotta go, babe,' Aidan said, giving me another quick kiss. 'One of these days we'll have time for something else, right?'

'Right,' I said, though I wasn't entirely sure I believed it as I dragged my tired body out of bed.

No time to shower before I had to drop the twins off at preschool and fight traffic to my teaching job at the middle school. Six o'clock in the morning and I was already promising myself I could go to bed early. It was going to be a long day.

* * *

Catherine was smiling. That in itself wasn't unusual, but since we were on first period lunch duty on a Friday and the kids were off the chain, her smiling meant she was either on drugs or had gotten laid. In either case, I was terribly jealous.

Her smile turned to stern teacher look as two sixth-grade boys pushed each other in the lunch line. She snapped her fingers and pointed to the tables. They grinned sheepishly and collected their lunch. If only it was always so easy.

I sidled up to her and leaned in close to be heard over the din. 'What are you so happy about?'

She tried to stop smiling and couldn't. 'It's Friday. Why aren't you happy?'

'I am,' I said.

She looked doubtful.

'Bad night. Bad morning. I'm tired,' I mumbled. 'I'll take two of whatever is making you smile like that and about twelve hours of sleep.'

'You don't need sleep, you need a good –' She glanced around and then whispered conspiratorially, '*You know.*'

'Know what?' Lexi joined us, looking as exhausted as I felt. 'Will this day ever be over?'

'Know what I need,' I said. 'And yeah, I *know*, I just can't do anything about it. Having two little ones around makes the *you know* difficult.'

Lexi snorted. 'Having no one to *you know* with makes it difficult, too.'

Catherine didn't have kids, so she could *you know* all she wanted with her hot, hunky mechanic husband. Lexi was single and childfree, so I didn't expect her to understand, either. I sighed and looked at my watch. Another fifteen minutes in the lunch period, another five hours in the work day. Then a fun-filled weekend of gardening and a trip to the zoo and endless rounds of 'Twinkle, Twinkle Little Star' and recorded episodes of *Sesame Street*. It was wonderful, it truly was, and I loved my weekends with my family – I just wanted a little alone time with Aidan to … *you know*.

'Let me take them for a night,' Catherine said.

I shook my head. 'I couldn't do that to you. They're toddlers. One is bad enough. Two of them together? You'd never survive.'

She laughed. 'I deal with this every day,' she said, sweeping her arm across the controlled chaos of the lunch room. 'I can deal with your little boys for one night.'

'Do it, Hannah,' Lexi stage-whispered. 'You can always find another friend – but who knows how long it'll be before you get to *you know* all night long again?'

She had a point. Not about finding another friend, but because doing what I wanted to do with Aidan wasn't just about being able to close the door. It was about being able to make noise. A lot of noise. Not just orgasmic noises, but screaming and crying and begging and the sound of being slapped and smacked ... Those weren't things we could do in a house with children, at least not until we could afford a bigger house and some sound-proofing for the walls.

'OK, if you're sure,' I said.

Catherine nodded. 'I'm sure. I have my own agenda. I'm kind of ready for one of my own. Just need to get Mark on board. One night with your kiddos and he'll be ready to *you know* me to a big pregnant baby belly.'

I opened my mouth to warn her about what might happen to all that *you knowing* she was doing if she decided to have a baby, but then I thought better of it. 'Thanks,' I said. 'You have *no* idea how much this means to me.'

'Just return the favour when I have a baby.'

I nodded absentmindedly, my mind not on babies at all.

* * *

208

Convincing Aidan to let Catherine and Mark take the twins overnight was easier than I thought. Thankfully, they lived just across the street so my motherly guilt was assuaged by the knowledge that if either of them got scared and wanted to come home, they could. I did feel a little guilty for hoping they *wouldn't* want to come home as I filled their backpacks with pyjamas, toys, books, videos and even a bedtime snack and walked them across the street the following Saturday evening. The twins acted like they were going to Disney World, probably because they loved hanging out with Mark while he worked on his classic Mustang. With a kiss and a wave, I walked back to the house feeling like a new woman.

The plan was dinner, just the two of us. And then ... well, I knew what I wanted, but we hadn't really had any time to discuss it. I smiled as I let myself back into the house. Aidan had volunteered to make dinner and the scent of simmering onions and garlic was heaven. Even better would be getting to eat his signature pasta marinara without having to scrape it off the ceiling afterward. I moved up behind him at the stove and wrapped my arms around his waist.

'That smells delicious,' I said, resting my head between his shoulder blades. 'I am so excited about tonight.'

'Me, too.' He added crushed tomatoes, chopped green pepper and mushrooms to the simmering pan. 'I rented the *Bourne* trilogy.'

I laughed. 'Uh huh. You're cute.'

He tilted his head. 'Did you want to watch something else? Maybe comedies instead? I'm not sure I can do a night of chick flicks, but *The Hangover* is on cable.'

I unwound my arms from around his waist. 'You're serious.'

'You said you wanted to catch up on things we hadn't done in a while,' he said, sounding confused. 'I can't remember the last time we sat down and watched an entire movie without one or both of us crashing out before the end.'

'You really *are* serious.'

I shook my head as I stepped back against the counter. It should have been funny. I should have laughed at the goody, confused expression on his face. Instead, I picked the pasta pot up from the counter and slammed it down.

'Are you *kidding* me?' I slammed the pot again. 'The first night we've been alone – completely *alone* – since the twins were born and all you want to do is watch vampire movies and eat pasta?'

He was staring at me as if I'd grown a second head. 'I – well, this was your idea. I thought you wanted a quiet dinner and to relax for awhile. I thought we'd go to bed early –'

'Let me guess, go to bed early and *sleep*,' I all but snarled. 'Maybe get eight or ten solid hours of *sleep* and then what? A quiet breakfast alone, too?'

'What the hell is wrong with you?' Aidan turned the burner off and pushed the sauce pot to the back of the stove. 'So you don't want to eat and you don't want to watch movies and you *obviously* don't want to sleep. What the hell do you *want* to do and why didn't I get the memo?'

'I want to fuck like we used to!'

As loudly as I screamed it, I was sure Catherine and Mark were now staring at each other and cranking up the cartoons to drown me out before one of the kids asked them what 'fuck' meant. I threw my hands up and walked out of the kitchen, heading for the bedroom. *Alone*. To *sleep*. Holy fuck, this was my life now? And Aidan wanted to know what was wrong with *me*?

I slammed the bedroom door and lay down on the bed, but I was too pissed off to sleep. Or cry. Or even relax. I was as rigid as an ironing board.

Aidan opened the bedroom door. 'Hannah? Why didn't you say something?'

I just shook my head. The anger was fading, replaced by soul-crushing depression.

He sat down on the edge of the bed. 'You should have said something,' he said, his voice firm. 'How am I supposed to know what you need if you don't *tell* me?'

He sounded angry. I started crying. This was definitely not how I envisioned us spending our first night alone in three years. 'You haven't said anything either. I'm not going to *make* you fuck me.'

'What? Baby, I've wanted you that way every day since the twins were born,' he said, his voice soft. 'But I didn't want to push you. I didn't know what you could, or wanted to, do and I didn't know what we could manage with them in the next room.'

'It's not like it's been so bad,' I amended. 'I just miss –'

'The kinky stuff,' he finished.

I nodded.

'Get undressed,' he ordered.

I shook my head, sniffling. 'I'm not in the mood any more.'

'I said get undressed. It wasn't a request.'

And it wasn't. His tone was something I hadn't heard in a long, long time. Demanding. Forceful. Aidan was the most gentle, easy-going guy I knew, so when he unleashed his dominant side, it brought out something dark and secret in me. A total submissiveness that was completely absent in every other part of my life. A submission I craved. It had been a very long dry spell and I was ready to release the floodgates.

And yet, despite knowing that he was serious, I still delayed. But now I was delaying as part of the game. *Our* game. I could already feel my anticipation building.

'I'm not in the mood,' I said again, but this time I threw in some attitude. Rolling over on my side, I presented him with my backside. 'Sorry.'

I waited for the smack I was sure that was coming, but it didn't come. Instead, I felt him stand up. For one panicky minute I thought he'd taken me seriously and was going to leave me alone. I needn't have worried. Aidan knew me too well for that.

Instead of smacking my ass, he put his hand on the nape of my neck, gathered all of my hair in his hand and tugged hard. Hard enough to make me arch my neck to look at him. Hard enough to make me gasp.

'I said,' he tugged at my hair for emphasis, 'get undressed. Now.'

I couldn't help myself. I whimpered. It had been so long since he'd pulled my hair. So long since he'd taken charge. I could feel myself letting go, slipping into that sub space that I loved so much and had been denied so long. It hadn't been his fault, or even mine, but I had missed it and now I was anxious to renew that part of myself.

'No,' I said defiantly, looking up into his face. Watching the way his eyelids hooded his eyes, lust and challenge flaring his nostrils. 'No.'

He pulled me up by my hair, forcing me to brace my hands on the bed to support myself. 'Did you just say *no* to me?'

I had never seen him so angry. His jaw was tight, teeth clenched. If I hadn't known him so well, if I hadn't trusted him so much, I might have been scared. Even despite those things, I shivered with my helplessness.

213

'Let's see if we can change your mind,' he said, still holding me by my hair as he unbuckled his belt and unzipped his jeans with the other hand.

I moaned as he pulled his cock free. He was already hard and heavy, ready for me. He held his cock in one hand and guided my head to it.

'Suck it and maybe you'll feel like getting naked,' he said. 'Suck it and maybe – maybe – I'll fuck you.'

He yanked hard at my hair, arching my neck over his crotch, and I opened my mouth to gasp at the twinge of pain. He took that opportunity to push the head of his cock into my mouth. Reflexively, I opened wider to take him in, covering my teeth with my lips, automatically drawing him into my throat.

He laughed. 'You say no, but you're still my slut, aren't you?'

The words, combined with his cock pushing into my mouth, had me soaking wet. I couldn't tell him that, though. Let him find out for himself. I shook my head, even while I sucked him deeper and ran my tongue over the sensitive underside.

'No? You're not my slut?'

I couldn't speak – he was flexing his hips and pushing his erection to the back of my throat. I shook my head again.

'We'll see about that,' he said, as much a promise as a threat. 'Before the night's over, you'll be my slut again.'

I swallowed the saliva pooling at the back of my throat, which served to make my throat ripple around his cock. He groaned and thrust again, making me gag. The sound aroused us both. I braced my hands on his thighs to control the depth while he put both hands on the back of my head and pulled me closer. It wasn't a struggle; he let me control it. But his hands on my head served to remind me who was in charge – if I wanted him to be. And I did. Oh, God, how I did.

'Suck it, baby,' he murmured. 'Suck me. God, your mouth is so fucking warm and wet.'

I sucked him like I meant it – intent on getting him to come as quickly as I could. It was part of the game, part of the power struggle. My submissive streak was a mile wide, but I also enjoyed pushing his buttons and seeing if I could turn the tables on him. He knew that and fought against it.

I reached up to fondle his balls, intent on making him come in my mouth. He might – it had been at least a week since we'd done anything sexual at all and since he hadn't known this was what I was planning for our night, there was no reason he would have masturbated beforehand to make sure he'd last. But just as I felt his cock swell, a sure sign that he was moments away from orgasm, he pulled me away by my hair.

'Bad girl,' he said sternly. 'You're not in charge here, I am.'

I giggled and licked my wet lips. They already felt tender and swollen. 'Then you're going to have to work harder,' I said defiantly.

He moved so fast that I didn't have time to do anything but gasp. One minute he was standing in front of me, cock waving in my face, the next he'd sat down on the bed and pulled me over his lap. He tried to get my jeans unfastened, but I was squirming too hard. So he gave up and just stared smacking my ass with the flat of his palm. A good old-fashioned spanking, the likes of which I hadn't had in three years. After the first couple of wallops that left my ass sore, I settled into the heat and sting of it and kind of wished I'd let him get my jeans off so I could really feel it.

'You *will* do what I say,' he said, smacking me hard and fast. There was no rubbing in-between smacks to soothe me, just the unrelenting slap of his hand on my jean-clad ass. 'Do you understand me?'

I didn't respond. I just kept trying to squirm away. He anchored me across his lap, his erection pressed to my stomach, his size and strength too much for me to fight against. Not that I didn't try. I wiggled forward, my head almost on the ground. But my ass was still within striking distance and he took advantage of it.

After over a dozen hard, quick smacks, I whimpered and squirmed. 'OK, OK, I'll do what you want!'

With one more slap across my sore ass, he let me go. 'Good girl.'.

I felt an irrational pride for having earned his praise. That's what being in sub space does for me – and I'd gotten there a hell of a lot quicker than I would have expected after so long away. I'd missed it, a lot. Knowing I could stay immersed in it and not have to shift to mommy mode probably had a lot to do with my mental state.

I slipped bonelessly to the floor, flushed and panting. And we hadn't even fucked yet. He helped me to my feet. Despite trembling hands, I got my jeans unfastened and pulled them, and my damp panties, down to my hips. I was feeling a little shaky – that endorphin rush of pain and pleasure messing with my balance – so I sat on the edge of the bed to take them the rest of the way off, followed by my socks. Still sitting on the bed, I pulled my T-shirt over my head, then unfastened my bra and added it to the pile of clothes on the floor. Then I sat there naked, looking at Aidan expectantly. He was still dressed, his cock as hard as ever and poking from his jeans.

Much to my disappointment, he tucked his erection back in his pants and zipped up. 'First things first,' he said. 'Where is the rope?'

'In my closet,' I whispered.

'Go get it.'

Our bag of bondage rope had been relegated to the back of my closet, behind a box of maternity clothes.

He knew where it was, too, but this was part of the game. Making me work for my own punishment and ultimate pleasure. Prolonging my release until I would be begging for it. And I *would* be begging. I knew that before we even began.

I retrieved the bag of rope and presented it to him. Without a word, he pointed to the bed. I knew what to do. Face down, spread-eagled, I waited. He quickly bound my wrists and ankles to the posts of the bed. Despite the fact that it had been nearly three years, he moved quickly and his knots were effective. Idly, I mused that maybe he had missed this as much as I had, after all.

Firmly tied and helpless, I already felt like I was floating even before I heard the *swoosh* of him pulling his belt through the loops on his jeans and the metal clack of his buckle as he doubled it in his hand. I tensed, waiting. Remembering. Knowing how it would feel before the first strike. Knowing it would hurt, knowing I would yelp from the sting of it, knowing I would tingle in that spot for a minute before the heat diffused throughout my tender ass. I knew all of it, remembered all of it, and I wanted it so badly I was making little whimpering noises in the back of my throat.

He said one word. 'Beg.'

Oh, how it wounds my stubborn ego to have to beg for what I want! Which is exactly why he does it. Aidan does everything for my pleasure, as he will remind me if I disobey in any way. Dare I rebel again, after the beating he just gave my ass? I wanted to play the brat, but his spanking had taken some of the rebellion out of me. Still, I didn't want to disappoint him.

'You know I want it,' I said, which was true enough – he did know. But it also wasn't what he'd demanded.

I felt the edge of the belt glide down the small of my back. He rested the end in the cleft of my cheeks. 'Beg, or I will leave you here and go take a nap in the guest room until you're ready to beg.'

He wouldn't. Would he? I didn't think he would – it wasn't like the old days when we had all the time in the world on the weekend. On the other hand, we did have until the next afternoon and he might very well take a nap and come back to me in two or three hours. I wasn't willing to risk it.

'Please,' I whispered.

'Again.'

'Please.'

He stroked my ass with the belt. 'Louder.'

'Please,' I said, though my voice was still soft. I had gotten used to keeping my voice low during sex. 'Please, Aidan.'

He rewarded me with a slap of the belt across my ass. It was hardly anything at all – more noise than sting – but it made me gasp anyway. Oh, that sound. How I had missed it.

'Please, Aidan,' I said, louder this time. I wiggled my ass in invitation, knowing it was already pinking up from the spanking. 'I need it.'

The second stroke was harder, across both cheeks. I whimpered and squirmed some more. He moved around the bed to the other side. The belt whistled through the air and in that instant before it struck me I knew this one was *really* going to hurt. I wasn't wrong. It caught me across the sensitive skin of my upper thigh, the belt curling inward to just tease the furled lips of my pussy. I yelped, bucking up from the bed as far as my restraints would allow.

'Oh, you liked that, did you?' he said, his voice amused. 'Does your pussy need a good whipping?'

Oh, God. It had been far too long since that particular torment and I wasn't sure I could take it in my current state. How was I supposed to answer? I shook my head. 'Not this time,' I whispered. 'Please.'

'OK. I guess your ass hasn't had enough yet,' he said, the belt whistling through the air for the fourth strike. 'You let me know when it has and maybe I'll stop. Maybe.'

Before I could even catch my breath from the soft scream I couldn't contain, he whipped me again. One, two, three more strikes in quick succession. My ass was on fire, my pussy was trickling wetness down to the sheets. I was rubbing against the bed, trying to get off that way even though I knew he'd never allow it. I was already so hot for it, so ready – I didn't know how much longer I could wait to come. *Until he wanted me to come* was the answer, of course, but I was too caught up in my own need to care.

'Stop moving,' he said, 'or I will stop everything.'

That was all it took for me to go completely still. Until the next stroke of the belt, of course. And then I was arching my back, trying to wiggle away from the next stroke. I couldn't get away from him, though, couldn't escape the next two, three, four slaps of the belt. He'd gentled the force – I couldn't take too many full-on strokes – but they were still hard enough to make me cry out, enough to make my ass throb. Enough to bring me to the brink of orgasm, clinging to the ropes and willing him to give me what I needed so desperately.

'Tell me what you want,' he said, moving around the bed as he struck me with the doubled belt. 'Tell me now.'

I opened my mouth to speak just as the edge of the belt caught me full across my wet, swollen pussy. All I could do was wail, a high-pitched sound that I didn't even recognise as my own voice. I wasn't sure he meant to hit me so squarely or so hard, but I knew he wouldn't say anything until afterwards. We were in this moment together and all I had to say was 'Enough' and he would stop. I knew that I was safe with him, always. And so I thrust my ass up to him, meeting the next stroke of the belt.

'Yes!' I cried out as leather came down on me, unapologetic and unrelenting. 'Yes!'

'Tell me,' he said again, his voice firm but gentle. 'Say it, Hannah.'

This time, I was done. My limit had been reached and he knew it.

'Fuck me,' I whispered, my throat rough and hoarse from my cries, though I didn't remember making that much noise. 'Please fuck me.'

I heard him drop the belt, followed by the rustle of his clothing joining mine on the floor. I was more ready for him than I had ever been as he knelt between my spread thighs and rubbed my fevered flesh with his hands.

'God, your ass is so gorgeous,' he murmured, squeezing and pinching the cheeks until I whimpered and wiggled. 'You should see the stripes the belt made. They won't go away anytime soon.'

That thought – knowing he'd marked me for a few days or even a week – was almost enough to make me come. I'd always loved that about our playtime, knowing that I would carry the memory of it not only in my imagination but on my body. In the shower I would lovingly finger every bruise and welt, touchstones of the passion we shared.

'Oh, good,' I breathed. 'I'm glad.'

I felt his cock probing my entrance and then, in one hard stroke, he was buried as far inside me as he could go. I didn't have to touch my pussy to know I was as wet as I had ever been. His groan of delight let me know it was a good thing.

'Damn, baby, your pussy is positively drooling for my cock,' he marvelled. 'You are a hot little slut for me, aren't you?'

I felt my face flush with embarrassment. It was true, all of it, but to hear him put it so crudely did something to my psyche. I wasn't Hannah the mommy or Hannah the teacher. I wasn't even Hannah the wife. I was Hannah, Aidan's slut. And God, how I had missed it.

He sat there, fully seated in my wetness, until I impatiently pushed back against him. My pussy was clenching around his cock, but I was so wet there was hardly any friction.

He chuckled. 'I might need to lick up all that wetness before I fuck you.'

The idea of him teasing and tormenting me with his mouth made me groan out loud. 'Fuck me, *please*,' I whimpered. 'I just need you to fuck me hard.'

He slapped my thigh hard. 'You're not in charge, sweetheart. I am.'

I made a sound of protest when I felt him withdraw, my pussy empty and achy without his cock to fill me. But then his tongue swept across my engorged labia and I cried out with the pleasure of it. He wasn't quiet about licking me – he slurped and sucked as if he were drinking a milkshake and had to get every last drop. I was blushing furiously, embarrassed by my out-of-control body and unladylike responses to such perverse pleasures. But I knew that was what he loved best about me in this situation – that I loved the kinky stuff and couldn't control my body's reaction.

He licked me from clit to asshole, until I was a quivering mass of nerve endings. I strained at my bindings, longing for him to flip me over so I could grab his cock and pull him into me. But I remained helpless to his whims. And that knowledge, along with the sensation of him sucking every inch of my pussy into his mouth before roughly stroking me with his fingers, was all it took for me to come. I writhed on the bed as he finger-fucked me, screaming and crying as I came.

'Fuck me,' I cried out again, all of my need in my plea. 'Please!'

And then he was in me again, feeling bigger now that there was less lubrication and my pussy was contracting in orgasm. He gripped my well-beaten ass in his hands as he thrust into me, driving me up inch by inch on the bed until I was nearly bumping against the headboard. I braced my hands against the wood and pushed back, giving as much as I could in this position, tightening my muscles around him, clenching my cheeks and thighs to drive him wild. I felt his thumb circling my asshole, massaging it, pressing just enough to make me squirm in remembrance of how it felt to have him inside me there. I nearly begged him to fuck my ass, but he felt too damned good in my pussy to stop now.

He groaned, thrusting into me as my undulations stroked his cock from every direction. 'Baby, you feel too damned good,' he said by way of apology as he flooded me, coming as he gripped my hips in his hands and bucked into me.

I tilted my hips up and back, the head of his cock angling down to my G-spot so that those long, rough strokes hit me just right. And then I was coming again too, adding to the flood. I cried out, gripping the ropes in my hands until my knuckles went white, riding his cock even as his orgasm crested. For several long moments, there was only wetness and tightness and cries and heavy breathing. My world. Right here, right now. With Aidan.

Slowly, I loosened my grip on the ropes at my wrists and sank back onto the bed, feeling the spread of moisture beneath me. Aidan was still kneeling behind me, though his erection had softened and slipped from my body. I was feeling relaxed and drowsy and wanted him to untie me and cuddle up on the bed.

Instead, he smacked my ass. Hard. I yelped, jerking at my bonds.

'What the hell was that for?' I asked, straining to see him over my shoulder.

He laughed. 'We have all night and you don't want to watch movies. You don't think I'm going to stop with just one round, do you?'

Despite my post-orgasmic bliss, I felt a shudder dance along my spine. 'Um, no?'

He moved from between my legs and stood up. I watched as he pulled on his jeans and tucked his damp cock into his pants. '"Um, no" is right,' he said, sounding very, very sure of himself. 'I'm not even *close* to being finished with you. I might have to call Catherine and see if she'll keep the boys tomorrow night, too.'

I knew he wouldn't do that. At least, I didn't *think* he would.

'What are you doing? Where are you going?' I asked, as he moved towards the door. My muscles strained as I twisted to see him, but he was just out of my line of sight.

'To finish making dinner for you,' he said. 'You're going to need your strength later. I promise.'

I groaned, and it was *almost* pure anticipatory pleasure. I'd unleashed a beast. I had no doubt he would make me regret it for just a little while before he let me revel in it.

Starting Over

'Shit, shit, shit!'

I couldn't see the person who was screaming, but I could hear her. Hell, everyone could hear her. It was a Friday night and the coffee shop was crowded and the line was out the door. No one was at the counter, but I assumed the voice belonged to the only person working.

'Have you been waiting long?'

I turned to the man behind me and shrugged. 'Not terribly. But I haven't seen anyone yet.'

He glanced at his watch. 'I don't have time for this,' he muttered, though I didn't think he was talking to me. 'I have a date.'

So did I, I thought, as he stalked around the growing line and out into the night. The woman who had been behind him just shrugged and we shared a commiserating smile.

'I'm sorry, can I take your order?'

The voice belonged to a young woman who looked as frustrated as she sounded. 'We're extremely short-staffed tonight.'

'I see. Don't worry about it, it happens.'

She nodded absently as she noted my order and rang me up. 'Yeah, and it keeps happening to me. We had one girl just take off for Florida a few weeks ago and, instead of firing her, the manager said he'd pick up her extra hours but then he got the flu or pneumonia or something and no one wants to work on Friday night ...'

She kept talking as she walked the length of the counter to the espresso machine, then talked through the making of my drink even though I couldn't hear her over the sound of the machine or the impatient crowd behind me. I wondered if the manager had any idea that his lone Friday-night employee was losing her mind.

I collected my drink from the end of the counter and found a seat at one of the tall tables along the bank of windows. I'd be able to see him coming – which sounded more ominous than it really was. But I was nervous as hell and needed the advance warning to collect myself.

Full dark had fallen while I'd waited for my coffee. Now I sat looking out at the streetlights and the headlights going by, my face reflected back to me. I wondered what others thought when they looked at me, what they saw that I didn't see. Long dark-blonde hair pulled back at the nape of my neck, my mother's high cheekbones and aquiline nose, my father's piercing blue eyes and long, lanky body. The only people who ever told me I was beautiful were the ones who had loved me – others said I was statuesque or striking. When I was in college, still awkward and coltish in my body, I'd been told by a photographer that I could be a model. But I think he'd only said that to get in my pants. It hadn't worked. I was many things, but I wasn't vain or easy. No, I was incredibly self-critical and stubborn.

Out of habit, I glanced at my wrist, forgetting once again that my mother's watch – which had belonged to her mother – was at the jeweller's, the clasp being repaired. I fished through my purse, hunting for my cell phone to check the time, when I heard his voice behind me.

'Sorry I'm late.'

His voice was a balm for my nerves, though I suppose it should have had the opposite effect. I smoothed my hands over my skirt and smiled. 'Hey. It's OK.'

Denny sat down next to me, looking the same as he had the day we split up. The same wavy brown hair that was a shade darker than his eyes. The same kind face, the same athletic body that looked as good in sweats as a suit. Seeing him was like letting my eyes settle on a field of wildflowers after a drive through the crowded city – comforting, soothing, familiar. It had only been six months, but I felt like he was a memory from another lifetime. I had been some other person then. But he hadn't changed at all.

He studied me and, unlike the musings about what strangers might see when they look at me, I knew what he saw. I was thinner than I had been, but not in a good way. Stress makes me forget to eat and, for the six months I'd been with him and the three months after we broke up, I'd steadily lost weight. I was better now, eating healthier, coming back to myself. It felt good.

I let him look his fill, waiting for the questions that would come. Of course he would have questions. I'd walked out on him after we'd had sex that last time and I hadn't looked back. Hadn't taken his calls or responded to his texts and emails. After a month, he gave up. I knew he would. Denny wasn't the type to chase after a woman once she made it clear she didn't want anything to do with him. And though I couldn't say the words, my actions said I was done.

'So, did you want to stay here or go someplace else?'

I blinked at him. I'd expected questions, but not that one. 'It's up to you. I thought this would be a good place to talk.'

Just then a group of seven or eight people came in,

filling the already crowded coffee shop to capacity as they squeezed in along the counter beside us and chattered about an art class they were taking. I nodded as Denny cocked his head toward the door. I followed him out, tossing my still hot coffee in the trash can. I hadn't wanted it anyway. I caught the eye of the poor lone barista as we left and mouthed, 'Good luck.' She shook her head and threw up her hands. I knew the feeling.

It took my eyes a moment to adjust to the darkness outside and I nearly bumped into Denny as he walked to the curb. 'Where are we going?'

He tucked my hand in the crook of his arm, a true gentleman in every sense of the word. 'I don't know. Let's start with my car. We can at least talk in peace there.'

We walked in silence to the parking lot tucked behind a row of restaurants and shops across the street. Denny keyed the remote to unlock the doors on his Land Rover, let me in on the passenger side and closed the door with a resounding thud. My heart responded with a jump-beat of its own. Nerves. Just nerves. This was both a reunion and a confrontation and it was impossible to tell from Denny's demeanour how it would turn out. I knew how I wanted it to go, but I also knew I didn't really deserve another chance.

Denny climbed into the driver seat, closed the door and put the key in the ignition. The stereo blared to life, a hard-driving rock song filling the interior of the SUV. He adjusted the volume until it was barely audible and looked at me.

'It's good to see you, Alanna.'

'Thanks.' I smoothed my hands down my skirt again. 'It's good to see you. I'm sorry for how I ended things.'

He cocked his head at me. 'I wouldn't say you ended it. You just disappeared.'

I couldn't argue with him. 'I know. And I'm sorry. I didn't handle it well. I'm sorry.'

He leaned his head back on the seat rest and closed his eyes. 'I don't need an apology. I just need to know why you're back.'

'I wanted to see you,' I said, though that didn't begin to describe what I wanted. 'I want you back in my life.'

There, I'd said it. Or at least the most important part of it. If he didn't want anything to do with me now – and I couldn't blame him if he didn't – he would tell me and I could walk away knowing it was truly a closed chapter in my life. And cursing myself for not doing things differently.

'OK. But how do I know you won't disappear again?'

I took a deep breath. 'Because I'm not married any more and have no reason to leave.'

I waited for an explosion, but it didn't come. He simply nodded slowly. 'You're a free woman now?'

'Yeah.' I stared at him, willing him to meet my eyes

and see how sorry I was. For everything. 'I'm sorry I never told you – it wasn't fair to you, or to him. But I didn't know what to do. I was miserable. Hell, he was miserable. I thought I just needed to have a little fun –'

He turned to look at me again. 'And I was the fun?'

I realised I was rambling on like the barista at City Coffee and closed my mouth before I made things worse. I nodded.

'Did you tell him about me?'

I shook my head.

'Why not?'

I held my hands up in a no-answer gesture. 'I thought you'd be gone after a few weeks. I thought maybe I could make peace with my marriage, with his lack of interest in ...'

'Sex?' he filled in.

'In me. He had no interest in me, in any way.'

'So I was the ego boost you needed and then you took off,' he surmised. 'But you ended up divorced anyway.'

'No, you weren't an ego boost,' I said.

He looked at me sharply, scepticism in his expression.

'OK, maybe at first. But after a little while –'

'We were together for six months,' he reminded me. 'At some point, didn't you think I should know you were married and unavailable? I thought you were just putting in a lot of hours at work.'

233

'I was!' I took a breath and let it out. I was getting defensive. 'I *was* working a lot. I didn't want to be at home and I didn't want to get in even deeper with you. So I stayed at the shop.'

It was true. The floral shop had taken off since I'd opened it two years ago and it had been easy enough to hide there, away from Richard, my husband of five years, and Denny, my lover who had become so much more. It had been the coward's way out of a difficult situation.

'Why didn't you tell me?' he asked quietly.

'I was ashamed.'

'I would have understood.'

I turned in the seat so that I was facing him. 'Denny, I didn't understand. I wasn't that person, that woman. That's not who I am.'

'Apparently, it is,' he said dryly.

'But I didn't want to be that person. I ended it with you and put my energy into trying to make my marriage work.'

'What happened?'

'Richard told me I was smothering him. Then he told me he had a girlfriend and wanted a divorce.' I laughed, sounding more bitter than relieved, though I had felt tremendous relief at the time.

'I'm sorry.'

'Don't be. I'm not. I am just sorry I hadn't had the

234

nerve to end my marriage myself when it was clear neither of us was happy.'

'Yeah, that probably would've been for the best.'

I hadn't known Denny long – but I had expected a stronger reaction from him. We'd been well on our way to getting serious, which had made my life even more complicated as I tried to dance around Denny's questions about why he couldn't spend the night at my house. I'd told him I lived with a roommate who wasn't comfortable with overnight guests. It hadn't been a lie – nothing I had ever told him had been a lie and he'd never asked me outright if I'd been married – and yet I'd been living a lie for the entire brief time we were together.

'You don't seem angry,' I said, wondering if I should say anything at all or leave well enough alone. 'You don't even seem surprised I was married.'

'I *was* angry,' he said. 'But first I was hurt and confused. Then I found out you were married and I was furious. Then I let it go.'

'You found out?' My voice was rising again. 'How? When? Why didn't you say something?'

He laughed. 'You know what I do, Alanna.'

I was confused. 'You work for the Department of Defence. So?'

'Sweetheart, I'm former Army Intelligence. I'm suspicious of everyone, everything,' he said. 'I knew something was up the first night you wouldn't let me come

235

over to your house. I just didn't want to believe it.'

'So you figured I was married and didn't bother to say anything?' It was completely irrational, but I felt like I'd been deceived. 'Why didn't you say something?'

'What was I going to say?' He shook his head. 'It was your burden to carry. If you'd wanted me to know, you would've told me. You forgot to take your rings off once, the night of that crazy rainstorm. I surprised you at the shop one night when you were closing and took you to dinner. You were wearing your rings when you let me in, then they were gone when you went in the back to get your stuff. Remember?'

I did remember. Not that he'd seen my rings, but the rainstorm. And after. We'd driven to his condo and walked to the Italian restaurant a couple of blocks away. The rain started coming down in sheets as we were leaving, making it impossible to even see the street. We waited for it to let up but it never did. We'd started making out there under the awning of the closed restaurant. I'd been anxious to get home before Richard started worrying, but Denny's kisses down my neck on the deserted street had set my blood on fire until I'd forgotten all about Richard. We'd made a run for it to his house, getting soaked in the process, and he'd stripped off my clothes as soon as we got in the door. My wedding rings had been tucked in my purse by then and I was his – all his. At least for another hour.

'Remember?' he asked again.

I nodded. 'I remember that night. And a lot of others. It was the best time I'd had in a long, long time.'

'You made a lot of mistakes,' he said. 'After a few weeks, I had a pretty good idea you were married. When you took off, I had to know for sure.'

I felt cold all of a sudden. 'What did you do?'

'I have a friend who's an attorney. Family law, divorces, stuff like that. He works with private investigators. I didn't want to be linked to it, so I asked Joe to look into it and let me know.'

'You had me followed?'

He laughed. 'I didn't have to. A simple records search turned up your marriage. The rest – like your real address – was just icing on the cake.'

'If you knew I was married before I left, why didn't you check up on me then?'

'I was in love with you. I wanted to trust you.'

His words slammed into me like a thousand-pound weight. He'd never even said he loved me and now he was saying he *had* been. Of course, I was no better.

'Oh.' I swallowed hard, willing myself not to cry. 'I'm sorry I did that to you.'

'Why didn't you tell me you were married? I'd like to say my morals would have made me end it, but I know it wouldn't have made a difference with you.'

I swallowed again. 'I was falling in love with you.'

'Seems like all the more reason to tell me,' he said.

'I couldn't. I couldn't even tell you I loved you.'

'I know. And I couldn't tell you because I knew you weren't free.'

Despite my best efforts, the tears started falling. 'I'm sorry, Denny.'

'Is that why you wanted to meet me tonight? To apologise?'

I reached across the space that separated us and cupped his cheek. I could feel the hint of stubble rough against my thumb as I stroked his jaw, willing him to relax. I needed this connection, the physical touch, even if it wasn't reciprocated.

'I am in love with you,' I said, staring into his eyes and willing him to see the truth. 'I never stopped loving you. I just needed to get my life in order before I could say the words and have them mean everything I want them to mean.'

There, I'd said it. Whatever happened now, I had said it. The words that I'd kept bottled up for all the time we were together, even though I could feel myself falling for him, feeling things I'd never felt with Richard or anyone else, knowing it was little more than emotional blackmail to confess my love to someone I'd been lying to. I'd thought a little fling would get me past a rough spot in my increasingly unhappy marriage. Instead, I'd found the love of my life and he didn't even know who I was.

The tears continued to roll down my cheeks, but I refused to break contact with him. If he pulled away, so be it, but I wouldn't leave this time. I wouldn't let go.

He opened his mouth to speak and in that moment before the words came out, I didn't know if it would be forgiveness or condemnation. I knew what it should be and I knew what I wanted it to be, but I also knew life didn't always go my way. So I held my breath and waited.

'So you're divorced now? You're free?'

I nodded, afraid to breathe or blink or say anything at all.

'And you want me? You love me?'

I nodded again. 'Yes, oh, yes.'

He moved so fast, gathering me up in his arms and dragging me across the console to straddle his lap, that I could do little more than squeak and hold on, my hands tucked against his chest where I could feel his heart hammering.

'You're not free,' he said, burying his face in my hair. 'You're *mine*. You're finally mine.'

Only then did I breathe, truly breathe. 'Yes, yes,' I murmured, kissing his temple, down his face to his jaw, kissing his mouth. 'Yours. I'm yours.'

His hands stroked down my back and up again, catching my hair in his fingers, twirling, tugging, like he couldn't get enough of touching me. Back down to my hips, spanning their narrow width, taking a measure of me. Judging by the growing bulge I felt pressing against me, he was very pleased.

'I've missed you,' he said against my mouth, his hands everywhere at once, touching me, memorising me. 'Missed you so damned much I was going out of my mind. I dreamed about you, damn it. I dreamed about fucking you, being inside of you every way we've done it and every way we never got a chance. I want that chance.'

'I know, I know,' I groaned, grinding on him now, relief and tenderness turning to desire. Unfettered, honest desire built on what we had, not on what I was missing with someone else. 'I missed you too. I thought this was best, I thought –'

He kissed me until I was breathless, then came up for air long enough to say, 'Stop thinking so damned much. Talk to me, tell me everything.'

I shook my head, my brain buzzing like I'd had too much caffeine even though I'd hardly touched my coffee. 'What – what do you want to know?'

He laughed, and it was the sweetest sound I'd ever heard. 'Not now, woman. Not *now*. For ever. Always. Tell me everything, always. We can deal with anything together.'

For ever. Always. So I wasn't the only hopeless romantic. I laughed along with him, fisting my hands in his shirt and kissing him long and hard.

'You're grinding on me,' he whispered against my mouth.

I was. I couldn't help it. 'Is that a problem?'

'Nope. As long as you don't mind fucking me right here and now.'

There was a time when I would have said no. When I would have worried about someone I knew seeing me and telling Richard. Now I didn't have those worries. Someone could still see us, of course, but what they'd see was two people who couldn't wait until they got home to be together – not a woman who hated herself for living a lie.

The words were barely out of his mouth before I was hiking up my skirt and tugging at my panties. I pushed back on my knees, flashing my panty-clad crotch at him. He groaned, bucking against me, the bulge in his pants all I needed to let me know he wanted me as much as I wanted him. I ached to feel him inside of me, filling me in that way only he could.

I reached for his belt and fumbled with the stiff leather in the tight confines of the car seat. He all but groaned as I awkwardly unfastened his trousers and palmed his full erection through the narrow opening. My heart leapt and I felt a corresponding throb in my pussy. I wanted him more than I had ever wanted anything in my life. I had spent so many sleepless nights fantasising about him even though I had no reason to think he would ever want to see me again.

He covered my hand with his and squeezed it over his hard cock. 'Feel that? I need you now, baby. It's been too damned long.'

'Yes,' I breathed, pulling his cock free, careful not to catch it in the zipper. 'I want you, too.'

He put his head back against the seat and moaned as I stroked him awkwardly, my arm tucked between us. I needed him inside of me as much as he needed to be inside of me. I gave up trying to get my panties off and just tugged them to the side. He went utterly still as I guided him toward my opening, spreading my knees as far as I could to accommodate him. The broad tip of his cock bumped against my swollen clit, sending shockwaves of pleasure through me. It *had* been too long, too long without this man who did things to my body, and to my heart, that I'd never experienced before. All I wanted was to fill the emptiness with everything he had to offer.

I adjusted the angle of his cock and then, just like that, he was inside of me in one long, wet stroke. He groaned and I echoed him, tightening my hips and curving my body over him. I anchored my hands on the metal supports of the headrest, rolling my hips so I could feel every inch of him inside of me. My pussy tightened convulsively around him, so full it almost hurt. I rose up slowly, as far as the roof of the car would allow, and slid back down just as slowly, the steering wheel rubbing against my ass. I was teasing us both, even though neither of us needed to be teased. Prolonging the pleasure because I could, because I didn't need to rush home or change my clothes or wash his scent from my body. Enjoying every inch, every second, every gasp and moan, because I had all the time in the world to fuck the man I loved.

He had other ideas, though. He cupped my face in his hands and pulled me down for a kiss. His lips slanted across mine, warm and wet and firm, tasting just the way I remembered. Then he thrust up into me. Hard. I gasped into his open mouth as he did it again. Hard. Harder. Fucking me in this confined space in quick, short, driving thrusts. One, two, three. Kissing me the entire time, taking my cries into his mouth, giving me his own moans of pleasure. One, two, three.

I clung to the headrest, my hair a curtain around both our heads, shielding my view of the outside, my existence contained within this car with this man. The whole world could be right outside staring at us and I didn't care, as long as he kept fucking me. Let them watch. Let them wish they were us.

'Yes,' I cried out, the angle of his cock hitting that swollen, sensitive spot inside of me. 'Fuck me, Denny.'

'Say it again,' he growled. 'Say my name again.'

I thrust down on him as hard as he was thrusting up against me. 'Denny, my Denny,' I cried out. 'Fuck me, Denny!'

He surged up into me and I bumped my head on the roof, but I didn't care. He was inside of me, he was mine. And I was his. He moaned, the sound primal and filled with longing, and I felt his cock pulse inside of me just as everything inside of me turned to liquid. I was laughing and crying and coming all at the same time, riding him wildly, milking his cock for every sweet drop as he pulled me down on him and filled me with his need.

Finally, I pulled back and looked at him. I couldn't help but giggle. 'This was ... wild. I never expected this to happen.'

'Are you sorry?'

'Not in the least. You?'

He looked into my eyes and smiled. There was no regret or hesitation when he said, 'I love you. I'll fuck you like this every night if you want me to. But I'd really prefer to get you naked in a bed – yours or mine – and make up for lost time.'

I got up the nerve to look around, but I couldn't see out the windows for the fog we'd generated with our body heat. My skirt was twisted around my waist, my hair was a tangled, damp mess and it felt like a river ran between my legs. I laughed again, shaking my head at the incongruity of it, the pure joy of it.

'Yeah, I think we should find a bed. Right now.'

'Good.' He pulled my face down for another kiss, whispering something against my lips. '*Mine.*'

Right As Rain

I once read that sex was only a big deal if you weren't getting it. Kind of like air or food. I guess I always felt that way about my own sex life – no big deal, except when I wasn't getting even my basic needs met. Sometimes I would wonder if there was something more to be had, something I was missing, if all the articles in the women's magazines on the grocery-store racks were to be believed. But I was getting enough to sustain me – like a strict diet would sustain me – and it seemed petty to complain when I didn't even know exactly what it was I was longing for.

Then I met Duncan and realised that I'd been settling for plain noodles when there was a gourmet meal to be had. They say sex isn't love. They're right – and wrong. Sex, really mind-shattering, soul-touching sex, can be a form of love. And once you've had that, there's no going back to a bland diet. Your body won't let you. And your heart? Well, your heart may be OK without sex, but it develops a fondness for the one who gives you everything you never knew you desired. My body longed for Duncan. And my heart was quickly following.

It seemed fitting that I met Duncan on a rainy day since things were always pretty wet once he was in my life. He moved in downstairs one soggy weekend in April. At the time, I was between jobs, colleges and relationships. I was living in a tiny apartment on the third floor of a sprawling apartment building right off the campus of George Washington University, planning to start my Master's in political science in the fall. I kept to myself most of the time – busy filling out financial aid forms and job applications – and I was used to my neighbours coming and going at all hours. The guy who lived next door had an older girlfriend with a rockin' bod who could shake the shingles off the roof with her orgasmic moans. I wondered sometimes, with curiosity and probably envy, if it was just an act or if it was all real. If it was real, well – maybe I needed to chat up Matthew Wheaton (the name on his mailbox) and find out his secrets. Did he have a ten-inch cock? A tongue that curled? Double-jointed fingers? A closet full of sex toys? Somehow, I didn't think his girlfriend would appreciate my inquiries, so I never said anything.

Other than the neighbourly waves and 'how are you?'s, I kept to myself, paid my bills on time and didn't play my music too loud. For the most part, my neighbours did the same. I'd never felt a compelling need to introduce myself to any of them until that rainy Sunday in April when I looked out my window and saw a lean, athletic, ginger-headed hottie in cutoffs and a SUNY sweatshirt trying to unload a surfboard in the rain off the top of a Jeep Cherokee with New York licence plates. Suddenly, I wanted to get to know my neighbour in a bad way.

'Hey, let me help you,' I said, a little breathless from running down three flights of stairs.

Duncan gave me that wary look of all people who've lived in a city, the one that says, 'Stay out of my personal space.' He gave me the once-over and I was suddenly painfully conscious of my lime-green 'Give Peas a Chance' T-shirt, purple tie-dyed yoga pants and mop of dark-brown bed-head hair. I might have looked a mess, but I guess I seemed harmless enough because he smiled.

'Thanks, but I've got it. I can't get the knots out because they've swollen up from the rain.'

I wasn't going to be so easily deterred. 'I grew up around boats and my hands are smaller than yours. Let me give it a try.'

He cocked his head to the side as if trying to determine who this crazy chick was, willing to get wet in the rain for a stranger, and then shrugged. 'OK, thanks.'

247

'Wendy,' I said, thrusting my smaller hand into his bigger one.

He laughed. 'Duncan. And a nice girl to help out a stranger. Or maybe you're a strange girl to be running around in the rain helping a stranger.'

'I like a challenge,' I said and left him to figure out whether I was talking about the surfboard or something else.

I didn't think I was strange. Granted, my technique was more than a little awkward compared to what I imagined he was used to – a bevy of college coeds and surfer girls fawning over him. Not that you could call my impulsive decision to abandon the dry warmth of my apartment for the wet April chill any kind of a technique, but I didn't really care at that point. He was talking to me and that was a start.

'These knots are a challenge,' he agreed, taking the high road. Or maybe offering me even more of a challenge?

I grinned, up for whatever he wanted to throw at me, and worked diligently on getting the surfboard untied. We both got drenched in the process. Five minutes later, with him working on one side and me working on the other, we got the board down. He hefted it on his shoulder and headed up the stairs to his apartment. I watched him go, thoroughly enraptured by his wet running shorts clinging to his taut ass and the sexy way his reddish-blond hair curled on the nape of his neck. Then I did the only thing I could do – I grabbed a surprisingly heavy box marked 'Media Shit' and followed him, feeling a little bit like a lost puppy following him home.

By the time we had unpacked his car, it was raining in great windy sheets and we were both soaked. Helping somebody move, even if it's only a few boxes, is a bonding experience. It speeds up the 'getting to know you' process. Or at least that was my justification as I invited Duncan up to my place for a drink. If it had been a Saturday night and I'd asked him to hit the clubs with me, it would have sounded like a come on. But it was a rainy Sunday, the rest of his stuff wouldn't get there until Monday morning and he was new to the city, so I was just being neighbourly. OK, so it was still a come on. But it was a neighbourly, friendly come on.

I made a pot of coffee to knock off the chill. Duncan had stripped off his wet sweatshirt and I nearly collapsed as I witnessed the unveiling of his flat, ripped stomach. It was smooth except for a reddish-brown sprinkling of hair that started a couple of inches below his belly button and disappeared into his running shorts. Thankfully, he was wearing a sleeveless muscle shirt under the sweatshirt, which he tugged down to cover his stomach and protect my poor heart. But the shirt left little to the imagination and accentuated his well-muscled arms. He hadn't needed my help carrying his stuff – he could have carried all of it and me, too, without breaking a sweat.

He flopped down on my futon by the window and watched the rain while I tried not to stare at his biceps or imagine licking a trail down the hair on his belly. He had a Celtic tattoo banded around his right arm. Most guys don't get the inner arm tattooed – it hurts like hell – but his went all the way around. He won bad-ass points for that. Not that he needed points. I was already counting the ways I wanted to devour his body and I hadn't even seen him naked yet.

He shifted around as if he was uncomfortable. His running shorts pulled taut over his crotch and I really had to make a concentrated effort not to stare. He reminded me of a greyhound, lean and muscular with awkward limbs that wouldn't seem to do what he wanted while he was sitting still. A greyhound with an amazing bulge. I grinned.

'What's so funny?'

I shook my head. 'Nothing.'

'Mmm. This is just what I needed,' he said, sipping from the mug I handed him. He looked up and narrowed his eyes at me, probably because I was still grinning like an idiot. 'C'mon. Tell me why you're laughing at me.'

I sat on the corner of the futon, as far away from him as I could be and still be sharing the same piece of furniture. I would have sat someplace else, but spending money on furniture hasn't exactly been a priority for me. Some people are funny about having their personal space invaded by a stranger, so I was trying to be polite even though I didn't think Duncan was like that. Or at least I was hoping he wasn't like that. On the other hand, I didn't think he'd appreciate it if I just plopped myself down in his lap, either. But the thought crossed my mind.

'I was just thinking that you look like a dog.' I realised how bad that sounded as soon as the words were out of my mouth. My face flushed hotly. I was always putting my foot in my mouth like that. Honesty may be the best policy, but if I'd learned anything from the guys I had dated, sometimes honesty needed a filter which I didn't seem to have. 'I mean, you look like a runner, someone who is more comfortable in motion.'

He laughed, no offence taken. 'Yeah, that's about right. I ran in high school and undergrad and played just about every sport my parents would let me play.' He thumped his chest. 'I'm still pissed my mom wouldn't let me play football. She was afraid I would get hurt. *Me*. Look at me!'

I didn't need an invitation to look. He certainly looked capable of handling a football. Or anything else. Like me, for instance. Especially me.

'And you surf,' I said. I was just filled with witty, insightful comments. 'I mean, you must have surfed at some point. Not a lot of surfing around here.'

I wanted to bang my head on the hardwood floor so the word 'surf' would stop falling out of my mouth. No wonder I didn't date much.

Duncan reached over and put his hand on my thigh. He had to lean towards me to do it, and his mug looked precariously close to spilling its contents all over my dry-clean-only futon, but I didn't give a damn. I stared at his hand on my leg, the long, tapered fingers with their short, neat nails, and I didn't care if he drenched the futon in coffee. My entire body tensed at that gentle touch. It was ridiculous, I'd just met him, but my brain had become detached from my body, which was quivering with pent-up anticipation.

'Don't try so hard,' he said softly.

'Huh? What?' It was as if my brain had not only shut down, it had packed a bag and left the country.

Duncan laughed and I decided I really liked the sound, even if it was at my expense. 'I like you, girlie. You're cute.'

'Uh, thanks, I think.' I wasn't entirely sure it was a compliment.

He set his mug on the floor and scooted closer to me. I couldn't have moved if there had been a fire in my kitchen. Or in my pants, which I was pretty sure there was. Duncan leaned over and I thought he was going to kiss me and I thought I was going to come in my panties if he did. Instead, he whispered in my ear, 'I love rain storms. They make me horny.'

It was a lame pick-up line. Seriously. Did he think that was all it took? Oh hell, who was I kidding? That *was* all it took. I'm not the type of girl who lets an opportunity slide by, especially when it looks so fucking delicious still wet from the rain. Still, I was a little annoyed he thought I was that easy.

I turned towards him, nearly kneeing him in the groin in the process, and took his face in my hands. 'Do you really think that's all it takes to get in a girl's pants? Or are the girls in New York just that easy?'

He smirked. 'Well, there aren't many girls who'd stand out in the rain helping me carry my shit and then offer me coffee. I figure you're either a really good Samaritan or you think I'm cute, too.'

'You *are* cute,' I said, rubbing my knuckles along his cheek. 'You have cute dimples.'

'I saw you staring at my stomach,' he said, mirroring my moves and rubbing my cheek. 'Aw, and now I've made you blush. So, should I apologise for the horny comment – or just work a little harder?'

I smiled. 'No need to apologise. I'm not as easy as you think I am, but I do think you're cute.'

'So I should work harder,' he said. 'OK, Wendy, I can do that.'

I couldn't stop staring at his mouth. His body had been so distracting, I hadn't noticed his beautiful, full lips. I licked my own bottom lip just at the thought of what his mouth must feel like.

'Can I kiss you?' I asked, saying exactly what I was

thinking about doing. See what I mean about not having a filter?

'Yeah,' he breathed into my mouth as I kissed him.

Kissing Duncan was better than his mouth even looked – and that was pretty damned good. His mouth was soft and warm and wet and he leaned into me as I kissed him deeper, his hands on my hips, bracing his weight so that I knew he was there, right *there*, practically in my lap, kissing me harder and deeper and wetter until I was panting raggedly into his mouth and we hadn't even touched or undressed yet.

He must have been thinking the same thing because he ran his hands up my arms to my shoulders and down again, grazing my breasts as he went. He wrapped his hands around my waist and shifted me so that I was sitting across his lap. I sighed, happy to go wherever he wanted to put me.

He yanked my T-shirt up, breaking our kiss only long enough to get my head through the neck hole. Then he was palming my bare breasts, kneading them almost as hard as he was kissing me, driving me to distraction so that I almost forgot he was still fully clothed. I quickly stripped his tank top off, admiring the nicely muscled chest and stomach that had been teasing me before. He was still very much the runner he had been in high school and college and didn't have an overly muscular upper body, but I liked it. I ran my fingertips over his pecs, twirled my finger in the scattering of reddish-brown curls on his chest, trailed my fingers down to those washboard abs that intrigued me so.

I nibbled my way down his collarbone to his chest, where I found the edge of one nipple and sucked it gently before switching to the other. My hand was on another mission, stroking circles around his belly button, scraping my nails across the flat plane of his stomach. I would have been quite content to spend the rest of the afternoon making out with Duncan if he hadn't gotten his hand down my yoga pants and found my pussy.

'God, you're wet,' he murmured as I nipped his shoulder in response to the fingers manipulating my folds. 'So fucking wet.'

I tried to get my hand in his shorts, but they were damp from the rain and too constricting. 'And you're hard,' I said, biting his shoulder a little harder. 'Get these damn shorts off so I can see.'

We fumbled our way out of the rest of our clothing, panting and laughing as we went, a tangle of limbs and damp hair and wet pussy and hard cock on my too-small futon. It never occurred to me to move the party to my bed. I didn't care about comfort or space or washable fabrics. I just wanted to get fucked. Fucked by Duncan.

'I want to see you. Naked.'

Duncan lay back on the futon, feet braced on the ground, thighs spread. He was stunning. I couldn't stop staring at him, from the sprinkle of light-red hair across his upper chest and his lower belly, to the flat, muscular stomach, to the triangle of darker red hair that framed his magnificently thick cock, to the thighs and legs rippling with corded muscle. He was a naked god. And he was naked on *my* futon.

'You are amazing.'

I didn't give him a chance to respond. I dropped my head between those lean thighs and licked his cock, top to bottom and back again. Slowly. So slowly. Until he was clutching at my hair and pushing his erection toward my mouth in anxious need for more than the torment I was offering him. The futon creaked as he pushed his hips up to meet my mouth and I enveloped the tip, stroking my tongue across it as I went. He moaned and made shallow thrusts as if he couldn't help himself. I wrapped my fingers around the base of his cock to keep from gagging and guided him back as far as I could take him. That seemed to be enough because he groaned and held my head. I swallowed around him, concentrating on breathing as I held him in my throat, enjoying the way his hips quivered under me.

I like being in charge during sex. I like going down on a man and feeling that power. And right now, with Duncan's cock at the back of my throat, I felt all powerful. I slowly slid off his cock, leaving a trail of moisture in my wake, and looked up at him. He was gone – so far into his lust that he couldn't even speak. He opened his mouth, shook his head and smiled. I kept staring into his eyes as I dragged my tongue across the engorged head of his cock. His eyes widened, as did his mouth, and all that came out was a groan and something that may or may not have been my name. Then I was taking him to the back of my throat again and he was doing his damnedest not to gag me as his hips starting pushing.

I stroked his cock in time to his hip thrusts, pulling him up to my mouth, taking him in a few inches, then sliding off. Up and down, I let him fuck my mouth while I controlled the motions – and things were getting frantic enough that my poor old futon was creaking. I had a moment's concern that we'd end up in a pile on the floor. Then he was coming, coming hard and wet in my mouth, and I couldn't think of anything else except how musky sweet he tasted and how his moans sounded like a Buddhist chant.

I teased the opening of his cock oh so gently, licking the wetness that leaked from him until he finally relaxed his grip on my head. I rested my head against his thigh, breathing him in. I'd never smelled anything in my entire life quite so good as fresh rain and wet Duncan. I ran the palm of my hand from his knee up to his groin, feeling him tremble under my touch. His cock rested against his thigh, softening but still impressively large. I was looking forward to seeing what else his magnificent dick could do. Hopefully soon.

Finally, Duncan sighed, pulled me up between his thighs and wrapped those long arms and legs around me. 'Come here,' he said. 'Come here and let me fuck you.'

I went willingly, but I knew it was all bravado. 'The mind may be willing, but the body needs a rest,' I said, stroking his cock gently.

I expected him to flip me over and go down on me until he was hard again. Instead, he reached down between us and slid two fingers into me. I gasped as his palm grazed my clit.

'Mmm, you're even wetter now,' he said. 'I wonder how wet you get?'

I tried to say something witty, or at least coherent, but all I could manage was to croak, 'Don't know. Find out.'

He angled his fingers up into me, cupping my cunt in his hand and squeezing on the outside while his fingers stroked me on the inside. It was an amazing sensation and I melted against him, my mouth instinctively going to his chest. I sucked as he fucked me, finding the rhythm he used on my cunt. Steady, steady, leaving red marks where I went, sucking his nipples, the whorls of hair, the muscular ridges of his chest and shoulders, sucking and nibbling as his fingers worked their magic.

I was wet, wetter than I'd ever been. I could tell by the wet, squishy noises his fingers made as they slid in and out of me. I rode his hand, fucking myself on his fingers, wanting him to rub my clit harder and make me come. Instead, Duncan rolled me off him and over onto the futon, flat on my back with him kneeling between my legs. He never took his fingers out of me. I closed my eyes and spread my legs wider, waiting for the feel of his tongue on my clit. It never came.

I opened my eyes and watched him leaning over me, his hand angled between my legs, stroking deep in my cunt. I could see my clit standing up, swollen and red and aching to be sucked. I whimpered, I moaned. I even tried to push his head down between my thighs. But Duncan never touched my clit, he just kept fucking me with his fingers.

I was starting to get annoyed. He felt good, so fucking good, but I couldn't come without him touching my clit. I propped myself up on my elbows, watching him watch me. Or, rather, watching him watch his fingers go into me. His cock was hardening again and that made me even wetter.

'I need your mouth,' I finally gasped. 'Please.'

'No, you don't,' he muttered, though it appeared he was talking to my clit, not me. 'You're going to come all over my hand in a minute. You're so fucking wet, baby. So wet. Just let it come.'

'Fuck me then,' I pleaded to the top of his head. 'I can't take any more of this.'

'Oh, yeah, you can,' he said, his mouth so close to where I wanted him that I could feel his breath.

His cock was right there for the taking and I was pretty sure he wouldn't say no if I pulled him on top of me, but I hesitated. I wanted to come, but I didn't think what he was doing was going to work. I wasn't even sure I had any condoms and, desperate as I was, I wasn't going to fuck him without one. I bit back a cry of frustration, grabbing at the fabric on the futon as I wiggled against his hand. I wanted his mouth or his cock, but all I was getting was his fingers.

'Just let it happen, baby,' he murmured again, rubbing that spot inside me that was at once intensely pleasurable and borderline uncomfortable.

'I don't think, I don't know,' I babbled, wanting what he was offering but not knowing how to get there. I felt suddenly inadequate, an inhibited woman who didn't have G-spot orgasms. I could feel my body tense, resisting him, rejecting the fingers stroking me in a steady, pumping rhythm.

Duncan looked up and the pure, naked lust on his face nearly made me groan. 'Don't, baby. Just relax and let me do this.' Then he leaned down and gently, oh so gently, licked my clit. 'I'll make you come. I promise.'

I don't know if it was his words, the look on his face or my clit anticipating his mouth, but I did relax. I lay back on the futon and closed my eyes and let him finger-fuck me with wet, squishy noises and soft, breathy words of encouragement.

'That's it, open for me,' he whispered. 'Your pussy is so wet and open. You're so beautiful like this. I have three fingers in you now, did you know that?'

I shook my head. I hadn't expected him to be a talker. He didn't *look* like a talker. I was usually chatty during sex but suddenly I couldn't speak. Didn't want to speak. It would ruin everything if I said something dumb right now. I kept my eyes closed and imagined his fingers, three of them, sliding deep into me before pulling out to pump just inside my opening, rubbing that spongy bump that was the source of this curious feeling. I was so wet, wetter than I'd ever been. I could feel it trickling down my ass. I was spread wide, opening to him, wanting more.

I didn't realise I'd verbalised my request until he asked, 'More? You want more, baby?'

'Yes, please. Yes.'

I was so wet, so fucking wet, I wouldn't have known he had four fingers inside of me if he hadn't said, 'That's four, baby.'

I'd never felt so full and so open at the same time. My hips moved against his thrusts without conscious thought. I raised myself up and fucked his fingers whenever he would go still inside me. I forgot about my clit and simply felt my cunt swell and grow wetter, wetter,

261

until something released me, like the knots I'd untied from the surfboard. Then it felt as if everything inside of me was gushing all over his hand. I'd tried to stop it, to clamp down on it, but he stroked me steadily and there was no stopping.

'That's it, baby,' he said, making shallow little thrusting motions in my cunt. 'That's it, let it go. Don't hold back, give it all to me. Yes, like that, just like that.'

'Oh, God, oh, God, oh, God,' I gasped, unable to find any other words.

I reached between my thighs and grasped his narrow wrist tightly. Whether to push him away or pull him closer, I wasn't sure. Thankfully, he wouldn't let me direct him. He just kept fucking me with quick, steady thrusts of those amazing fingers.

I felt it again. A rise, a quiver, a gush. And again. Every time he pulled his fingers to my opening, I gushed around him. He stroked me over and over as I came, wetness flowing out of me like a fountain on a switch. I arched my back and cried out, every muscle in my body taut, all feeling and sensation centred on my cunt.

I opened my eyes and looked down at him, his fingers buried in my pussy, his gaze between my legs. My clit stood up as hard and red as before, but I was coming, coming, coming and it didn't matter how. Then he lowered his mouth and flicked my rigid clit with just the tip of his tongue. It felt amazing, delicious, but just a part of the experience of being fucked by Duncan, not the main course. I stroked his head softly, running my fingers through his hair that was now damp with perspiration and not just rain. Who was this redheaded demon I'd let into my apartment? I didn't really have time to ponder it – and I really didn't care. I was still caught up in the incredible sensations he was causing to ripple through my exhausted body.

Duncan gently eased his fingers out of me and it was almost painful, leaving me feeling empty and open after so much exquisite fullness. He looked up into my eyes as he slowly licked his fingers, making my entire body quiver at the expression of pure lust on his face.

'Told you,' he said, looking smug and lustful all at the same time.

I laughed in lighthearted joy. Much as I hated the cliché of having been taught a sex lesson about my own body, he was entitled to be smug. He was absolutely right. He'd pushed me to feel something I'd never fully explored with anyone else and hadn't thought to try on my own.

'You're incredible. I've never ... wow.' My pulse was settling back to normal speed and I was able to speak again, even if I couldn't form a coherent sentence. 'Uh, thanks,' I added, laughing. 'Thanks a lot.'

'You don't have to thank me. The pleasure was mutual,' he said graciously, though I knew there was no way what

I'd done to him could even come close to the experience he had just given me. 'But I think we ruined your futon.'

I reached under my ass and felt the wetness that was spreading beneath me. 'I think you're right.'

'Sorry.'

'Fuck it,' I said. 'I'm not sorry. I'll buy a new one. It was totally worth it.'

I pulled him up until he stretched out on top of me, his cock pressing hard and insistent against my stomach. There wasn't enough room for us to lie side-by-side, but I didn't care. I liked the weight of his damp body on mine. Besides, it didn't seem fair to make him lie in the big wet spot, even if he had caused me to make it.

'Uh, yeah, so I haven't had a boyfriend in a while and I don't think I have any condoms,' I said by way of addressing his increasingly noticeable erection. 'You wouldn't happen to have any packed away in one of those boxes, do you?'

'Maybe. If not, I can go to the store,' he said. 'But first, I have a confession to make.'

There it was. The sound of the other shoe falling. He looked down at me and my heart nearly stopped. Of course he had to be too good to be true. A guy who could get me off like that had to have a major flaw. I braced myself for the worst. He had a girlfriend. He was gay and just experimenting. He never fucked a girl more than once.

I swallowed. 'Yes?' I asked past the knot of disappointment in my throat.

'I don't surf.'

I studied him, trying to keep the ridiculously goofy smile off my face and failing miserably. 'Oh, that's too bad. I only let you get into my pants because I thought you were a hot surfer dude.'

'Damn. Really?' He nuzzled my neck. 'I'll have to learn to surf then.'

We laughed and held each other while the rain fell and the wet spot grew cold underneath me. Duncan never did learn to surf, but I bought a new futon. With a washable cover.

Joe for Breakfast

I'm in town for 3 days. Want to get together for dinner?

I didn't include my name in the text. I was counting on the fact that even after ten years Joe wouldn't have deleted me out of his phone. I also neglected to mention that my plane had just touched down when I sent the text. He didn't need to know that. He might think I was overeager to see him.

Wasn't I?

If I was, apparently so was he. Before I'd even collected my luggage, my phone dinged in response.

Definitely! My schedule is tight. Meet for breakfast?

Huh. A breakfast date. That didn't sound promising. At least not for what I had in mind. Still, I did want to see him. And maybe he just wanted an escape plan if things didn't go well. On the other hand, if things *did* go well, there was always the potential for dinner later. Right? Maybe. That's what I told myself anyway as I texted him back.

Sure. I'm staying at the Marriott.

His response made me rethink my entire plan.

OK. I can meet you at the restaurant at 6.15.

This was ridiculous. Six fifteen? A.m.? Six fucking fifteen in the morning? For breakfast? That wasn't any kind of date. That was an attempt to brush me off without actually saying he didn't want to see me.

Seriously? I don't get up that early for anything. I was so annoyed as I walked and texted that I nearly ran into the man in front of me at the taxi stand.

It'll be worth it. And I promise you can go back to bed after breakfast.

Damn. Joe had me spinning and I hadn't even checked into my hotel yet. Was he worth getting up for at 6.15? Correction, 5.15 so I could make myself presentable. I thought back to the brief time I'd known Joe. We'd both been summer interns at Ballard, Mendel & Stuart, each of us struggling to set ourselves apart from every other idealistic law student. We'd fallen into bed – or the uncomfortable couch in one of the offices, rather – one late night after reading briefs until we thought our eyes would bleed. And then it became a near-nightly event, at his apartment or mine or back on one of the uncomfortable couches, or a desk, or the parking garage. When we weren't working, we were fucking. It wasn't really a relationship, we'd never gone down that road and I knew Joe would never be monogamous (mostly because he told me so), but it was a hell of friendship with benefits.

Joe had been the one to get me through that summer, otherwise I would've lost my mind. Then he got me through the application and interview process of finding a job that would utilise my specialities of maritime and immigration law while I kept his spirits up (and other things) as he decided he really did want to do family law, after all.

'Joe, you're the most cynical person I've ever met when it comes to marriage and kids. Why the hell would you want to do family law?' I'd asked him.

'*Because* I'm cynical about marriage and kids,' he had said. 'I won't get jaded dealing with other people's misery. I'm already there.'

And so I'd gotten a job in Miami doing what I loved and he'd settled somewhere near Washington, D.C., doing what he was already jaded about, though I wasn't sure he loved it. Joe was an attorney because he was very good at it. Joe fucked as many people as he could because he was good at it. He was charming and witty and attractive and garnered attention wherever he went. I was pretty sure that hadn't changed, hence the reason for a breakfast date. I kicked myself for not giving him a heads-up sooner – but I'd been nervous about seeing him. Ten years is a long time and I had changed a lot. It never crossed my mind that he might have changed, too.

OK. I'll see you at 6.15.

It was already after 10 p.m. and just texting that made my head hurt. But he said it would be worth it and, knowing Joe and what he was capable of, I believed him. I checked into my hotel, did a little work, requested a 5 a.m. wake-up call (I figured I'd need the extra time just to wake up) and went to bed. My dreams were filled with legal briefs and the memory of Joe's naked body.

* * *

The phone ringing startled me from a sound sleep and I groggily woke up with that 'Where am I?' feeling. I quickly came to awareness and cursed Joe for making me get up this early. It crossed my mind to just bail and text him that I couldn't make it. Was an old fuck buddy worth getting up for this early when there was no guarantee of any fucking in the first place? He'd said he was worth it. That wasn't a promise of sex, it was just the conceit of a man who knew how good he was in bed.

I contemplated that for a moment – along with the reality that I hadn't had sex in six months – and dragged

269

myself out of bed. *It will be worth it*, I reminded myself. In more ways than one, if I was lucky.

'It better be,' I muttered as I padded naked to the bathroom.

A quick shower refreshed me enough that I was only mildly annoyed by the fact that I was up before the sun. I didn't want to appear desperate, so I opted for a Friday casual work outfit. Cream-coloured blouse, too sheer for work without a jacket but perfect for a hotel breakfast date, sky-blue skirt that had just enough swish to make me feel sexy and yet still appear professional, low heels and my hair down and loose. I'd put some thought into my underwear, just in case this turned into more than breakfast, and wore a lacy bra that peeked out from the shadow of my cleavage and a matching thong. Sexy and classy, that was my goal. Remind him that he was dealing with a lady, but give him enough of a hint that I was still the woman he used to know – if he wanted to renew our acquaintance. And why else would he want to get together if not to *get together*?

I was in the dining room of the well-appointed restaurant by six o'clock. I wanted to get some coffee in me before Joe showed up. I wasn't nervous. At least, I didn't feel nervous until I was actually sitting there, sipping my coffee and wondering if Joe had changed since I last saw him. I certainly had, I thought, nervously rubbing my right thumb over my left ring finger. There was no ring there – not any more – but a faint tan line remained. I had become cynical the hard way. Trial by fire.

I caught movement out of the corner of my eye and looked up just in time to see Joe lean in to kiss me. He brushed my cheek rather than my lips, and smiled.

'Hey, beautiful. Long time no see.'

'Smooth as ever.' I smiled. 'You're looking good.'

And he was. He'd always had the enviable ability to eat anything he wanted and maintain a lean runner's body. Not generally my type, even when I had been thinner myself, but for some reason it worked with him. He had a narrow frame that was perfect for the drape of the expensive Italian suits he had coveted in law school and apparently now could afford. But, despite the fancy suit, he was still Joe. His blue eyes still crinkled – actually a little bit more – when he smiled; he still played with his cufflinks and tapped his leg with that nervous energy that said he was ready to go, somewhere, anywhere, as long as it was fun. He had been one of the most ambitious young men I'd ever known. I wondered if that had changed.

He sat down across from me and poured a cup of coffee from the French press I had ordered.

'So, I don't know whether to ask why the last-minute surprise or why I haven't seen you in ten years,' he said finally, after savouring the first sip of his coffee.

I'd always liked the way Joe could immerse himself in an experience. Whether it was coffee or sex, the whole world stopped for the moment he was enjoying it. I smiled, thinking I could learn a thing or two about life from Joe, even now.

'I've been busy,' I said, keeping my tone light. 'Work eats up my time.'

He took another long sip of his coffee. 'I know the feeling, but there's always time to play.'

Bingo. He was still the same guy. I smiled.

'Well, my phone wasn't exactly blowing up with calls from you,' I said.

He nodded. 'I heard you got married. I didn't want to … intrude.'

I could feel my face flush hotly. I should've known someone in the grapevine of law-school friends and legal colleagues would have passed the information along. Now I felt like a jackass for not telling him myself.

'Oh, you heard that, did you?'

'Read it, actually. I was in Miami – when, five, six years ago? – and came across your wedding announcement in the *Herald*. You were a pretty bride.' He tilted his head toward my hand.

I shrugged. 'It was a pretty show. But that's all it was. I'm divorced now.'

He nodded without comment. This conversation was taking a decidedly non-cheerful turn.

'But I'm happy and life is good,' I said brightly. 'How about you?'

He blinked long and slow, and there was something mildly seductive about it. 'You know me, love. Still catting around with anyone who'll have me.'

'Players play,' I said, though I wondered when players *stopped* playing. Did they? 'So, no wifey and rug rats tucked away somewhere?'

'No.'

I'd expected a joke of the cynical variety, but that was the extent of his response. I shifted nervously and glanced at my watch. We hadn't even ordered breakfast yet.

'I, um, I wanted to catch up,' I said, trying to infuse my words with meaning. 'I've been thinking about you a lot.'

'Me or my wang?' he said with a grin, bouncing back to his old, flirty self. 'As I recall, you liked him even more than me.'

'Maybe we can get reacquainted and find out?' The words made me cringe, but I was anxious to get past our pasts and see if there was a chance of something happening. 'I know you said you're busy, but maybe dinner tonight?'

'Why not now?'

So much for working our way up to it. 'Really? Now?'

He shrugged. 'Why not? We're both here, you have a room, I don't have to be in court until ten. I assume your schedule is flexible?'

I nodded. 'Somewhat. Lunch meeting with a client,' I

273

murmured absentmindedly. This felt more like a business deal than a seduction.

'OK, then,' he said, standing. 'We can order room service afterward. Let your client pay for it.' He flashed me a quick smile as he took my hand.

For some odd reason, I felt like the prey instead of the hunter.

Joe rested his hand on the base of my neck as we walked from the elevator to my room. It felt nice, if proprietary. I wondered how many breakfast 'dates' he had – not that it was any of my business. But still, this was just all too smooth ... like he did this all the time. I started to ask him and then thought better of it. That wasn't why I was here. Judging Joe's sex life had nothing to do with anything. And if not for his proclivities, I might not have called him at all.

'I'm glad you called,' he murmured as I swiped the key card in the door, as if reading my mind. He dropped a kiss on the curve of my neck as I let us into the room. 'I'm looking forward to this.'

I dropped my purse on the vanity in the foyer and turned to him, suddenly uncertain if this was a good idea. 'Hey, um, I don't want you to think I just wanted to see you because I wanted to have sex,' I said.

Liar, a little voice screamed in my head, but I ignored it. I didn't want Joe to think he was a piece of meat to me – even though he didn't seem to mind.

He slipped his arms around my waist and kissed me for the first time in a decade. Despite being married for half of it, I had kissed a lot of men in those in-between years, but I still remembered the way Joe kissed. Soft at first, with increasing intensity. Like him. So easy-going on the surface, but with a heat and drive like no other. My train of thought was immediately derailed as he pressed his body against me, moulding my curves to his planes.

'Sweetheart, you don't have to explain anything to me,' he said, cupping my ass in his hands. 'Once a man whore, always a man whore, right?'

I was thrown into an emotional and physical conflict. My body was responding to his touch, the press of his erection against my belly, his fingers kneading the cheeks of my ass. My mind, though, was horrified that he thought of himself as just a piece of ass – or of me as someone who would treat him that way. The fact that I was actually treating him that way, or had intended to, didn't really matter.

Not without some reluctance, I pulled away from him and took a few steps back. That helped clear my head, even if it did nothing to ease the dull throb in my cunt. I licked my bottom lip, already swollen and tender from his rough kisses.

'Joe, you don't seriously feel that way, do you?' I asked, hearing how breathless I sounded. 'I don't think you're a … a man whore and I didn't want to see you just for sex.'

He sat on the edge of the bed and leaned back, bracing himself on his elbows. The position perfectly framed the erection straining against the front of his expensive trousers.

'Everyone knows I'm a man whore, love. I'm who you call when you need to get your pipes cleaned,' he said. He was smiling, but I could hear the bitterness in his voice. 'It's OK. It's a reputation I've built for myself. Might as well enjoy the … perks, right?'

I felt like crying. I didn't much care what Joe did, as long as he was happy. But he was so clearly *not* happy – why didn't everyone else see it? Or was it only with a decade's worth of distance that I could? Or was I looking for something that simply wasn't there?

I sat down next to him, but left enough space between us to keep my head in charge of the conversation. 'No way in hell you really feel that way,' I said softly. 'Maybe you did once, but you're not that guy now.'

He smiled, but it didn't reach his eyes. 'Aren't I? Would you change your mind if you knew I'd had a very kinky threesome in this very hotel just a couple of months ago?'

'No.' And I said it with all the conviction I felt. 'You may have done that, and you may have slept with a lot of people, but you're not just a … a piece of meat. I'm sorry if I ever acted like you were.'

'It's OK. I did it to myself.' He sighed and lay back on the bed, hands behind his head, staring up at the ceiling like he was going to find the answers to the world's problems in the white expanse. 'I love sex, Danica, always have and always will.'

I laughed. 'There is *nothing* wrong with that.'

'No, but I'm starting to realise that there's more to life.'

'That's good, right?'

He turned his head to look at me. 'Come down here. I can't talk with you hovering over me.'

I lay on the bed next to him, our shoulders touching, studying the same expanse of ceiling he was. 'OK.'

'Don't laugh at me,' he said, sounding for all the world like he really believed I might laugh. 'But as much as I love sex, I'm thinking I might actually want to be in love.'

Part of me was happy for him. Happy that my old friend was still the same guy I knew and loved and also evolving into someone who wanted to make a connection with another person. Another part of me was oddly disappointed.

'I fall for girls I can't have,' he went on, oblivious to my warring emotions. 'Oh, I can fuck them, if I want. But I can't *have* them. They don't want me – Joe the player – or they already belong to someone else and I'm just the dessert they want but that's bad for them.'

277

'So find a girl who is available and doesn't care about your history,' I said, realising how idealistic – and unlikely – it sounded even before he snorted. 'Fall in love.'

He rolled to his side and looked at me. 'Is it really that easy?'

I sighed, thinking about everything I'd been through, everything I had wanted that always seemed just beyond my grasp. 'No. It's not. If it was, I'd have everything I want.'

He nodded. 'What is it you want?'

'I wanted to fall in love and get married and have babies,' I said. 'I fell in love, I got married, he decided he didn't want children complicating his lifestyle. I decided I couldn't live my life with someone so utterly selfish, we divorced, I gave up on love but I still want a baby.'

I expected him to bolt off the bed and run. He didn't. 'That's sad,' he said. 'You shouldn't give up on love. Plus, it makes it hard for you to convincingly give me relationship advice.'

I laughed. 'You're right. But men seem to smell the maternal desperation on me and run for the hills. I figured I'd have the baby and then deal with finding love.'

'Kind of ass-backwards, but I get it.'

I sighed. He didn't get it entirely and I was cursing myself for feeling the need to tell him. 'I'm ovulating,' I said. 'I was kind of hoping you'd get me pregnant.'

That did make him sit up, though to his credit he actually stayed in the room. His eyes narrowed, as if he was waiting for me to say I was joking. I stared at him, unblinking, until he shook his head.

'You're serious.'

'Yeah. Sorry.'

'Were you planning on telling me before, after or not at all?'

I hesitated. 'Honestly? I don't know. I think I would have told you after. I don't think it would be fair not to tell you.'

'Wow.' He lay back on the bed next to me. 'That's ... wow.'

I shifted so I could look at him. 'Are you mad?'

He studied the ceiling for another long minute. 'No, I don't think so. It seems oddly flattering in some way. Why me?'

I'd thought about that a lot in the past few months. It wasn't like there were a shortage of men willing to fuck me, no strings attached. But in my mind I kept coming back to Joe. My imaginary child, having his good looks and ambition, not to mention his sense of right and wrong and gentle personality.

I shrugged. 'You're one of the smartest, kindest men I've ever known. Why not you? We were close once, I've never stopped caring about you, I'd consider myself lucky to have a child who was like you.'

'Aw, love, you have a very strange way of talking a man out of his pants.'

'I'm being honest, Joe,' I said, trying to convey to him how earnest I was. 'When my marriage fell apart, I was as cynical as you'd always been about love. But I couldn't let go of the idea of being a mother, having a child, making a family, even if it didn't include true love. And you kept popping into my head.'

'I'm honoured. I wish you would have discussed it with me first, but I'm honoured I was your choice.' He turned on his side and stroked the side of my face with the back of his hand. 'You'd make an amazing mother, Danica.'

I swallowed my sadness. 'Maybe one day.'

His thumb stroked over my bottom lip. 'Why not now?'

I stared at him. 'Are you serious? You just said you wanted to fall in love. Don't you think getting me pregnant might … complicate things for you?' Not that he had to tell a prospective girlfriend, since I had fully intended to raise any child I had on my own without asking for any assistance, but Joe wasn't the kind of guy to abandon his own baby – even one he hadn't planned on having.

And then it hit me – that's why I'd chosen Joe. I caught my breath at the epiphany. I'd been so caught up in my desire to become a mother that I hadn't really examined my reasons for choosing Joe as the potential sperm donor, other than he was a good guy. But part of his goodness stemmed from the fact that he was a responsible and honourable man, too. His man whoring, as he called it, had always been with willing partners and full disclosure on his part that he wasn't exclusive to anyone. Even in that, he handled himself with integrity.

'I couldn't just knock you up and walk away,' he said softly.

'I know. I'm sorry.'

I could feel a single hot tear slip from under my lid and roll down my cheek. He caught it on his fingertip.

'Why? I'm not.'

He leaned over and kissed me, and it wasn't like the way he'd kissed me before. It wasn't intense and sexual, it was soft and tender. It was passionate. It was better. I wrapped my arms around his neck and kissed him back, feeling my body respond just as quickly as it had before. No one had ever had that effect on me, not even my ex when we'd first gotten together. Joe knew how to kiss a woman and make her feel it everywhere. Or maybe it was just *me* he knew how to kiss so effectively.

I moaned into his mouth, wanting everything he was offering me in that kiss. But my attorney's mind was thinking of loopholes and contingencies and, before I could fall too far off the cliff, I needed to know what he meant. I pulled back just enough to look into his eyes,

281

the blue of his irises flecked with green, an ocean for me to drown in if only I would let myself.

He shifted his weight over me, the length of his erection finding a home pressed between my thighs. We both moaned then, me bucking my hips up to feel him and him reaching under me to grab my ass and pull me up against him. My skirt slipped up my thighs as I wrapped my legs around his hips. Hardly ladylike, but I wasn't feeling particularly ladylike at the moment.

'You've got a great ass,' he murmured.

I laughed, feeling suddenly self-conscious. 'It's bigger than it used to be.'

'I like it just the way it is,' he growled as he ground against me, letting me know just how much he liked it. 'I like your curves. You're sexy as hell.'

I wanted to respond, but he was nibbling his way down my cleavage, popping buttons on my blouse as he went, slipping his tongue under the edge of my bra and soothing the warm flesh he exposed. My nipples were pressing against the silk of my bra, aching for his mouth. I reached between us, finishing the job he'd started on my blouse, struggling out of it even as he slid his hand under me and popped the clasp, releasing my ample cleavage into his warm, firm hands.

I moaned as he pressed my breasts together and licked up between the crease, his thumbs pressing and massaging my nipples into hard, needy points. He sucked each in turn, wetting them with his mouth, making them ache even more in the cool air of the room. I was writhing against him, my skirt a tangle of fabric around my hips, my thong soaked through.

'You'd better get your pants off,' I gasped, as he nipped at my nipple. 'Before I get them wet.'

He chuckled. 'That wouldn't be good.'

Standing, he kept his gaze on me as he stripped off his suit and laid it over the chair next to the bed. I stretched, feeling desirable and utterly shameless lying there in nothing but my skirt, thong and heels. I kicked off the shoes, letting them fall beside the bed, and shimmied out of the skirt. I left the thong for him to deal with. Which he did, kneeling between my spread thighs.

'Nice,' he breathed, running his finger up the seam, pressing it into *my* seam. 'So wet.'

'Don't tease me,' I groaned, bucking up against that determined finger as he stroked me up and down, brushing my clit through the lace. 'Not now.'

He chuckled. 'Oh, love, it will only make it that much better.'

Even if he was right, I didn't care. I wanted him inside me. Now. All thoughts about why I'd wanted to have sex with Joe had flown out the window. Now it was all about feeling him, touching him, fucking him. I hooked my fingers in my thong and dragged it down my hips. If he wouldn't take it off, I would.

'Impatient wench,' he said, smacking my ass as I lifted my legs to free myself from the damp lace. 'I would've done that.'

I flung my underwear across the room and spread my legs. Running my hands up and down the inside of my thighs, I framed my wet pussy with my hands. 'I have something else you can do.'

'Soon, sweet girl, very soon.'

He jack-knifed between my thighs and his mouth pressed to the core of me. I cried out, shifting my hands from my thighs to the back of his head, pressing him into me for fear he was only teasing me again. But no, Joe was no tease once he committed himself. He licked me with long, unhurried strokes, circling my clit before slipping down and applying his tongue to my opening. I felt my muscles tighten, searching for something to squeeze down on, and I whimpered. He followed that path again and again, until my clit was throbbing and my entire body was slicked with sweat.

'Oh, God,' I moaned, bending my knees and pushing my feet down on the bed so that his tongue could go deeper. 'Joe!'

He sucked my clit between his lips and that was all it took for my over-sensitised cunt to come. I clamped my thighs around his head, holding him in place as he continued to suck my clit and wring every last sensation from that hard little nub. I was bucking against him so hard I was afraid I was going to knock him unconscious, but I couldn't stop.

He surged up over me and put his mouth on mine at the same time as he pushed his cock into me. I could taste myself – sweet and salty – and it only served to intensify the sensation of being filled. I wrapped my arms and legs around him, pulling him down and into me, my body tight around him as he eased into me as far as he could go.

Flushed and damp, his body on top of mine made it feel like we were in a furnace. But there was no way in hell I was going to ask him to get off of me. Not yet. Not until I'd enjoyed everything he had to give.

Slowly, so slowly I would have screamed in frustration if I hadn't just come like fireworks, he moved inside of me. He raised up to look at me, smiling slightly as he pulled out to the thick tip and then slid home again.

'I've heard that a woman's orgasm can facilitate conception,' he said.

I giggled. 'I know it's crazy, but you have no idea how sexy that sounds.'

'Yeah, I do,' he said, and then his eyes fluttered closed.

He was lost in his own sensations, his long, slow strokes for his pleasure, not for mine. For some reason, that only served to arouse me – knowing that he was enjoying my body as much as I had enjoyed his mouth. I rocked my hips, as slow as his strokes, finding a rhythm that was just this side of the Zen music I favoured at bedtime. But it was enough to arouse me all over again, the long strokes touching every inch of my engorged pussy, and I was the one who picked up the pace, swirling my hips so that I could intensify the sensation for both of us.

He moaned in appreciation as I shimmied against him, and dug his fingers into the cheeks of my ass as he pulled me up hard on his cock. I gasped as he moved faster, going into me in hard, shallow strokes. It was almost too much for me to bear, but then it shifted to pure pleasure, my pussy tightening around him on every down stroke as another orgasm tightened my belly.

He was close, I could see it in the way his jaw clenched and his body tightened. I pulled his head down and kissed him, rocking my hips on him, in time with his strokes, my tongue in his mouth as he groaned into me and released his seed. I hooked my legs up high on his back, keeping everything he offered in the well of my pussy, kissing him and stroking him as my own orgasm moved through me, all sensation focused on where our bodies connected.

We gasped and moaned as we kissed, our sounds filling the quiet room over the hum of the air conditioner. I held him to me, as hot and damp as I was now, but I didn't mind. It felt ... right. This was why I had come to see him. But I was taking away so much more, no matter what happened.

He shifted his weight off of me, rising on arms and knees to look into my face. 'You are so fucking amazing,' he said. 'And you're going to be an amazing mother in nine months.'

'It doesn't always happen the first time,' I said, feeling suddenly shy as he moved to lie beside me, the cool air drying my skin and making me shiver. 'It can take months sometimes, even if the timing is right.'

'I can live with that. I'll be on call until the deed is done.' He kissed the top of my head. 'You would have had to tell me what you were planning, you know. Otherwise, I never would have forgone using a condom.'

I hadn't thought about that. I should have, of course, Even for all his sleeping around – maybe *because* of all his sleeping around – Joe would be careful.

'I don't think I could *not* have told you, but I hadn't thought of that.'

He cuddled me close, though I sensed our time was running out. At least for now. Court and clients awaited. I wanted nothing more than to close my eyes and take a nap in his arms. And then wake up and do what we'd just done all over again until we were both exhausted. I laughed at myself.

'What?' he asked, sounding just as drowsy as I was.

'I was just thinking how this wasn't at all how I expected this to go,' I said. 'It's so much better.'

'Just wait until the baby comes.' He sighed, as if it

was already a reality. 'And you really have everything you want.'

I wanted to say that I'd held back – that I wanted the same thing he did, to fall in love. But that was too much to hope for. Hell, this was too much to hope for. Even if I got pregnant the first time out of the gate, Joe hadn't really had time to process everything. He could still change his mind and I wouldn't – couldn't – blame him at all.

'Are you sure about this, Joe? I mean, really?' I didn't want to talk him out of it, but I couldn't in good conscience let us just do this thing and have him deal with the consequences later. 'I had fully intended not to involve you, or at least that's what I told myself, but I think part of the reason I chose you was because I knew you'd be a good father.'

He laughed. 'Honey, I'm scared to the marrow, but knowing you believe in me is conquering all kinds of fears.'

'There's no obligation on your part,' I hurried on, before I lost my nerve. 'You can be as involved – or not – as you choose to be.'

He put his fingers over my lips. 'These are the weirdest vows I've ever heard. Just stop. I know what I'm getting into. I want to do this.' He paused and kissed me hard. 'I want to give you the child you want – on one condition.'

My heart sank. Of course there would be strings. Of course he would want something out of the deal. Visitation, maybe? Or a contractual agreement that I wouldn't sue him for child support? That didn't seem like Joe, but then I hadn't really expected he would agree to father my child, either.

'What?'

'Date me,' he said, stroking my bare thigh in a distracting way. 'Date me, Danica. I'd be lying if I said I hadn't thought about what it would be like to have a little one running around. I just didn't think I'd find a woman who wanted to have a kid with me. The fact that you do – well, I want to date you. I want to see what's possible.'

I shook my head, trying to clear both my analytical thoughts and the haze of lust that was growing increasingly impatient and wasn't helped by Joe pressing his damp cock against my hip. He was hardening again and my body was already responding.

'What does that even mean?'

'Just that. I know we live in different cities, but date me. Date me while you're here trying to make a baby, date me long distance when you go back to Miami. I have some vacation time coming up, I'll come down and hang out with you. Just ... date me. More than sex, more than baby-making. Date me. Exclusive, at least on my part.'

I stared at him. It was incongruous. Ridiculous. And ridiculously sweet.

'Joe, you're not in love with me.'

'No,' he agreed, guiding me on top of him and settling me over his fully renewed erection. 'I'm not. And you're not in love with me.'

I gasped, losing all hope of being able to speak coherently. And maybe that was his plan.

'But we once had a connection that went beyond sex and I was too absorbed in my own life to pursue it,' he said, rubbing his cock back and forth against my already sensitive pussy. 'I've had ten years to do my running around and I got tired of it at least three years ago. And here you are now, asking me to get you pregnant, so obviously there's something about me that you think is special. So, let's date and see what it is. Worst case scenario, we're incompatible and go back to being friends raising a child together.'

That didn't sound like such a horrible thing, markedly better than raising a child on my own. Plus, it came with the added perk of what he was doing to me right now. I tilted my hips and he slid home.

'And best case scenario?' I gasped.

'We fall in love and raise a child together.'

It sounded like a good plan to me.

Word Games

My phone beeped, letting me know my opponent had made a move. I studiously ignored it and finished marking the sixth-grade history report in front of me. Just as I scrawled a B+ on the paper, my phone beeped again. The five-minute reminder warning. I squirmed in my seat, the anticipation almost more than I could handle.

I got through two more history reports before I couldn't take it any more. Like an addict in need of a hit, I thumbed the slider bar on my phone and the Word Games screen popped up. Like Scrabble for a smartphone, it displayed a board with letters laid out like tiles. The board was nearly filled with words. Beautiful, glorious words.

I'm a word slut. I love words. I love language. I love

dictionaries – and thesauri. I love the way certain words roll off the tongue. *Undulate*. There's a word for you. It sounds like what it is. Ripples of energy flowing off the curves of my tongue to fill the air with that beautiful sound, the mouth forming a perfect 'oh' in the middle. *Undulate*. Ohhh.

I'd played *undulate* in this game already, using all seven of my tiles and the *d* in *audacity* that he had played earlier. I didn't know who my opponent was. I use the random player selector and the game assigns me a partner. I assumed it was a man, though his screen name – InkSlinger – could've been a woman, too. But for some reason, I just knew it was a man. My screen name was less ambiguous – Lexigirl, a play on my name, Alexandra, and 'lexicon'. We'd been assigned as random opponents twice and that seemed enough of a coincidence that I now sought him out every time we finished a game.

Do you want to challenge InkSlinger to a new game?

The answer was yes. Always yes. Because the only thing better than words is someone who knows how to use them. I love a man with a clever mind, who knows how to engage in wordplay as well as foreplay. Sometimes wordplay *is* foreplay for me. And InkSlinger was stroking my mind the way I liked my body stroked. Slowly, confidently and with the occasional surprise just to keep me on my toes. It felt like foreplay, except the pay-off was not nearly as satisfying as real foreplay.

The addiction, and I really had to admit that after only a month of Word Games it had become an addiction, had now taken on a special place in my day-to-day life because I had an opponent who not only had a good vocabulary but understood the strategy of the game. It wasn't always about big words. Big was good, of course, and using all of your letters garnered you extra points – but sometimes a short word would do even better. *Lick*, when placed strategically, could land you with thirty points or more. The same with *suck*. K is a nice letter. It can be used in so many deliciously naughty words. Unfortunately, Word Games wouldn't allow me to play *fuck* or *dick*, but it was fine with *cock*. I played *cock* a lot. I love cock. In Word Games, I mean.

InkSlinger was fond of certain words, too. My *suck* became his *suckled*. He used the *l* in my *lick* for *nipples* and I used the *e* in *nipples* for *ecstasy*. We had both played *oh* and *yes* many times, taking advantage of triple letter scores for both the *h* and the *y*. Sometimes our game board looked more like a jumbled erotic story than a word game. I loved it. Sad to say, it was the only erotic thing about my life, which included teaching sixth graders at Willow Oaks Middle School about the American Revolution, coaching high-school girls' softball after school and on the weekends and taking care of my parents' two dogs while they were off on yet another of their exotic trips. And I had InkSlinger. I wasn't so far gone that I was masturbating to our games, but waiting for him to reply and hearing the 'beep' of my phone was enough to make my breath quicken. And sometimes his words ... well, they did have a certain affect on me.

We built on each other's words, lining up tiles adjacent to each other in vertical, horizontal and perpendicular positions. The words were bad enough to ignite my fevered imagination – *tease* and *me* right there next to *stroke* and *lust* – but I started to imagine the tiles as bodies – his and mine – engaged in various sexual positions. It was ridiculous. It was sad. It was what kept me going through endless hours of grading history reports and endless nights going to bed alone.

I probably would've gone on like that for ever, or at least until summer came and I was free of my commitments and lonely enough to consider online dating, but then in the middle of a game I was winning, a little blue bubble popped up at the top of my screen. Apparently Word Games had a chat function I hadn't noticed before. Maybe because there hadn't ever been anyone I wanted to chat with before.

I opened the bubble and saw the first words from InkSlinger that were in an actual sentence. *Hey Lexigirl, I like playing with you.*

Then, *The game, I mean.*

I thought for a moment, wondering whether to further

the tone of our games or let it drop. I didn't know him and he didn't know me; I could just find someone else to play with. Or not play at all. But it was rare to find someone who had a good vocabulary, a knack for strategy, a sense of humour and a dirty mind. Or maybe I was just projecting these qualities onto him because they were things that were important to me.

Thanks. I like playing with you too. I like the way your mind works.

I started to amend it the way he had, make sure I was clear that I didn't mean it in a suggestive way. But I did mean it in a suggestive way. And flirting with a stranger over a word game seemed about as innocuous as playing dirty Scrabble with co-workers. What was the harm?

What was the harm, indeed. It didn't take long before we were messaging as much as we were gaming. It felt natural to play a word like *sexy* and then ask him how his day had been. We talked about work in general terms; I had no idea what he did besides something that involved writing and I just told him I was a teacher, but everything else was fair game. We messaged about movies and books and what we were going to do over the summer. I didn't have plans other than *not work*, but his goals included renting a house in the Outer Banks of North Carolina and learning to surf. *But I have to keep working*, he messaged.

Like strangers meeting at a party, we kept the banter

light and stayed away from politics and religion, though sex came up. And up, and up. While our games were fun and somewhat arousing but never enough to get me there, our messaging *did* fuel my fantasies. We danced on the line of propriety, pretending to be word geeks playing a game, but – for me at least – it was the most erotic chat I was getting in my life.

I've heard that you can tell how good someone is in bed by the way they dance, he messaged. *But I think it's by how well they use words.*

I smiled. *A love of language makes for an inquisitive and passionate mind.*

Oh, how I love your passion.

And so it went for another few weeks, with the conversations taking twists and turns but always staying somewhat anonymous. I was both content and frustrated with the situation. It was lovely to have someone like him around to entertain me while I was standing in line at the grocery store or post office, or when I couldn't sleep at night, but chatting with him was like the first taste of a decadent piece of chocolate cake – I wanted more. Then one night he offered me more.

Feel like playing? he messaged, after playing the word *strip* off of my word *poker.*

We're already playing.

A pause, and then: *Not what I meant.*

I blushed, knowing exactly what he meant, and

squirmed in my bed. How in the world could such an innocent flirtation arouse me? But arouse me it did.

I don't know how to play, I confessed.

We need to create a version of Strip Word Games.

I laughed out loud. *That's too geeky for words.*

So? Geeks are sexy.

Oh, hell, yes, they were. Or *he* was, anyway. Sexy with his wordplay. I wondered idly if it would translate to sexy in real life.

We seem to be a perfect match. Maybe we should meet up sometime and play in real life.

Whoa. Not what I expected, at all. It wasn't creepy; I felt like I knew him, and I didn't feel threatened. It was actually kind of flattering because I'd been thinking the same thing, but –

Yeah, I couldn't think of a reason that it might be a bad thing to indulge his little fantasy, either.

That would be intriguing and probably explosive in a variety of ways. I typed. But w*hat are the odds of us being anywhere close to each other?*

The odds are pretty good. The random matches are based on geographic location. Didn't you know that? Word Games wants word geeks to find each other!

Crap, I didn't know that. I was having second thoughts about this game. But then …

OK, I'll bite. Where are you? I figured I was safe – basing a game on geographic locations could mean

297

anything. The east coast was a geographic location, but that wouldn't make meeting feasible. Or he could be four hours away in North Carolina since he'd mentioned renting a house in the Outer Banks. And I didn't have to tell him where *I* was, right?

Just outside D.C., suburb called Willow Oaks.

Meep. We lived in the same neighbourhood. This game was a better GPS than the one in my car.

Are you going to tell me where you are, Lexigirl?

I closed the Word Games program without answering.

* * *

Like most addicts, I couldn't stay away. I didn't finish the game with InkSlinger and I ignored his requests to start a new game. I let Word Games match me up with other random players, always aware that these new strangers might live around the corner or next door. There was no temptation to flirt. Especially when I played the word *erotic* and my most recent opponent, with the uninspired name Luv_My_Kids, messaged me *That's dirty!* and promptly quit the game. I longed for InkSlinger. Did it matter that he lived in the same neighbourhood I did? It wasn't likely that some psycho would use Word Games to lure in his victim, right? I was being paranoid, watching too many episodes of *CSI*. And doing what my sister Valerie always accused me of doing – making excuses to be alone. But Valerie was the pretty, confident older sister; she could take her clothes off to model for a room full of strangers taking an art class, while I could barely speak in front of the Parent Teacher Association.

Late one night, about a week after I found out InkSlinger lived nearby, I logged back into the game and sent him a game request. From my tray of seven tiles, I made my first word. *Sorry*. Then I sent him a message.

It kind of freaked me out that you live so close. Sorry. It would be cool to meet. If you still want to.

He didn't respond that night. But the next night, as I was just falling asleep, my phone beeped. He'd played *lovely* off of my *y*.

Whenever you'd like, he messaged, *just let me know.*

I took a deep breath. What the hell, right? Might as well take a leap of faith and see where it took me.

How about Thursday night?

It was Tuesday night, so Thursday seemed soon enough that I wouldn't chicken out. It also wasn't a traditional date night, so no undue pressure to make this blind date – if you could even call it that – into something more than two gamers meeting in real life. On the other hand, if we hit it off (what were the odds?), there was a chance of a real weekend date. I was proud of myself for this little logistical move.

Sure. Time? Place?

299

How about 8 o'clock? Do you know City Coffee in City Village?

Sure, he messaged, *that works. I prefer a busy public place. Just in case you turn out to be a psycho.*

Alone in my bed, I laughed out loud. InkSlinger might end up disappointing me in person, but here – confined to my phone – he was funny and charming and smart.

Fair enough. Good night, InkSlinger.

Call me Sam, he messaged. And then he was gone.

* * *

Sam. Sam. Samuel. Or Sampson? Maybe just Sam. I hadn't even told him my name, but his name was a mantra in my head for the next two days. We finished the game I had started with an apology – he beat me by 27 points – and had played a couple of new games since then. My favourite word so far had been *luscious*. He'd played it off of the *c* in *creamy*. I was pleased to see we'd slipped back to our usual suggestive word banter, though it still made me a little nervous. I didn't know why – other than it felt like he knew more about me than I really wanted a stranger to know on a first date. Even if it wasn't a date.

I kept going back and forth over that. I didn't know anything about him. He could have a girlfriend. Be engaged. Or married. Or, hell, he could be seventeen and

I could be breaking the law having sexual fantasies about some high-school kid who just had a good vocabulary. My nerves were getting the best of me. At my lunch break on Thursday, I hid in the teachers' work room and opened Word Games on my phone.

Please tell me you're at least eighteen.

I didn't expect a response, but within a minute he messaged me.

I'm thirty-four. I'm single. I have a job. I pay taxes. I'm not a criminal. I'm normal, Lexigirl. OK?

Man, this guy was too good to be true. I laughed again.

'What so funny?' Catherine asked from the doorway. 'And where's Hannah?'

I played *crazy* in Word Games and closed the programme. 'Hannah took the day off. Her substitute is losing her mind with those wild kids of hers. They won't listen to anyone but Hannah.'

'Hannah took the day off?' Catherine looked flabbergasted. 'What's wrong with her?'

I laughed. 'She's horny.'

Hannah and her husband Aidan had been renewing their sexual vows, so to speak, after a long dry spell that had been broken when Catherine had volunteered to keep their almost-three-year-old twins one night last month. I'd been terribly jealous that she actually *had* someone to have sex with, though I couldn't

301

very well tell her that when she'd been complaining about how sex had gone out the window post-babies. In any case, I was now jealous she was actually getting it on during work hours – not that administration knew that. Hannah's sick day was keeping her in bed all day, all right, but not for the reason the principal thought.

Catherine shook her head in mock surprise and offered me half of her sub. We ate and chatted for the next fifteen minutes, but my mind was on my sort-of-date with a guy named Sam, who was over eighteen and gainfully employed. I felt like I'd won the lottery, but I hadn't seen the check yet to know exactly how much I'd won.

* * *

City Coffee was quiet on a Thursday night – though the barista behind the counter looked like she needed a break. I absentmindedly listened to her lamenting how short-staffed they were as she made my iced mocha. I'd been caught in traffic and was a couple of minutes late, so I'd cast a look around for Sam expecting to see someone who looked like an InkSlinger (whatever that looked like), but the only other people in the coffee shop were a fifty-something couple with their heads bent over a stack of travel guides and a cute young cop who appeared to be doing some paperwork. I wondered for half a minute if he could be Sam, though he didn't look anywhere close to thirty-four, but then his radio chirped to life. He murmured something into the mike before collecting his paperwork and leaving without so much as a backward glance. OK, so Sam wasn't a cop and he wasn't one half of the travelling duo. I swirled my straw in my iced coffee and waited.

At seven-fifteen I was feeling like I'd been stood up. It was only fifteen minutes, and I'd been a little late myself, but good grief, my nerves were on edge. Then my phone beeped – a message from InkSlinger in Word Games.

So sorry. Crisis at work. I won't be able to get out of here for at least another hour.

I wanted to believe him, I really did. But I'm not Valerie. I'm just not that trusting of men. But still, he'd been pretty straightforward with me so far and I didn't have to be a bitch about it.

That's cool, maybe another time.

No! I really want to see you tonight. Please?

I hesitated. Then, *OK. I'll wait another hour. Maybe I'll find someone else to play Word Games with.*

Fair enough, he messaged, *but only until I'm done here, OK?*

OK.

He was gone and I didn't really feel like playing Word Games. So I bought a copy of the *Post* and nursed my coffee. An hour later, there was still no sign or word from Sam and the lone barista was busily scrubbing every surface around me, hinting that it was time for me to leave.

I sighed, messaged *I'm going home* to Sam and did just that. So much for taking a leap of faith. I'd landed in the rocks.

* * *

My phone beeped as I was getting into the bed. I looked at the time. 11.03. Was he kidding? I had to get up for work in less than seven hours. It crossed my mind to ignore it, but then my brain started going down the *CSI* path. What if something had happened to him? I picked up my phone and read his message.

I'm so sorry. I'm in advertising. I'm the head copy-writer on a major account. The client wanted a last minute meeting and I couldn't get out.

While I appreciated how forthcoming he was about his career, it didn't sway me.

I'm going to bed.

Please, Lexigirl. I'm grovelling here. And I'm driving around the streets of Willow Oaks.

So, go home, I messaged.

Let's at least meet. Just ten minutes? So we can say we did.

I didn't see the point, but I didn't tell him that. I turned my phone over and over in my hand, thinking. Did I really want to get up, get dressed and drive somewhere to meet some guy I didn't really know? Not really.

On the next flip, my phone beeped again.

I'm going to start yelling, 'Lexigirl, where are you?' out my car window.

I smiled. The guy was a nut, but maybe in a good way. I played a mental round of 'What would Valerie do?' and came up with the usual answer. She'd go for it.

Fine, I will give you my address. You can come over, but you cannot come inside. We'll sit on the front porch for ten minutes. Then I let out a long slow breath and carefully typed in my street address.

You're something else, Lexigirl. I'll be there in ten minutes, tops.

Because I was having second thoughts the minute I messaged him, I sent a group text to Valerie, Catherine and Hannah that said, *Meeting a guy I play Word Games with. His name is Sam, he's thirty-four and a writer of some kind. I don't think he's crazy.* I left out the part that I was letting him come to the house after eleven o'clock on a school night. I giggled at the notion.

Good for you! Valerie responded. *Go for it, little sis!*

Catherine was equally enthused. *Woo hoo, it's about time you got laid. Have fun and be careful.*

I didn't bother to correct her misguided assumption

305

that there would be sex. I was just relieved that I wasn't alone in this. I had a cheering section.

Ever the mother hen, Hannah's response was a little more cautious. *Text me back in exactly two hours with the names of my twins or I'm calling the police and reporting you missing.*

Hannah watched as much *CSI* as I did. And ever-cautious me was taking another leap of faith. I pulled my mess of blonde hair up into a ponytail, threw my robe on over my T-shirt and panties, turned the porch light on and sat on the steps.

I thought my heart would hammer out of my chest when headlights flooded the driveway, temporarily blinding me. They quickly dimmed and the car door slammed. I let out the breath I was holding as he approached – little more than a silhouette to my night-blinded eyes.

'Hey, Lexigirl,' he said, his voice deeper than I'd imagined.

'Hey.'

I looked up at him and smiled. We'd never met, but he felt oddly familiar. It was hard to gauge his height at this angle, but he had a stocky build – solid, my mother would have said – reddish-blond hair and an easy smile.

He sat down on the step next to me. And nodded. 'Yeah, this was the right thing to do.'

I laughed, my voice sounding loud on the quiet street. 'You were having second thoughts, too?'

He shrugged. 'Sure. I was afraid I'd show up at the wrong address – or find the police waiting for me.'

I hadn't even considered that he might feel uncomfortable. I had to give him points for taking a leap of faith, too.

'Right address and no cops,' I said, spreading my arms to take in the deserted street of small bungalow houses.

My thinking had been that, if we sat outside, my neighbours would hear me if I started screaming. My next-door neighbour Caitlin lived alone, too, so I knew she'd be the first to call the police if I raised the alarm. But now it actually felt kind of silly, sitting outside like this when I had perfectly comfortable furniture inside.

'So, I know where you live. Do I get to know your name?'

'Alexandra,' I said. 'But everyone calls me Lexi.'

'Well, Alexandra, I'm going to kiss you now because it's pretty much all I've been thinking about for the past month.'

I probably should have said, 'No.' A three point word. But instead I said, 'Yes.' Because five points beats three points.

And then the man I only knew as InkSlinger and Sam, who was a stranger and yet somehow not, kissed me. And there were so many points in that kiss that I couldn't even figure out how to add them all up. His lips were soft and fit so perfectly against my own I wanted to comment on it, but I was too busy kissing him. His face had the rough stubble of a long work day and he smelled like coffee and smoke. I leaned into him, only our mouths touching as we sat on my front stoop and kissed.

He slid an inch closer so that our hips touched and I turned into him, my robe coming loose. It was a cool night for this time of year and I shivered, but my chill quickly dissipated when he slipped his arms around my waist and kissed me harder. I realised I had grabbed the front of his shirt – now when had I done that? – and let go, smoothing out the fabric before I put one arm around his neck and held him to me, intensifying the kiss. I could leap with the best of them, I thought hazily as he tugged the belt of my robe and kept me anchored to him.

'What's your last name, Sam?' I whispered against his lips.

'Haverty.'

'Mmm, nice word count,' I said. 'But not as good as Zambruski.'

He leaned back to stare at me. 'Stop playing Word Games and kiss me.'

I laughed. 'I am kissing you. I am,' and I went back to proving it.

I hadn't intended anything more than kissing. Hell, I hadn't even intended that. But this didn't feel like a first date, the previous ignorance of last names notwithstanding. I knew him. I knew his words, I knew how he thought. I knew that he was outgoing and fun, things I wanted to be. I knew he was lonely, like me. And, despite how we had started, this wasn't a game any more.

'Let's go inside.'

He seemed as surprised by my overture as I was. He pulled back and looked into my eyes. I felt flushed, aroused. I licked my bottom lip self-consciously and he groaned.

'Are you sure? I didn't come over here for that. You know that, right?'

I smiled. 'What would Valerie do?'

'Huh?'

I'd told him about my mental game whenever faced with a decision, but I hadn't told him my sister's name.

'Valerie. My sister.'

He nodded. 'Gotcha. Well, this isn't about Valerie. This is about Alexandra. And what she *wants* to do.'

I didn't hesitate. 'I want to go inside.'

That seemed to be all the answer he needed. He stood up, took my hand and helped me to my feet – turns out he was about two inches taller than my five-foot-seven – and let me lead the way inside.

I paused, debating whether to actually take him to the bedroom now that I'd committed to this, but he interrupted my decision-making process by taking me in his arms again and nudging me down to sit in the upholstered chair by the front door.

Kneeling in front of me like a man about to propose, he took my hands. 'Thank you for trusting me,' he said. 'Believe it or not, I'm scared to death.'

I laughed gently, both at his position and the stark wide-eyed expression he gave me to accompany his words. 'So let's treat it like the game,' I said. 'However this round turns out, there will always be another chance.'

I didn't know where that came from, but it seemed right. It must have seemed right to him, too, because he nodded.

And then he kissed me again and I forgot about Word Games and speaking in general. He parted my robe and ran his hands up and down my bare thighs, up to the hem of my long T-shirt and back down to my knees. I spread my knees a bit further, allowing him to scoot closer into the space between them and deepen the kiss. His shift pressed my breasts up tight against his hard chest and I let out a soft sigh at the intimate contact. His breath quickened, signalling that he could feel my hard nipples through the thin cotton shirt.

I ran my hands up and down his back, up through his longish red-blond hair and down across his shoulders. I couldn't get enough of touching him. I'd never slept with anyone on a first date, but I kept marvelling how this didn't feel like someone I'd just met.

I broke the kiss, feeling dizzy with lust. 'Is this crazy?'

He cupped my face in his hands and stared into my

eyes. 'Yes. Of course it's crazy. But I've never known anyone like you, who just *got* me, who could match me in wit and intelligence, who seemed so much like me and so much like someone I want to know.'

It was a good speech. Smooth. It felt true, too.

'Besides,' he added, 'we've been making out verbally for weeks. I like foreplay, but God, I want to find out what else we do well.'

And that felt true, too. So instead of playing 'What would Valerie do?' I played 'What does Alexandra want?' I reached down between us, slipped my fingers into the sides of my panties and slid them down my thighs. He groaned as he watched me, rocking back on his heels to give me room. His gaze was riveted to the shadowy place between my thighs, the spot my T-shirt just barely hid.

'You are one incredible tease, Alexandra Zambruski.'

'Who's teasing?' I breathed, hooking a finger in the neck of his button-down shirt and pulling him closer. 'You can have me.'

I'd intended to kiss him, but his head veered south. I felt the press of his mouth over the hem of my T-shirt, so close to my pussy all I could do was slide down lower in the seat to facilitate direct contact. But he slid with me, keeping his mouth just over that bit of fabric.

'Who's teasing now?' I groaned.

And then he put me out of my misery. Or ramped it up, depending on how you look at it. His mouth slipped under my T-shirt and zeroed in on the wet spot he had created. I let out a very unladylike yelp as he tongued my pussy in broad strokes, not missing an inch of wet, sensitive flesh. My clit throbbed against the velvety softness of his tongue. I tightened my fingers in his hair, holding his mouth to me, begging with my hands and my clenched thighs for him to never stop.

He licked until I was trickling wetness down my ass to the chair. I felt like an ice cube melting to boiling water, all boneless, liquid heat. I was whimpering, unable to stay quiet and very, very happy we'd taken this party inside. I distantly heard the rasp of a zipper and jerked against his mouth in anticipation. I had already been close to orgasm, but thinking about him fucking me, feeling his cock inside me – oh, God, please let him be as solid there as everywhere else – was sending me into oblivion.

And then he pulled his mouth away.

I groaned in frustration and stared at him. 'Don't stop,' I commanded, sounding far more forceful than my poor lust-weak body felt. 'Please.'

'I'm sorry, I'm sorry,' he said, looking embarrassed. 'But, I, well, I wasn't expecting this. At all, and I'm not ready.'

'Ready?' I was trying to make sense of his words. I leaned down and felt his erection peeking out from his trousers. 'Yes, you are. Very ready. So am I, oh, God, am I ready.'

He caught my hands in his. 'Stop that before I come,' he growled. 'You're driving me crazy and I'm very, very ready to be inside you, but I'm not *prepared*, I should've said.'

It dawned on me what he meant. Oh, hell. I thought frantically. 'Wait!'

I stood up on legs that felt like cooked spaghetti and hurried down the hall to the bathroom. 'Please, please, please,' I muttered. Then I hit the mother lode. I checked the expiration on the package – three months to spare – and dashed back to the living room where he still knelt in front of the chair, looking dazed.

'Here, now you're prepared,' I said, thrusting the unopened box of condoms at him. And I was oh so grateful that he was.

He took the box and nudged me back into the chair. 'Thanks. Now let me finish what I started.'

With no embarrassment whatsoever, I plopped my ass back on the chair that was feeling decidedly damp, spread my thighs and raised the hem of my T-shirt, baring my wet pussy to his gaze and his hungry mouth.

'Be my guest,' I said. And he was.

I went from zero to sixty in nothing flat, my brief detour doing nothing to slow down my growing passion. His mouth devoured my pussy like a succulent delicacy, licking and nibbling my inner and outer labia, teasing around my clit before sucking it wholly in his mouth. And I could

313

feel myself coming, everything tightening inside of me as his mouth sent me over the edge. And just to make it more intense, he slid a finger inside of my wetness, rubbing my G-spot in steady strokes as he sucked my clit, everything turning to liquid inside of me and gushing across his tongue as I held his shoulders and screamed.

He took everything I gave him, his mouth never leaving my wetness, lapping and tonguing at my opening, rubbing my G-spot with a finger inside of me, then two, while he alternated licking and rubbing my clit with his thumb. I was a bundle of exposed nerve endings, so far gone that I didn't notice when he took his hands away and used only his mouth on me. I realised why when he surged up against me and pressed his condom-sheathed cock to my pussy.

I slid lower, taking the head inside of me with just that small motion. It was enough penetration to make him groan.

'Damn, oh damn,' he gasped as he pushed forward and slid the rest of the way into my wetness. 'You feel so good, Alexandra.'

The use of my full name seemed more intimate somehow than calling me Lexi and I whimpered at both the feeling of fullness his cock gave me and the sense of closeness I felt to this man. And then all thoughts flitted away as sensation took over and he rocked into me, pushing me back into the chair and then pulling me forward onto his cock, over and over, in a sinuous rhythm that reminded me of a seesaw. Back and forth, his hands hooked under my thighs, anchoring me to him, pulling me on and off him as I stretched my hands above my head and held tight to the top of the chair.

My breasts strained against my T-shirt as I arched my back and pushed my hips forward, and their prominence was an invitation for Sam to nibble them. He sucked my nipples through the fabric, wetting my T-shirt and drawing them up into even tighter points than before. I could feel his cock swelling inside of me, the added friction of the condom stroking my already sensitised pussy. Then his hands tightened on my thighs and he was coming, thrusting into me, pressing me back hard into the chair as his body went rigid and his cock pulsed inside of me.

I pulled him to me, wrapped my arms around him, drew him down over me, feeling every twitch and throb of his damp body against mine, his breath harsh and ragged in my ear.

'You're amazing, Alexandra Zambruski,' he whispered, nipping at my earlobe. 'After all these weeks of foreplay, I knew you would be.'

'Foreplay. One of my favourite words. I wonder if Word Games will allow it.'

He laughed, his chest rising and falling against me. 'We have plenty of time to find out.'

I cradled his face in my hands and kissed him hard. 'Maybe in the morning,' I said. 'I can think of better things to do right now.'

Then I whispered words in his ear that Word Games would never, ever allow.

The Path Not Taken

We all grow up with the idea that someday we'll be the captains of our own fates and we will be happy. I knew what I wanted – the husband, the house, the kids, the white picket fence, the job I adored as much as I loved my family. I never thought that someday I would wake up alone in a house with a mortgage that was killing me, a sixty-hour work week at a job I hated and no relationship prospects on the near (or distant) horizon. But here I was. A travel agent who had never travelled *anywhere*, working in a college town where everybody was from someplace else and everyone else's life was more exciting, more interesting, more *alive* than mine.

Depression is a wily creature. It sneaks up on you with

its long and twisting tendrils wrapping around you in a way that at first feels comfortable and familiar and not altogether bad. You feel vindicated. You're sad and you deserve to be sad. But those tendrils start tightening pretty quickly and, the next thing you know, you're strangling. And you're too tired and sad to fight it.

I was fighting it. Damn it, I was fighting it. Which is why, at the ripe old age of thirty-three, I quit my job, sold the house at a slight profit, broke even on the car and sold or gave away everything else I owned except a few clothes, my laptop, my books, my bike and a few pieces of furniture that I couldn't bear to part with, and bought a one-way ticket to Ireland. The bike, most of the books and all of the furniture went into storage in my parents' basement. I bought a three-piece set of luggage to replace the ones I'd had since high school and had donated to Goodwill, and packed everything I had in them right before I handed my house keys over to the realtor and caught a cab to the airport.

The house had made me feel like such a grown-up when I'd bought it and had ended up feeling like an albatross strangling me – and as it grew smaller and smaller in the rear window, I felt as if I was getting lighter and lighter. I looked at my shiny new red luggage on the seat next to me. My life, condensed into a roll-on bag, a duffel bag and a backpack. I didn't know if I was exhilarated or terrified. Maybe a little of both.

Why Ireland? I don't have a clue, other than I'd always wanted to visit it and I had just booked a one-month vacation for a couple who were going there on their divorcemoon. That's what they called it, too. A divorcemoon. After thirty years of marriage, they'd gotten divorced and realised they were still in love. They'd already sold their house and packed their belongings, so they decided to take leaves of absence from their jobs and take off on a trip. He was a professor and she ran a bookstore over in the City Village shops, so June was the perfect time for them to take off. One month in Ireland, to start. A Greek island cruise after that, maybe. Or Australia. They really didn't know. They were going to travel for a year and decide what they wanted to do next. It sounded exciting – and romantic. They seemed like carefree teenagers, not a couple in their fifties. They also seemed a lot younger – and a lot happier – than me. So I'd decided, if Ireland was the place they were going to start over, it was good enough for me.

It doesn't hurt that my name is Caitlin and I have naturally red hair. My mother's parents were originally from Ireland, so maybe it was in my bones to make Ireland my first destination when I finally got up the nerve to overcome my fear of flying, get on a plane and leave the United States. Whatever it was, I was going. The wheels had been set in motion and I was really and truly starting my life over. Or running away from my very boring life. I guess it depends on your perspective. All I know is that when the plane touched down in Dublin, all I could think was, 'I'm home.'

I wasn't quite sure what I was going to do in Ireland. There would be things to take care of – getting a job, getting a temporary work visa to stay in the country, taking care of the paperwork and minutiae of being a foreigner setting up a life there – but I figured I would worry about all of that after I took a real and proper vacation.

At thirty-three, I could honestly say I'd never been on a vacation as an adult. I'd gone to Disney World and Busch Gardens and the Grand Canyon with my family when I was a kid. I'd done the spring break thing with my friends when I'd been an undergrad at the College of Charleston and I had hazy memories of Cozumel and Lake Tahoe. But since graduating from college with a very useless degree in history, I hadn't been anywhere. I'd come back home, job-hunted with the optimistic goal of landing a position at the Smithsonian or another museum, decided that writing might be fun and applied to every history periodical that existed, ended up with a gig at a niche travel magazine that specialised in historical trips and then, when it inevitably folded, slid into a job at a travel agency while occasionally freelancing for more lucrative travel magazines. I wasn't anywhere close to where I'd wanted to be and only a few miles from where

I started – first living in my parents' house, then taking the small inheritance my grandmother had left me and buying a small bungalow just a few miles from where I grew up. I no longer knew where I wanted to be, but I knew I didn't want to be there any more.

And here I was. In Dublin. Not knowing a soul, not having a job, with a few thousand in the bank, a small flat that I had rented for a month and enough clothes to get me through the summer. The rest would come, or so I hoped. What I really wanted, more than a home or a job, was some clarity. A sense of belonging. I wasn't sure I'd find it in Ireland, but it seemed as good a place as any. So I found my way to the small, ugly apartment building near Trinity College, feeling as if I'd just flown several thousand miles to start over in exactly the kind of place I'd just left, and fell asleep on a pillow that was too flat to be called a pillow, with city noises right outside my window. I felt suddenly, horribly lonely.

'What have I done?' I whispered as I fell asleep.

* * *

Pounding. Loud, unrelenting pounding. That's what I awoke to the next morning, with sunlight just creeping in the window. I pulled the flat pillow over my head, desperate to get more sleep. My internal clock was not on Irish time yet, but I'd slept very little the past couple of weeks and hadn't been able to sleep on the plane at all, so I had known, once my head hit an unmoving target, I was going to sleep until I was rested. Except the person who was doing the pound-pound-pounding seemed determined to make sure I didn't sleep.

The pillow wasn't helping. Neither were my fingers in my ears. I'd gotten in so late – or early, since it had been about dawn when the cab had dropped me off – that I hadn't really had a chance to look around my new home. The keys had been on the sill of the transom window above the door, as promised, and I'd simply let myself in, stripped down to my underwear and fallen into bed. Now I uncovered my head and looked around the small apartment that would be home until I found something else.

The pictures on the walls – vaguely pastoral in their faded ugliness – literally rattled on the walls from the pounding. Whoever it was, they had to be pounding on the other side of my bedroom wall.

'What the hell?' I muttered to myself, followed by a string of more colourful cursing as the noise continued.

I felt like my teeth were going to rattle out of my head as I crawled from under the faded quilt and struggled to get back into my sweater and jeans, feeling clumsy and sore from so many hours of travel and a lack of sleep. Finally dressed, I unlocked my door and popped my head out. No one there. The noise had to be coming from the apartment next door, judging by the way my interior walls were rattling.

The pounding continued as I walked to the door, unrelenting. What the *hell* were they doing in there?

I knocked on the door. 'Hello? Excuse me? You are banging on my wall and I can't sleep.'

The pounding stopped. I heard someone walking to the door. I braced myself for an angry confrontation with my new neighbour. The door opened and I blinked. I knew him.

'Greg?'

He held a hammer in his hand and gave me a mock salute with it – coming awfully close to cracking himself in the head. 'Hey, Caitlin! How are you?'

I shook my head. Greg Hemmingson was my brother Landon's friend. I'd met him at a few of Landon's parties and was never very impressed. Oh, he was cute and charming – always the centre of attention – but he never struck me as terribly deep. Landon said I wasn't being fair, but my brother always manages to find the best in people that turn me cold, including his ex-girlfriend Candace. I was secretly relieved they'd broken up and he was dating Katie, a girl he worked with. Not that it was any of my business whom he dated – or befriended. I was one to talk, after all. My dating history was a mishmash of blind dates and one-off events that never went anywhere.

What's funny is that Greg's dating history sounded a lot like mine, at least to hear Landon tell it. But what's embarrassing for a woman is something to be proud of when you're a man, I guess. Or maybe I was just too sensitive to the fact that all of my friends were settling down and getting married. Maybe Greg was my single soul mate. Maybe I needed some more sleep.

'What are you *doing* here, Greg?'

He shrugged. 'Work. We're setting up an Ireland office and I'm part of the start-up team. The company set me up here –' he made a sweeping gesture behind him '– because they're cheap bastards. Just trying to make it home.'

I sighed. I left the country to start my life over and here one of the less than wonderful parts of my life was 'trying to make it home' at dawn. 'Do you know what time it is?'

He shifted from one foot to the other and had the good grace to look sheepish. 'Sorry. I've been here a couple of weeks and thought the apartment next door was empty.'

'I just got in a couple of hours ago. Literally. And I'm wiped out, so –' I mimicked his sweeping gesture '– could you make it home at a more reasonable hour?'

I was already wondering how difficult it would be to get out of my contract and move somewhere else. But that seemed impractical, since I'd end up forfeiting a month's rent and I was only planning to stay a month anyway. I sighed.

'Sure, no problem,' Greg said, grinning. 'Maybe we can get a drink later? When you're awake and, um, put together?'

I shuffled back to my own un-homey apartment. 'This is as together as I'm ever going to be,' I muttered, closing the door on his question.

* * *

I woke up some time later and squinted bleary-eyed at the clock by the bed. It was nearly 6 p.m. I groaned. I'd never get on Irish time this way. Greg was pounding again, but this time it sounded like he was outside my door. I was still wearing my clothes from when he'd forced me to get dressed earlier and I climbed out of bed and made my way to the door. I scowled at his smile.

'Are you still sleeping? You're never going to adjust to the time change this way,' he said, pushing his way past me. 'Go get a shower and put on something that doesn't smell like stale airplane.'

I shook my head. 'Thanks, but I'm just going to stay in –'

'Shower, clothes, now,' he said, nudging me toward the bathroom. 'Please.'

I was annoyed. I'd never much liked Greg – and I was

liking him even less on this side of the pond. 'Why should I?' I said, sounding like a petulant child and not really caring. This was *Greg*, not someone I wanted to impress.

I expected some snappy comeback, or at least another insult about my maturity or how pathetic I was, but his expression was stark. 'Because I'm lonely and you're the first friendly face I've seen in two weeks.'

I probably looked like a fish gaping open-mouthed in the bottom of a boat. I gave up trying to think of a response and headed for the shower. If it was a line, it was a good one. He'd hooked me.

* * *

Dublin may be known for its pubs but, in the stark little neighbourhood where we were, the closest was a dingy little hole in the wall with the unlikely name of Pungo's Pub. Pungo, I surmised, was the owner's dog: a photo of the homely mutt with his name scrawled underneath sat propped in the window and the creature – a curious mix of what looked to be bulldog, some kind of terrier and a Muppet – snored in front of the small brick fireplace.

I took a seat at one of three small tables, appreciative of the warmth of the fire while keeping my eye on the sleeping animal. A run-in with the neighbours' dog when I was a kid had left me with a scar on the back of my hand and a distrust of all dogs.

Speaking of which, Greg was making his way back from the bar, two pints of dark beer in his hands. He put one in front of me and took a seat, scraping his chair loudly enough to rouse the snoozing canine. The dog gave us sleepy eyes before dropping his head back to the floor.

'I ordered the ubiquitous fish and chips for you,' he said. 'Your first meal in Ireland has to be fish and chips.'

'Thanks,' I muttered, not sounding or feeling thankful at all.

I resented him ordering for me. I resented him disturbing my sleep. I resented him even being in the country. I was supposed to be escaping. Running away. Starting over. Doing something new. Watching Greg relax in his chair and drink his beer made me feel like I was back home at one of Landon's parties, feeling envious of my brother and his friends, all of whom seemed to have the lives they wanted, with jobs they loved and relationships they deserved.

I sipped my beer and stared at the fire until our food was brought over. I had to admit, the fish looked good, as did Greg's meal, some kind of meat pie with a flaky crust. Hunger got the better of me and I had downed almost my entire pint and half a plate of food before I even looked up to see Greg smiling at me.

'What?'

'Nothing, just really glad you're here.'

I felt compelled to be nice. He had, after all, been nice to me. 'So, how long are you here?'

He shrugged. 'As long as they need me. Not my preference, but since I was the only one who was single and had nothing really tying me to home –'

There was that expression again. I really didn't want to delve too deeply. I didn't need to know his issues; I had issues of my own to sort out.

'So, not dating anyone this week?' I said it lightly, but the way he drew back made me regret it. 'Sorry. It's not like I'm here with my husband and three kids.' I made a sweeping gesture taking in the entire pub. 'Nope, it's just me, you, the guy behind the bar and that thing.'

'Don't like dogs?'

I was grateful he ignored my question. 'Not especially. I don't trust them.'

'Or men?'

Ouch. He wasn't ignoring it after all. 'I trust men. Or I don't have any reason not to trust them as an entire group,' I said, swallowing the rest of my beer.

'Ah, I see,' he said, though I doubt he did. 'You just don't like me.'

I nearly choked on my fish. 'What? No! I mean, I don't *not* like you,' I said, trying very hard not to cough while also keeping my foot out of my mouth. Doing both at the same time proved difficult. 'I don't even really know you.'

'We should change that.' He stood up. 'I'm going to get us another round.'

I didn't think it was a good idea, but then I tamped down that voice in my head that hadn't thought anything was a good idea until now. Maybe I needed to just do the opposite of whatever the voice in my head said. Take the path less travelled, the road not taken. All that. Be the different person I'd come to a different country to be. Or maybe that was just the Guinness talking.

In any case, when Greg returned with another two pints, I took mine and smiled graciously. 'Thanks for asking me out,' I said, though he hadn't asked me at all. 'I know I haven't been very nice.'

'Not very,' he said dryly. 'Why do you think I'm trying to get you drunk?'

I laughed, a honest-to-goodness full-bellied laugh. Whatever I knew and had judged about Greg, I liked his honesty. I liked how it made me feel to be with someone who was utterly without pretence. I wanted to be like that. I wanted to feel that free from awkwardness and discomfort.

'Sounds like a plan,' I said, taking a long swallow of my beer. It was tasting better the second time around, a sure sign I should stop. And true to my new promise, I ignored that little voice and took another long swallow. 'So tell me, Greg, are you planning on taking me to bed tonight or are you going to take it slow and wait until tomorrow night?'

Watching his eyes bulge, and hearing the bizarre snorting noise he made that had even the dog staring at him, was worth the interrupted sleep. I laughed again. I laughed like I hadn't laughed in a long time. I didn't know what great cosmic mystery had brought the two of us together here, but I was going to enjoy it.

'If I had thought I had even half a chance with you, I would've sprung for the cab fare and taken you someplace nicer,' he said.

'Damn, my loss.' I didn't feel like I'd lost out on a thing. In fact, I felt like I was right where I was supposed to be.

'Maybe tomorrow, now that I know it's an option,' he said, the laugh lines around his eyes holding a fascination I'd never noticed before. 'I have time to make it up to you, right?'

'We'll see.'

The funny thing about me is that it may take me for ever to make a decision, but once I do, I'm fully committed. I was committed to enjoying this night with Greg, to being someone who wasn't unhappy and lonely and jealous of everyone else. To be the woman I'd come here to be. And so we laughed and we talked and, though I finished my second pint and started on a third, I was far from drunk. I felt good, as if the weight I'd been carrying on my shoulders had truly been left behind.

'Ready to go?'

I hadn't realised how long we'd been sitting there until Greg glanced at the brass-rimmed clock on the wall. I was still on East Coast time, but the clock said it was nearly midnight. Had we really sat there that long?

The temperature had dipped and I shivered as we made our way out to the street. After being warmed by the fire, not to mention the beer, I felt chilled. I didn't complain when Greg put his arm around me, and I didn't take it as a come-on. He was just being nice. I wasn't entirely sure how I felt about that.

It wasn't far to the apartment building and we walked in a comfortable silence. I had no idea what Greg was thinking about, but I was contemplating those laugh lines around his eyes and how they crinkled when I said something he thought was funny. By the time we'd walked up the three flights of stairs to our floor, I was starting to be a little obsessive about those lines in the corners of his eyes. What were they called, other than laugh lines?

He stopped at my door, the one closest to the stairs, and I stared up at him, trying to remember that other name. The one my mother used to scowl about when she was using cover-up on hers.

'Crow's feet!' I said triumphantly, while Greg looked at me as if I'd lost my mind. 'That's what they are.'

'Frog's balls!' he exclaimed, his voice carrying down the hall.

I laughed, quickly fitted my key in the lock and opened the door. I dragged him into the entryway, intent on quieting him. And then, standing there in the darkness because I hadn't remembered to turn on a light before we had headed out, I was intent on kissing those lines at the corners of his friendly blue eyes.

I put my hands on either side of his face and stood on tiptoe, turning his face so that I could kiss one set of crow's feet, then the other. 'They're called crow's feet,' I murmured, staring into his eyes. 'But yours are laugh lines. I like them.'

He nodded and held me away from him. 'OK. Now, can you walk a straight line?'

It was my turn to stare and wonder what was wrong with him. 'Huh?'

'Can you walk a straight line?'

I turned away and demonstrated that I could, taking careful strides down the darkened hall of my small new home. 'Yes. Why?'

'And recite the alphabet forward and backward?'

I laughed. 'I doubt I can do it backward. What is wrong with you?'

He crossed the distance between us and put his arms around me. 'I want to make sure you're not drunk before I do this.'

'Do wha –'

He kissed me. Long, slow, tasting like Guinness and

the mint I'd given him when I complained I had vinegar breath. It wasn't what I had expected. It was better. I reached up and put my arms around his neck, liking his height even though it meant I had to arch my neck to kiss him back. I gave as good as I got, sweeping my tongue along his bottom lip before sucking it, then nipping it. We stood there kissing in my dark apartment for a long time, with only the wet sounds of our mouths and the faint noises of late-night street traffic to fill the quiet.

After several minutes of kissing him like that, when I could feel his arousal pressing against me and my own need building low in my belly, I pulled back.

'I am not drunk,' I said softly. 'And if you don't take me to bed tonight, I fully expect you to take me to bed tomorrow night.'

It wasn't me. It wasn't something I would say, it wasn't something I would do. Which was exactly why I was saying it and doing it. I didn't want to be someone else, I just wanted to be the Caitlin Morrow I had always been too afraid to be. The one who went for what she wanted. The one who ignored the little voice in her head that said something was a bad idea or that something was going to hurt her. I wanted to be the Caitlin that made Greg laugh. That made Greg hard just by kissing him.

'Yeah?' he asked, rubbing his thumb across my bottom lip. 'What about tonight *and* tomorrow night?'

I laughed. 'I like your confidence. I like it a lot.'

Then I took his hand and led him to my bedroom with the unmade bed and the luggage still mostly packed and piled in the corner. I turned on the light, because it was something the old Caitlin would never do, and I slowly stripped. Sweater, blouse, bra, I let each piece of clothing fall to the floor, my gaze never wavering from his. Topless, I kicked off my shoes, bent to take off my socks, then unhooked my trousers and peeled them down my legs. My panties were the last to go – a brand-new pair of turquoise boy shorts, a style I never wore, in a colour that was too bright for the old Caitlin. I stripped them off and tossed them at Greg's chest. Then I stood there naked, trying not to feel self-conscious about my weight or my breasts or my thighs or freckles. Watching him, watching the way his expression changed from amusement to desire to something even more insistent and needy, it wasn't hard at all. He wanted me. Me. This body, this woman. Me.

'Now you,' I whispered.

He stripped quicker than I did, sweater and jeans and boxer briefs piled on top of socks and shoes. His erection was beautiful and heavy, and I wasn't embarrassed to stare at him, to admire him like that instead of pretending to look at his face or somewhere else.

I sat on the edge of the bed and beckoned him closer. He stood in front of me, his cock bobbing in an amusing and arousing way at once. And then I slowly licked from the heavy tip of him to the base where dark hair curled. Slowly, like I was painting him with my tongue, I licked strips up his cock. He stood there, arms at his side, head thrown back, and he let me. He didn't urge me to take him in my mouth, he didn't put his hands on my head to guide me, he simply let me do what I wanted. And so I did.

I licked his cock again, then took it in my hand and licked the underside. I ran the flat of my tongue along his heavy balls, noting the way they drew up against his body, the way he gasped in surprise and pleasure. I cupped them in my hand and stroked them gently, marvelling at their weight and softness. When his cock twitched of its own accord, I took it in my mouth and sucked softly, then harder. I liked the way he responded, with appreciative noises and a tremor in his narrow thighs.

I pulled my mouth from him and lay back on the edge of the bed. Legs spread and raised, I put my feet around him and pulled him closer. 'Come here,' I whispered, drawing him down on top of me. 'I want you inside of me. Now.'

'Yes, ma'am,' was all he said. Then he was sliding into me with one long stroke.

I groaned as my wetness engulfed him, but there was no sense of discomfort or need for adjustment. It was as if he was always meant to be inside me. He slid me further across the bed so he could stretch out on top of me, and hooked his hands under my hips so he could go deeper into me while I wrapped my legs high around his back. And then we were as close as we could be, his cock buried inside me, my pelvic bone pressed against him so that his wiry curls rubbed my clit in the most intensely delicious way. He leaned up to look in my eyes as we moved together, staring at me as if he were memorising my face, and every moment of this experience.

'You're something else, Caitlin,' he whispered, lowering his mouth to kiss me again.

He filled me, absorbing my moans and whimpers into his mouth, teasing me with slow strokes, then thrusting harder, driving me across the bed until my hair cascaded over the side and I was gripping him with hands and nails and nipping at his shoulder to make him fuck me harder. He moaned and tensed against me and I thought he was coming, but no, he was only controlling himself. Making it last. Making it better for me.

Knowing that, knowing he was thinking about my pleasure, was enough to make me come. And I did, rubbing my clit sinuously against his belly, wetting him with my juices, clenching around his cock. Clinging to him, arms and legs and cunt, until he was filling me with his own wetness, holding me to him with his hands cupping my ass, pulling me up against him, filling me and filling me until I was whimpering and crying at the myriad sensations.

We lay damp and panting, him still on top of me, my head hanging off the edge of the bed until I started feeling light-headed and nudged him back. Then he pulled me up and sideways, so we could rest our heads on the pillows that smelled of lavender soap and my hair conditioner. And then we were both laughing and rolling on the bed, damp bodies rubbing against each other as if we'd done this a thousand times, the lamplight seeming suddenly brighter and more intense. I got up and padded naked to the light switch and turned it off, not out of embarrassment but because I wanted to lie with him in the darkness.

As I crawled back into bed, he took me in his arms and kissed the top of my head. 'What the hell is this we're doing?'

'That's my line,' I giggled, tucking in close to him, even though I was wet and warm. 'But does it matter?'

He lowered his head to my ear and his breath tickled. 'Nah. We have tomorrow night to figure it out,' he said.

I nodded. Tomorrow night. And the night after that.

'Hell, why limit ourselves to a night or two? I have the rest of my life, if you're interested.' I didn't care that it sounded like some kind of drunken proposal. I'd never felt more clear-headed in my life.

'Yeah, I think maybe I am,' he said. 'Very interested.'

And in that moment, with this man, it was the best answer in the world.

THE SILVER CHAIN – PRIMULA BOND

Good things come to those who wait…

After a chance meeting one evening, mysterious entrepreneur Gustav Levi and photographer Serena Folkes agree to a very special contract.

Gustav will launch Serena's photographic career at his gallery, but only if Serena agrees to become his companion.

To mark their agreement, Gustav gives Serena a bracelet and silver chain which binds them physically and symbolically. A sign that Serena is under Gustav's power.

As their passionate relationship intensifies, the silver chain pulls them closer together. But will Gustav's past tear them apart?

A passionate, unforgettable erotic romance for fans of *50 Shades of Grey* and Sylvia Day's *Crossfire Trilogy*.

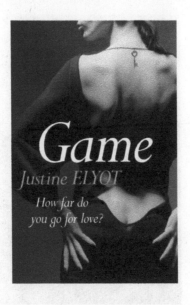

POWER PLAY – CHARLOTTE STEIN

Now she's the boss, everything that once seemed forbidden is possible…

Meet Eleanor Harding, a woman who loves to be in control and who puts Anastasia Steele in the shade.

When Eleanor is promoted, she loses two very important things: the heated relationship she had with her boss, and control over her own desires.

She finds herself suddenly craving something very different – and office junior, Ben, seems like just the sort of man to fulfil her needs. He's willing to show her all of the things she's been missing – namely, what it's like to be the one in charge.

Now all Eleanor has to do is decide…is Ben calling the kinky shots, or is she?

Find out more at www.mischiefbooks.com

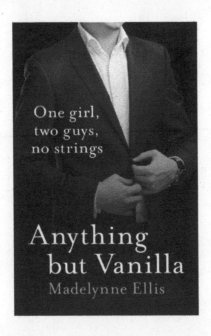

ANYTHING BUT VANILLA
MADELYNNE ELLIS

One girl, two guys, no strings.

Kara North is on the run. Fleeing from her controlling fiancé and a wedding she never wanted, she accepts the chance offer of refuge on Liddell Island, where she soon catches the eye of the island's owner, erotic photographer Ric Liddell.

But pleasure comes in more than one flavour when Zachary Blackwater, the charming ice-cream vendor also takes an interest, and wants more than just a tumble in the surf.

When Kara learns that the two men have been unlikely lovers for years, she becomes obsessed with the idea of a threesome.

Soon Kara is wondering how she ever considered committing herself to just one man.

Find out more at www.mischiefbooks.com

www.ingramcontent.com/pod-product-compliance
Ingram Content Group UK Ltd.
Pitfield, Milton Keynes, MK11 3LW, UK
UKHW022247180325
456436UK00001B/44